Reality's Fire

R. L. Copple

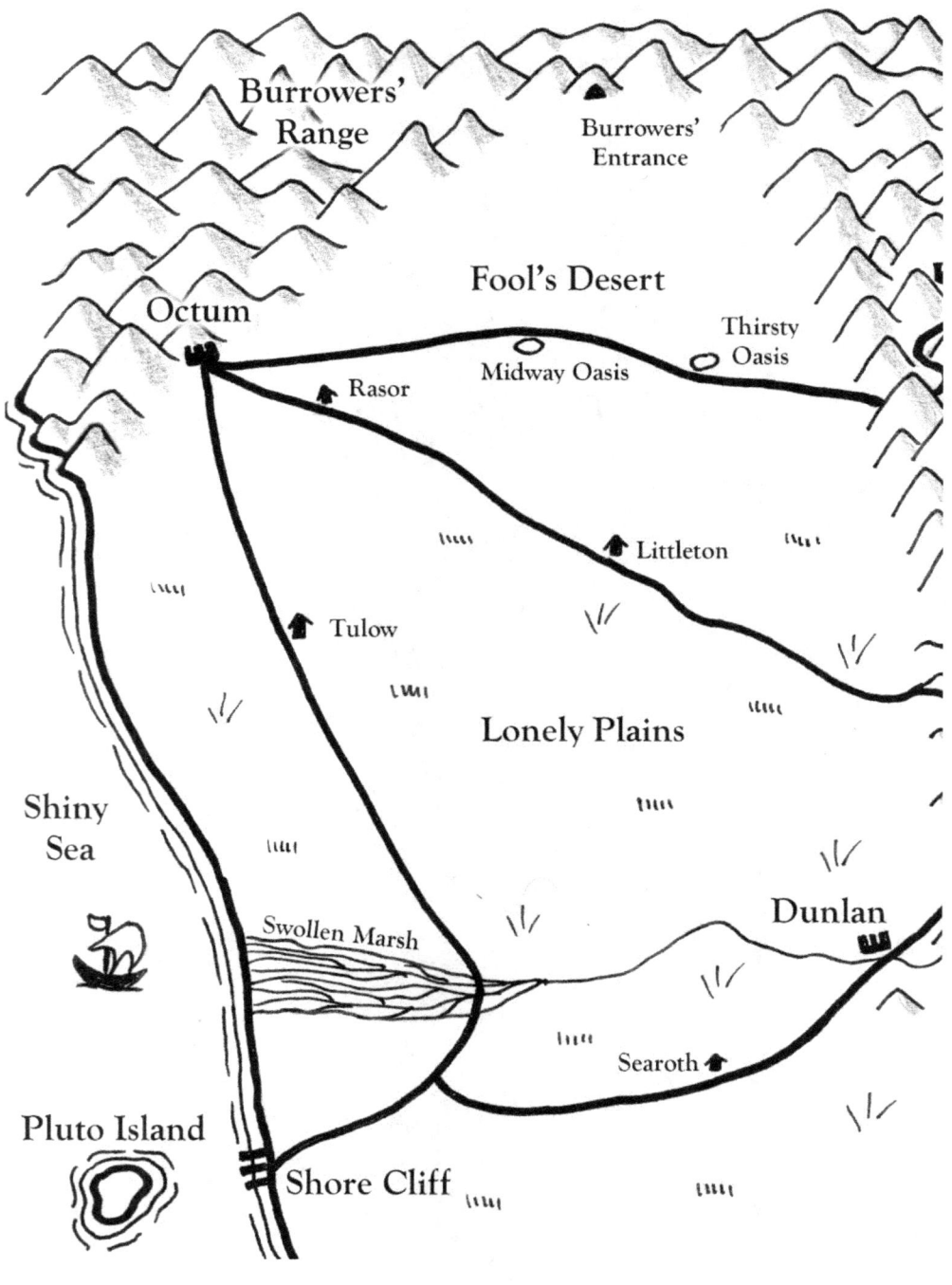

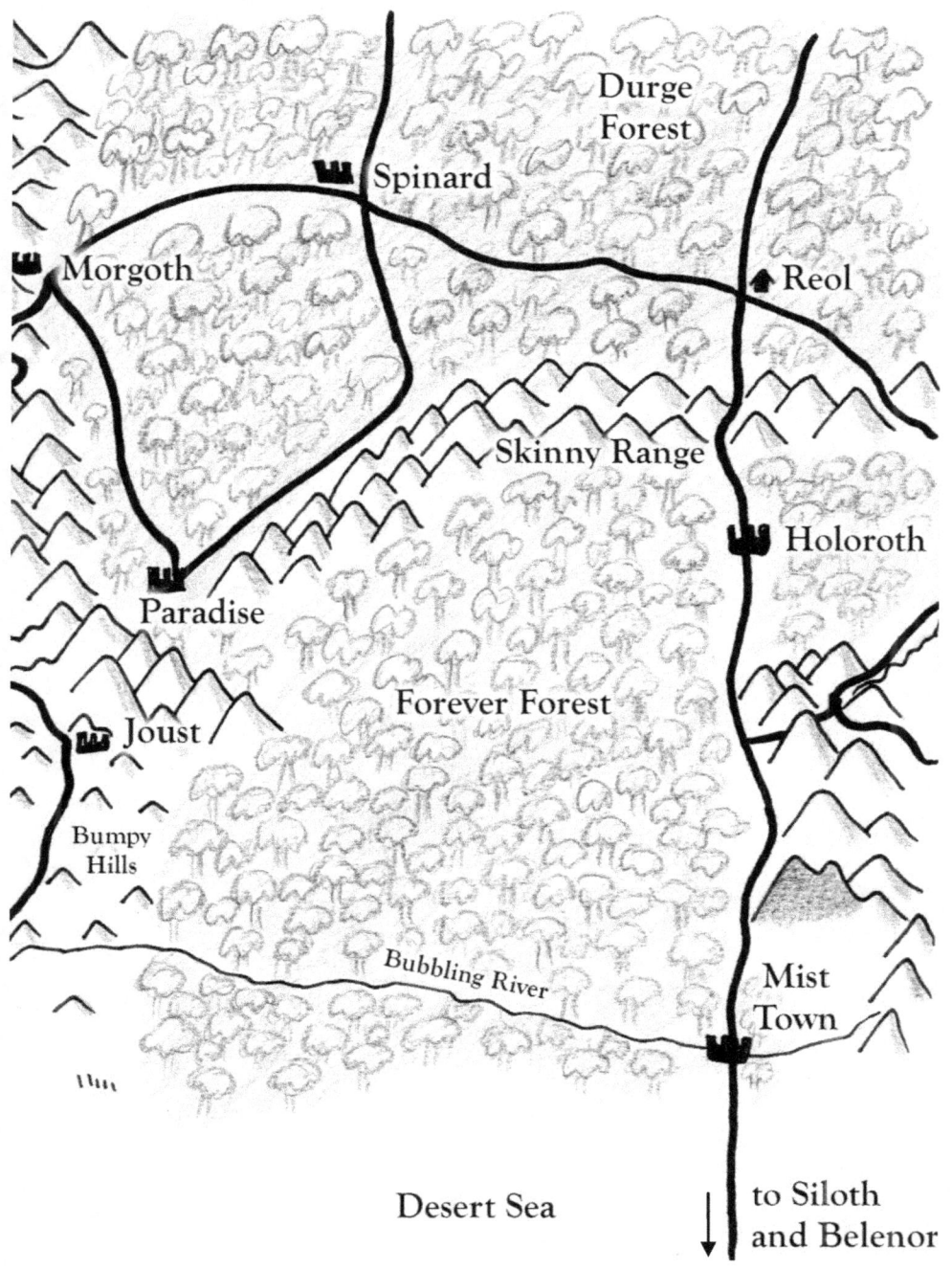

Reality's Fire

R. L. COPPLE

ISBN: 978-1-927154-24-3
Splashdown Books, New Zealand
http://www.splashdownbooks.com

Books by R. L. Copple:

The Reality Chronicles:
Reality's Dawn
Reality's Ascent
Reality's Fire

The Virtual Reality Chronicles:
Mind Game
Hero Game

www.rlcopple.com

Crystal teetered on the brink of madness. Imprisoned in her own mind and body, she could only watch as she stood by Nathan before a priest. The poor boy thought he was marrying her, but she wasn't in control. Beltrid, the demon, directed her actions and words.

She'd grown to love Nathan even through Beltrid's deception. His loyalty to her, despite his father and sister's warnings, impressed her. She sensed a deep love flowing in his soul. But did the love flow for her? Or did Beltrid's grip on him squeeze it out against his will? The boy proved too gullible to the demon's illusion.

She screamed in her mind, "Don't do this, Beltrid! He deserves better."

Often the demon ignored her, but occasionally he would respond. "Hurts, doesn't it—to see your lover tricked into marrying a demon? Or are you afraid of what he'll think if he finds out?" His smirking tone spoke of the joy he derived from her pain.

Crystal wanted to cry, but her body wouldn't respond. "He'll find out, and he'll save me when he does."

The demon laughed. "Him? Save you? He doesn't even know you. Nor does he have the power to free anyone from demonic possession, even if he knew."

"His father will. Sisko has power you don't."

"Sisko! Yes he does, but it will soon be mine. When he hands it to Nathan, I will control the ring. Through you, I'll gradually gain possession of him as well."

"Not if I have anything to say about it!"

Beltrid laughed again. "You have no say. But this priest does. And he's about to marry me to this boy. So enjoy the wedding. This is the closest you'll get to it."

Crystal struggled in her mind to move her lips, to say "stop," to do anything. But Beltrid's grip proved too strong.

The priest opened a book. "Have you, Nathan, a good, free, and unconstrained will and a firm intention to take unto yourself to wife this demon, Beltrid, whom you see here before you?"

"I..." Nathan's eyes narrowed. "What did you say?"

"Sorry, I have to be accurate or the service is no good. You have to know who you are marrying. The proper response is, 'I have.'"

Crystal leaped for joy inside her mind. The priest could see the truth! But would Nathan believe him?

Then Nathan turned toward her and his eyes grew wide. Nathan backed away, shock spilling off his face. His mouth hung open and his limbs shook. He saw the reality of Beltrid.

The bridesmaid pulled her veil off and ran to his side. Crystal's heart warmed. Kaylee, Nathan's sister, had somehow arrived here ahead of them. Beltrid wouldn't get his way now. He had failed.

Beltrid's rage burned inside of her as he spoke to her mind, "Failed? I think not. A minor setback. But for the moment, I'm done with you."

The scene before her wavered. She felt a wind whirling about her, fracturing the picture. "No, you can't do this!" She watched as Nathan and Kaylee huddled in a corner. Then Beltrid's control left her. She caught Nathan's eyes and wanted to yell, "I'm not Beltrid, I love you," but pain flooded her body. A fire-infested landscape overlaid the narthex of the church. She screamed as the world faded and the fires of Hades became reality.

She sat atop a small plateau, surrounded by fire and molten rock. In the distance, she could see other pillars jutting out from the fiery abyss with other poor souls languishing upon them. She stood and paced the rock, glad to at last have control over her own body. But her thoughts turned toward Nathan. She had no clue what Beltrid would do next. She offered up a prayer for his safety.

"This is what I get for giving into my passions." It felt good to say her thoughts aloud. Her father's words echoed in her mind, "If you don't control yourself, someone else will." She had discovered too late the truth of his words.

Now tears did push their way onto her cheeks. She collapsed onto the hot rock. Guilt welled up within her, turning her stomach. If only she could go back and start over. She'd do things differently. She wiped the wetness from her eyes and stared into the blackness above her. "God, if you're up there, I'm ready to listen."

"Then there's hope."

She jerked around but no one else stood on her rock. Could God hear and speak in this place? But it had to be Him. No demon would give her hope, least of all, Beltrid.

She lay on the ground. Time meant little in this unchanging Hell. How many days and nights cycled in Nathan's world? Did time even apply here? Whole lifetimes could have passed for all she knew as she sat, walked, took in every detail she could make out, and lay, sometimes sleeping. Nathan could have died by now. Beltrid was right. How could Nathan find her here? What chance did he have against a demon?

"I have a mission for you, my dear."

Crystal jerked up to see Beltrid standing before her. His stench rose above the smell of Hades' cauldron. "I'm no longer yours. Let me go."

He wagged a finger. "Not so fast. I've not released you and you have no say in the matter. I'm sending you to a new prison. One that will torment both you and Nathan for his entire life."

"What are you talking about?"

A wide smile slid across his face. "He thinks I wore a disguise to appear like you. You broke his heart, I'm afraid. He's none too happy about the deception you played upon him."

"You deceived him, not I."

Beltrid pointed a finger at her. "That doesn't matter. What he thinks is what matters. Please give the boy my regards...oh, wait. You'll not be able to speak except what I allow you to say." He grinned.

"You're not going to possess me again, are you?" She thought that would be pointless.

"You'll figure it out soon enough." He waved his hand, and the inferno transitioned to a forest. Birds winged their way through the tree branches, waving in a gentle breeze. The wind caressed her face, and the colors glowed with pastel brightness.

This is a prison?

3

Her feet moved, as if having a mind of their own, and she approached a clearing. She paused at the edge and watched. Out of thin air, Nathan materialized in the middle of it. His eyes soaked in the surroundings.

Crystal smiled outside, but leaped for joy inside. This wasn't a prison; this was paradise! Her feet moved her into the clearing; anticipation burst forth within her soul. She'd finally get to hold him as herself, and not as a demon-controlled puppet.

Nathan fixed his eyes on her, but instead of joy, his face grew red and the veins in his neck protruded. He drew his sword and sped toward her.

Her paradise morphed into a nightmare. She backed up, wanting to say something, but nothing would come out. She held a hand up as he stepped into striking range. He thrust his blade toward her. She tried to dodge it, but it plunged into her chest and through her heart. Numbing pain spread across her body; she fell to her knees.

She reached out a hand to him. "But, Nathan, I love you."

He clinched his teeth. "You don't love me, you used me! You tricked me. I was nothing more than a pawn in your hands. You couldn't possibly love me." He pulled the sword out.

Crystal fell to the ground, blood pooling around her. "No, I did love you. Whether you believe it or not."

The landscape dimmed, but Nathan's face remained solid. "Die, demon of my soul, and never return."

Blackness encroached from the edges of her vision. Death marched toward her, and she welcomed it. At least she would be released from this life. Some plan God had for her, to be killed by the one person in her life she really cared about.

The blackness swallowed Nathan's face, his piercing, angry eyes the last to vanish into the gloom of death. But Crystal still felt awareness. The darkness lightened, and trees, fuzzy at first, then growing sharp and clear, formed before her.

The forest, again? Was it the same one? Her feet stepped toward a clearing as before. She paused again to see Nathan appear in the clearing.

Outside she smiled, but inside she screamed as Beltrid's plan dawned upon her.

He'd trapped her in Nathan's mind. Not only his mind, but his dream. A nightmare of death. Once was bad enough. Now she'd be killed by him over and over. Within herself, she cried out, "Beltrid, I hate you! Hate, hate, hate you!"

She heard laughing in the distance as her feet pushed her into the clearing once again.

Crystal watched from the trees as Nathan's body materialized. For the hundredth time—in truth she'd lost count—Nathan scanned the area, waiting for her to appear.

Yet this time something was different. A different expression graced his face, as if confused about something. In all the replays of this dream, the least little difference stood out like a lonely tree on a plain. Could it be this time her fate would change? Would she have the chance to break out of this dream trap in his head?

She'd find out soon enough. Without willing it, she stepped forward from the trees as if on cue. She smiled as she had hundreds of times before, but her hopes crashed when he reacted as always.

His frown deepened upon seeing her, and his face turned red. He pulled the sword from his side, and raced toward her. She attempted to dodge his thrust, but as always, it plunged deep into her chest, piercing more than her heart. Her knees gave way, and she crumpled to the ground in a scream. No, nothing had changed.

From the ground she found the strength to reach up her hand to him. "But, Nathan, I love you." She'd said it so many times and it never made a difference. Would it this time? Maybe there was hope.

He snarled. "You don't love me, you used me! You tricked me. I was nothing more than a pawn in your hands. You couldn't possibly love me."

Pain raced through her body as blood fell upon the ground. The world grew even more dreamlike. But Crystal replied over and over as many times as her brain could muster, "No, I did love you. Whether you believe it or not."

He answered her pleas with, "Die, demon of my soul, and never return."

The barbs of his hate drained her soul as life drained from her body. But she noticed another difference as life ebbed away. Nathan acted as if he talked to an internal voice. His expressions were not the same as they'd been before. What could this mean? Maybe next time she appeared, it would be even more different. At least it had changed, and that offered hope.

Life vanished, and she expected to appear again outside the edge of the trees and repeat the dream. Yet, when the scene materialized around her, she didn't stand among the trees. She still lay on the ground. But Nathan wrapped her bloody body in his arms, held her close to his chest, and wept as she'd never seen him do before.

Joy raced through her soul. He had broken through the hate! She wrapped her arms around him and kissed him on the cheek. "Thank you, Nathan. I will always love you. You've freed me."

He smiled through the tears, and she nearly giggled with delight. He would be healed of his hate, and she could look forward to freedom. Then the whole scene vanished into blackness.

She eagerly waited for what would appear next. If it was the trees in his dream, she would be greatly disappointed. If it was anything else, she would rejoice.

The darkness swirled with red flames, then blew apart, leaving her standing in what appeared to be a cavern. A large hole in the center swirled with a bluish-red light. A man caught her attention, dressed in white that nearly blinded her eyes. Another man stood next to him, staring at her from a kindly face and black hair. She'd never seen either of them before.

The bright one smiled upon seeing her. "So, you've finally been freed from Beltrid's trap. Right on time, I might say."

Though relieved to be out of the dream trap, she sensed the time for rejoicing would still eluded her grasp. "Who are you?"

The man laughed. "I go by many names. But for you, let's just say I worked with Beltrid."

Her gut twisted. Not another demon! Yet, this demon radiated like a morning star. She suspected he didn't tell her the whole truth.

The bottom line, however, is she still wasn't free from this nightmare. "What happened to Beltrid?"

"The fool demon vanished into the void. He had his uses, but his approach lacked a more discreet mode of operation." The bright one turned to the man next to him. "We can use her as bait. Even now they are making plans to search for her. We can use her to trap the woman into violating her beliefs, and when she does, the ring will be ours."

The man glanced at Crystal and back to his master. "How can we use her for that?"

"I have a plan, but I need to tie up some dangling ends before I can say. Return to your post. I will send word when they approach."

Crystal scanned the area as they planned how they'd use her. An opening lay at one end of the cavern. Stairs ascended until she could see no more. It could be a way out.

She inched toward the door. The pair didn't appear to notice her progress, so she stepped further toward it. She reached halfway; the demon glanced her way, and then did a double-take.

She jumped and sped toward the opening. Before she could reach it, her feet left the stony floor and she hovered in mid-air. "Let me go! I can offer you nothing!"

He shook his head. "No, my dear, you cannot. That is why you are nothing more than a worm on a hook. I own you and have not released you. If you end up catching the ring for me though, you will have offered me everything."

"I won't help you do anything!" She jerked about helplessly.

"Does a worm will to be bait? I think not." He spread his arms.

Lightning arced across her body, sending her into a numbing consciousness. She opened her mouth to scream, but no sound arose from her throat. The fabric of her soul and body ripped thread by thread as if someone stabbed searing hot pins into every inch of her flesh. The cavern wavered and split in two. It took a couple of seconds through the pain before it dawned on her that she saw the scene from two sets of eyes.

When the ripping finished, her body collapsed onto the floor of the cavern and her soul hovered above it. She watched from her soul as her body rose. A blank stare shot from her eyes, and her face lost all expression.

The demon grinned. "Your soul will remain in Hades, while we use your body to lure them here." He turned to the man by his side. "Take her to Circo who lives several miles outside Spinard. Tell him she's his reward for the service he provided the last time. Her soul I will keep here."

"Yes, master." He grabbed Crystal's hand and her body followed him as if she were a horse led with a bit.

The bright one examined her for a moment. "You will join the rest of the souls. I may call for you later." He flung a hand toward the pit.

A force sucked her into the glowing hole—a swirling vortex of souls trapped in a blue-red tunnel leading deep into...wherever she was. Death sank over her; despair filled her being as if something of substance. Hopelessness cascaded across her. She would have cried if it were possible for a soul.

Another soul brushed against her. Sadness filled his eyes. *Don't give up hope. There is one who can free us.*

She only stared, but didn't respond. She could think of nothing to say, but she recognized faith when she saw it. Nathan held that kind of undying faith, and his sister, Kaylee. But would he find her here?

Nathan placed his hand on my shoulder. "Kaylee, are you sure you're all right going in there alone?"

I eyed the ring on my finger. "I'll be fine. The ring will protect me." Already it had protected me from death several times, just as it had Dad all the years he wore it.

Nathan stepped onto the wooden walkway as a horse trotted past us, kicking up dust. The low rumble of chatting voices among the clusters of buyers, sellers, and onlookers caused us to raise our voices to talk.

Nathan pointed at me. "It better. I'd hate to lose you."

I smiled. "Oh really? I didn't know you cared."

He winked. "Me? Care? You misunderstand, Sis. We're a team. I need you to help me find Crystal."

"In other words, all I'm good for is turning you into a winged horse, eh?"

He chuckled. "All right! I care!" His smile faded. "But seriously, if you need—"

I held my hand up. "I told you, I'll be fine." I patted my sword. "I can fend for myself. Besides, the sun will dip below the horizon soon and we still have two taverns left to check. If we finish them tonight and find news of Crystal's whereabouts, we can leave first thing in the morning."

He sighed. "You're right. I do hope we can find a lead on her. I'm tired of dead-ends. I fear for her if we're too late."

I laid my hand on his shoulder. "With Beltrid out of the way, she's probably fine. It's just a matter of catching up to her."

Nathan's face grew dark at the mention of Beltrid's name. "Beltrid's not the only demon in Satan's control. I can't rest until I know she's really free."

"Of course. I didn't mean to make light—"

"Say no more. I know you were trying to help." He glanced down the road. "I'll meet you back at the inn." He turned and dodged the crowd as he progressed to the north end of Spinard.

I spun around and spotted a sign a few feet down the street that read *Wagon Wheel Tavern*. I flowed with the bodies to the building and entered.

Half the tables lay empty. As I stepped across the floor the chatter died down and several eyes followed me. I tried to ignore them, but their stares bored into my back. I approached the bar and glanced around. The chatter resumed and most of the patrons returned to their mugs and conversation.

"I'm honored to have such a sweet damsel visit our fine tavern."

I spun my gaze back to the bar.

A young man, not much older than twenty-one, grinned at me from across the counter. He placed a hand over his heart. "Can I get you something? Ale? Whiskey? A good time in bed? The last would be on the house." He leaned over, his eyebrows raised high as if trying to charm me.

I released a breath slowly. Why did I have to be subjected to such men? "Just information if you have it. I'm searching for a girl. Long, midnight-black hair. Eyes of coal. A slender figure and a thin face."

He plopped his chin into upraised hands, his elbows resting on the counter. "You're the only girl I can think of. What's your name?"

I sighed. Some people didn't know when to quit! I'd have to take a firmer hand with this one. I grabbed the edge of the counter and swung my feet into the air as my back rolled across the top of the bar. I kicked his chest with my falling feet and landed on his side of the bar. He staggered back, giving me time to wrap my arm around his throat from behind.

I squeezed and he choked. He tried to pry my arm off. "Lady, please!"

I smiled. "Oh, am I a lady now?"

I applied more pressure and he wheezed out, "I can't breathe."

A nice shade of red spread across his face. I glanced around to see several watching the spectacle. As long as they didn't interfere, I didn't care.

I relaxed my grip so he could talk. "Now, about that information I requested..."

He coughed a couple of times. "Lady, do you know how many travelers come through here each week? There's about five I recall that could fit that description of late."

"She goes by the name of Crystal."

He paused. "Yes, I do recall a man and woman in here not too long ago. I believe he called her Crystal."

"Go on."

He answered in an apologetic tone. "That's all I recall. He didn't say his name or where they were going."

I flexed my muscles again. He coughed but managed to say, "I don't know anything else."

A voice sounded over the bar. "Ma'am, if you'll stop choking that kid, I'll give you more information on this girl you're seeking."

I turned to meet his eyes. A man of medium build and black beard stood watching me. He held a mug of ale in one hand and a pipe in the other with which he pointed out the door. "I did some business with this man. His name's Circo."

I smiled at the man. "Gladly." I grabbed the barkeep's hair, then released my hold and tossed him away. "Next time it will be my sword to your neck. It's not as forgiving as my arm."

He stumbled back and rubbed his throat. His eyes stared at me as if sizing up my words. He nodded. "Would you like an ale? On the house."

I swung myself back over the bar. "No thanks. I'm not thirsty."

The man led me to his table. I sat and listened to his story, asking questions at key spots. He had seen Crystal and knew where they had gone. Nathan would be excited to hear this. But politeness demanded we chatted for a good hour and a half before I felt comfortable excusing myself. He appeared to enjoy my company, and I felt I owed him that much at least.

Nathan set a cup in front of me, coffee from the kitchen. He sipped his brew; the mug clicked on the wooden table as he set it down. "Kaylee, I felt you were in trouble."

"Brother-sister link, I guess. Just a very forward barkeep. I dealt with him well enough."

"No, more than that. I felt it, could almost see it. I think it's the bracelets. They link us together. Especially when you put yours on, I can sense where you are all the time. But even when yours isn't on, I can still sense you, feel your fear when it becomes strong."

I glanced at the bracelet on his wrist. "Makes sense. If you lose the ability to be a winged horse five miles away from me, you'd better know where I am when you're flying around."

He smiled. "I guess so." He pointed at the ring on my finger. "But I didn't come to help. You said the ring would protect you."

I held it up. The candle-light flickered off the gold surface, highlighting the Hebrew inscription, "It is more blessed to give than to receive." Dad had received it from the steam house in Reol, and for a time it had given him the ability to do miracles for those who needed it. But then he passed it on to me. Memories of Dad flashed through me, especially his joy when he left us for Paradise. Thinking about him calmed me.

I breathed deep. "It prevents anyone from taking it, or killing me, but it doesn't mean it will prevent bad things from happening." I sat up straighter. "However, I discovered some news about Crystal."

His eyes widened. "Really? What?"

"I described her to the barkeep in the tavern, and he recalls seeing her with a man who called her Crystal. Another man in the tavern had chatted with a man named Circo who owns her. He said Crystal's expression looked odd."

"Odd? In what way?"

"That's all he said about it. Oh, and he remembered the man saying something about heading to Paradise."

He wrinkled his brow. "Paradise?"

"A town named Paradise, not the real thing."

"Oh." Nathan stared blankly at the wall.

I waited for a reaction, but he only stared. I knocked on the table. "I thought you'd be more excited."

He jerked his head back and blinked. "I am."

"Something's on your mind. What gives?"

He glanced at me before staring at the wall again. "Just remembering that dream where you helped me free Crystal from my hate."

I placed a hand on his. "You feel guilty?"

He breathed in. "How can I not? Killing her over and over, hating her. If it hadn't been for you and the ring coming into my dream, I might still be killing her in my sleep now."

"You didn't know. Beltrid's deception is to blame, not you."

He frowned. "I suppose you're right. Still, the feeling is there all the same. And it's why I need to find her, make sure she's really free." He turned his head to face me. "One thing I've been meaning to ask you, is how did you know? What did I miss?"

My mind returned to the scene in the dream. "Her eyes."

He raised an eyebrow. "Her eyes? What did you see?"

"Remember when Beltrid had possessed her and you nearly married Beltrid thinking you were marrying Crystal?"

He nodded.

"When Beltrid 'changed' from her into himself, for a brief second her eyes softened and a genuine horror flashed from them before his form overtook hers. I didn't know what it meant at the time, but when I saw Crystal again in your dream, with that same expression, I realized that she wasn't an illusion of Beltrid, but a real person he'd possessed."

Nathan nodded and refocused on the wall. "You have a knack for noticing details like that." He sighed. "Wish I did."

I placed a hand on his shoulder. "Whatever the case, we have to let the past be the past. Focus on the future. And right now, that future says we have a solid lead on where Crystal is for the first time. You should forgive yourself, rejoice, not wallow in guilt."

A smile creased his lips. "Yes, you are right. Tomorrow we'll leave Spinard behind us and head toward Paradise. I hope this lead turns out to be her."

"Me too. I'll be glad when we've found her and know she's safe."

He rose from his chair. "Then I suggest we get some sleep. We'll head out first thing in the morning. Right after we find out where Paradise is."

My legs felt firm as I stood up. "Paradise is just one quick blow of my sword away, Brother."

He chuckled. "But you'd have to get past my sword first."

Gabrielle clutched Josh's arm as the priest said, "From dust you came, and to dust you will return." Had her life come down to dust? Empty and pointless? She glanced at Jake. He had taken care of his parents for so long. She'd only helped him a little more than a month and a half. How much harder for him to watch his own parents buried? Yet, he didn't show it on his face.

And Josh, her dead husband's best friend, had protected them for many years while Sisko and she had lived miles away. His eyes drooped more than usual, but like Jake, he stared into the empty void of death with stoic bravery. Or shock.

The pall bearers lowered the bodies into the earth. Father Jonah said the final words as dirt fell upon the caskets. She whispered to them, "May your journey to Paradise be swift and sweet."

Death—she grew tired of its intrusion into her life of late. First her husband and now his parents. Who would be next? Must she watch as everyone she cared for dive into the next life ahead of her?

Josh nudged her arm. "Why don't we go back to the house now?"

Gabrielle nodded. As they strolled toward the village, she turned and caught Josh's eyes. "What now? Why am I here?"

He frowned. "Don't talk like that. You sound as if you're ready to die yourself."

"I stayed in Reol to help Jake care for his parents. Now they're gone, and I don't feel I have much reason to be here."

"You'll find something."

"You don't understand. All my life I've taken care of someone. First my father and brother who flew into uncontrollable rages. Then Sisko, then the kids. Sisko's passed on to the next life, the kids are out running around the countryside. Sisko's parents were the last in my care. Now, I've no one."

He paused on the hillside, overlooking Reol. Gabrielle's eyes surveyed the green forest, blocking the chill of the wind. The buildings barely peeked through the trees. Wooden houses and other buildings filled the quaint village.

Josh sighed. "You haven't gotten over Sisko's death yet. It is to be expected, it will take time."

"Does one ever get over such things?" She shook her head. "I know what you're saying, but while I'm sad he's not with me, I'm happy for him because I know he's where he wanted to be. What I'm talking about is what am I supposed to do now? Sitting here is pointless, waiting for death to pounce to my door and swallow me up. I can't simply hang around and wait for the end of this life."

Josh pulled her around to face him. He studied her eyes. "You're sort of old for this, but perhaps you should consider entering the steam house."

Gabrielle felt a wave of shivers roll over her. She'd never considered entering it. She feared what it would do to her. But the more she thought about it, the more right it grew. "You might be right. It could show me my purpose, even as it did for Sisko and my children."

He nodded. "Think about it."

Gabrielle knocked on the door of the rectory, and it opened to reveal Father Jonah's big smile.

"Ah, Gabrielle. What can I do for you?"

She held out her hand for a blessing, and he laid his in hers and blessed her as she kissed it.

"Father, thank you for seeing me on short notice."

"I'm always available, child. Come on in and sit down."

Gabrielle sat at the small table while Father Jonah busied himself making tea.

She watched as he pulled a pot off the fire and poured hot water into cups. "First, I want to thank you for the funeral. Your words were a comfort."

"All for my Master."

She drew a breath. "And I wanted your blessing to enter the steam house."

He raised an eyebrow as he placed tea leaves in the cups. "The steam house, eh?"

She nodded. "Now that Sisko's parents have died, an emptiness has settled over me. An emptiness that cries for me to fill it, to accomplish an unfulfilled task. But I don't know what it might be. It's left me very restless."

He fingered his beard. "And so you think the steam house will reveal what you should be doing?"

"That's my hope."

"You know the purpose of the steam house?"

Gabrielle nodded. "Sisko often talked about it, and I've heard the story of his experience in there more than once. If I understand it right, it reveals the strengths and weaknesses of one's character."

"Yes." Father Jonah touched his chest. "We often keep hidden the demons that reside deep within because we don't want to see them. We don't want to deal with them. The steam house brings those to the surface and forces one to face them. And potentially cleanse them if one's heart is open to it."

He removed the leaves from the cups and set one before her, but said before releasing it, "Are you prepared to see the demons within yourself?"

She chewed on her lower lip. "I...I think I am."

He shook his head as he sat. "Not good enough. If you're scared of what's inside, it will bite you. If you face it with trust in God, it can be cast out and healed."

Gabrielle sipped the tea. Its warmth strengthened her will. She focused on Father Jonah's eyes. "I do want to go in the steam house. If I'm to die, I want to die working on my sins or fulfilling God's calling. Please give me your blessing."

He studied her face and took a sip of tea. Then he closed his eyes and faced the ceiling as if communicating directly with God. And for all Gabrielle knew, he did.

While he stayed in this posture for at least a minute, Gabrielle drank her tea and waited. Would God approve, or decide she should live out the rest of her life sitting around, doing nothing? She hoped not the latter.

Father Jonah opened his eyes and stared at her. "It is good that you came to me first."

"I knew enough that such an encounter shouldn't be done on one's own will. That inserts pride into the mix right from the beginning."

He nodded and smiled. "Sisko always was a great judge of character. It shouldn't be surprising that he would chose a wife who is his equal." Father's smile faded and his jaw set. "What you'll find in the steam house will be a purpose, but you'll not find it pleasant or easy. Yet the role you'll play will be of eternal significance to many people."

Gabrielle sat back in her chair. Eternal significance? Could one person really have such an impact? "How can I do such a great task? I've no powers like Sisko, or skill with magic like Josh."

A smile broke through his beard. "You would be surprised at how a small act can have eternal significance. You need not worry about how, only follow what God shows you to do." He leaned over the table. "The steam house will reveal how to spend your life for Him. But it will not be what you expect, and the road before you is hard."

She blew into the cup and sipped as she pondered his words, then sat up in her chair. "What can I say, Father? If so many depend on my actions, how can I say no? I must go, no matter how hard it is."

He nodded slowly and extended his hand. "You've spoken well. May God give you strength and courage." He signed the cross as he said, "You have my blessing to enter the steam house, and my prayers go with you."

Relief swept over her; she'd stepped closer to ending this emptiness. But she felt a weight settling upon her as well. Up until this point, such a purpose had always been the domain of Sisko, and now Kaylee and Nathan. What part she would play in all this remained a mystery, but she resolved to follow what the steam house revealed. Nothing would stand in her way.

3

The demon peered into steaming water at his servant. "She's on her way. Get her to violate her beliefs, then bring me the ring."

"Yes, my Lord. But what if she will not?"

He gritted his teeth. "Have you ever heard of temptation? You provide the motivation. Convince her through pride. It never fails."

"Ah, there was that one time—"

"Enough! Don't fail." He ended the connection and gnawed on a fingernail. "How dare he bring up that one exception." The man wouldn't last long.

I never tired of flying with Nathan. The village of Spinard fell into the distance as Nathan carried me through the heavens. Flirting with the clouds and birds soothed my fears. Trees and hills filled the landscape below us, hiding behind clouds passing under us. Rivers and lakes sparkled in the late morning sunlight. The narrow road below guided us.

Flying horses were rare. A creation of magic. Even deep magic. Ever since Joel had provided winged horses to escape the flying island, I'd wanted one. But I never imagined my brother would become one. But he did, thanks to the steam house, and my dream became reality.

After a couple of hours, a city appeared on the horizon. Its brilliance surprised me. I figured it must be the way the sun shone off it. I patted Nathan's thick, white neck as his wings beat out a steady rhythm, often pausing to glide a ways on an updraft.

"Looks like Paradise ahead. You should find a place to set down soon."

Already picked out a spot, Sis.

We realized early on that flying into a city created too much attention, especially when Nathan changed from a winged horse back into his human form. Fewer problems resulted from landing well outside of town to effect the change.

I leaned over to whisper in his right ear. "Of course, I wouldn't mind staying up here longer if you want to fly around a bit more."

But Crystal—

"I know, if she's there, we'll find her." I patted his left thigh. The funny thought struck me that a similar action done to the human Nathan would have resulted in a more unpleasant reaction.

He glided downward. Details of the trees grew distinct, and the landscape took on character. We flew over a lone traveler on the road who bolted for the trees upon seeing us. I couldn't help but laugh wondering what thoughts ran through his mind.

In a few minutes, the brilliance of the city sank into the horizon before Nathan's hooves touched the ground. He galloped as he folded his wings back, then slowed to a halt. I slid off him and stepped a few feet away. His change always resulted in a very bright light, and I had learned to keep my distance when it happened.

I snapped the bracelet off my wrist. I shielded my eyes as a whiteness flashed around Nathan and dimmed, leaving my brother in human form standing before me.

He flung his shoulder length hair behind him and scratched his short beard. "Changing always feels a little strange. Sort of like getting stretched out and snapped back into place."

"I can only imagine." I winked at him. "Are you hungry? I am. How about let's pause to eat before we get into town. I have some dried meats and cheese in my pack."

"Sounds good."

We found a stump on the side of the road to sit on, and soon chewed on smoked meat and cheese, downing it with wine. My joy in flying through the sky had hidden my growing hunger. We ate without

19

conversation.

The sound of shuffling pots and pans echoed down the road and a man pulling a horse loaded with supplies rounded a corner.

As he approached, he stopped and bowed. "Servantes at your service. Trader of fine wares and supplies. You two perhaps need anything I can provide?"

Nathan shook his head. "No thanks. We're fine."

He cocked his head to one side. "Where are you headed, if you don't mind my asking?"

I glanced at Nathan. We didn't intend to keep our intentions a secret. The more we ask, the more information we might obtain. I met Servantes' eyes. "We're headed to Paradise."

His mouth fell open, and his eyes widened. "Oh, I wouldn't go there if I were you."

"But you are. Why not?"

"I'm going around Paradise, not through it. Those are strange people. I'd stay away from them. You're as likely to end up dead as trapped there."

I wondered if they called the town Paradise for how fast it could get one there. "But we're tracking a girl named Crystal. Dark hair flowing down past her shoulders, narrow face, black eyes. Last we heard, she traveled with a man of bulky build. Have you seen them?"

He shook his head. "No, can't say I have. I did see a winged horse flying overhead a mile or two back. Scared the living daylights out of me. Did you see it?"

I suppressed a laugh. "No, we didn't." After all, we didn't see it. We were it.

Nathan swallowed the last of his cheese. "We have reason to believe that this girl we're tracking is in Paradise. So in we will go."

He clicked his tongue. "I don't envy you then. But it's your life."

I stood and shouldered my pack. "Mind if we travel with you, at least until our trails part?"

He smiled. "I'll be glad for the company."

We headed down the dusty trail, chatting about the news abroad, of which he held many opinions.

Servantes departed down a well-traveled road that he said led around the town. The road into Paradise narrowed. Grass grew up on the trail as if few ever ventured this way. Branches from the trees overhung the path, creating a tunnel toward the city. Sparkles flashed through the branches and I realized that the sun didn't provide its brightness. The angle we approached from should have us in the shadow of its walls, but light beamed all around us.

Nathan and I said nothing as we drew near. The tunnel of trees ended at a clearing, and a few feet away a city wall glowed with colors. Blues, reds, yellows and greens, all shone with a light of their own. Whites especially blasted forth, as if radiance exuded from its being.

I broke the silence. "I guess this is why they call the place Paradise."

Nathan nodded as we entered the open gate. "Yet, something's missing. It doesn't feel the same as what I felt from Father in the steam house."

"You're right." He had spoken what lay under my thoughts. "This isn't real. It feels...artificial." My mind returned to the events a little over two months ago, when Nathan and I had entered the steam house in hopes of freeing Dad from the demon Beltrid. Instead Beltrid had killed him. But within the steam house, his death had revealed the glory of Paradise within him. And with it, Beltrid had vanished into the abyss. But the memory of the divine light flowing over me would never leave, and the brightness of this city simply didn't measure up to the real thing.

Yet, I kept wondering how such a radiance could shine from a city like this. Magic? Or maybe some very unusual paint? Every house blasted brilliance around me; colors literally jumped at me. Instead of feeling like I could never get enough like I did in the steam house, this had already become tiresome. But to find Crystal, we would endure it.

Several people moved about, and like the buildings, their clothing radiated brilliance. I squinted simply to avoid running into something or someone. Yet the people ignored us, as if we didn't exist.

"Mister?"

I swung my head around to the source of the voice and saw a child tugging on Nathan's trousers. Everyone ignored us, except for this kid.

Nathan jumped, and then addressed the boy. "Yes, son?"

"Why are you so dull?"

A giggle escaped my lips, though I knew what the boy meant. We did stand out amongst all this brightness like a sore thumb.

Nathan knelt. "We're not from here, but we're searching for a girl. Have you seen a strange girl around here? Maybe as dull as we are?"

He pointed at me. "You don't belong here."

Nathan met my eyes and shrugged.

"John Zolo, you get over here right now!"

A stern-faced woman in a brilliant blue dress, her hair tied back into a bun, stomped toward us.

"Mommy, are these the bad people?"

She grabbed John's arm and pulled him away, glaring at us over her shoulder.

Nathan stepped forward to follow her. "Ma'am, please. Can you tell me if a girl has been here recently?"

She turned her head and I knew Nathan wouldn't be getting an answer from her. "Come on, let's see if we can find a priest in this place."

He grunted and pointed. "Don't suppose he could be around the big, shiny, golden dome with a cross on it over there?"

I winked at him. "I think you're onto something."

We strolled through the streets toward the church building. A few people glanced sideways at us and hurried on their way. Servantes was right. These people were awfully strange. But I wondered in what way the town threatened our lives? So far, nothing suggested that.

"Strangers, what brings you to our city?" a voice behind us said.

I spun around to find a priest with several others. I squinted at them. Despite their cold greeting, at least someone finally decided to say hi instead of avoiding us.

Nathan bowed to the priest. "We are in search of a woman named Crystal. About twenty years old, dark hair, narrow fa—"

"Yes, she's been here."

Nathan's eyes brightened. "Can you tell me where she is?"

The priest strolled up toward Nathan to examine him closer. "Are you affiliated with that woman?"

Nathan sighed. "Long story, but I guess the short answer is yes. I'm desperate to find her. I'm afraid for her safety."

The priest turned his gaze toward me. "And you are a strange girl. Have you carried a sword all your life?"

His question took me by surprise. "Uh, well, yeah. Most of my life since about thirteen."

"And do you ever wear dresses?"

I glanced at Nathan who appeared as confused as I felt. "Only when I have to. Sort of hard to ride a horse in one."

Nathan breathed deep. "Father, please. Can you tell me where Crystal is. I must find her."

He answered Nathan without meeting his eyes. "The man with her, we put to death."

I gasped. "Why? What did he do?"

The priest stared at me. "He wasn't perfect. Much like yourself."

A glimpse of what Servantes meant sank in. I stared at the priest in shock.

"The girl," he continued. "We sold her as a slave to a passing caravan outside the city."

Nathan scowled. "Why the man and not the girl?"

The priest frowned. "We are not in the habit of killing innocents who know not what they do."

"What do you mean by that?"

The priest pointed at us. "She is not the issue here. You two are. We must remain pure of those who do not shine with the light of God."

I raised an eyebrow. "And how exactly do we do that?"

He paused for a second, staring into my eyes, before he answered. His lips twitched on the edges ever so slightly. "You go through the dipping ritual."

"Baptism? I've already been baptized."

He shook his head. "No, you have not. Not until you've been baptized here!" He spread his hands outward. "And once done, you live your remaining days within the perfection of these walls. In the next life, you'll notice no difference."

Nathan stomped his foot. "You'll notice a difference all right. A big difference!"

The priest drew closer. "And how would you know, dull as you are?"

Nathan's eyes blazed with energy and a smile crept across his lips. "Because I've experienced the real thing. This is a fake!"

The priest's face grew red. "I'll not be lectured by a false prophet! You will die for your blasphemy!"

Nathan laid his hand on his sword. But he hesitated for the same reason I did. It didn't feel right to pull a sword on a priest.

The priest motioned to the men around him. "Arrest these two. They will be put to death. They are not perfect."

I cried out, "Who is?"

He squinted at me. "Why, we are of course. Shouldn't that be obvious? That you can't see it is evidence enough."

Arms held my hands behind my back and they pulled my sword from its sheath. Three men also bound Nathan's hands.

"Please, Father," I pleaded. "We're on a mission from God. I'm a healer. Don't make this mistake."

He huffed. "Would God give such a gift to a woman? I think not. Your trickery ends here."

The men yanked us down the street. I glanced at Nathan who struggled helplessly against them. I knew they couldn't kill me, but if they executed Nathan while I was bound and couldn't heal him, he would die. I prayed God would help me stop this injustice.

As if a spell had turned us visible, the people gathered along the street staring at us with beady eyes and scowls. Some shouted, "Kill the imperfect." Others said, "Eradicate the contagion!" They chanted with such precision and unity that I wondered if someone behind a curtain somewhere pulled their strings.

Among the yells and cries of the gathering crowd, I saw the kid we'd met earlier, staring wide-eyed at me. I couldn't help but wonder what he thought of these proceedings, but I feared this served as an example of what happened to the "imperfect" ones who didn't conform to the group and their way of thinking.

They pulled us into town square, and in the midst of the opening stood four blocks. They shoved us down on two of them and latched our heads in place as we knelt over them.

The crowd fell silent when the priest raised his hand. "The Holy Book says that a sickness must be fully purged if the whole is to remain sound." He pointed a finger at us. "These two are not part of our perfection. They radiate no light, the girl wears provocative clothing and carries a sword, and claims to be working for God!"

The crowd burst into murmurs, and heads nodded in agreement.

The priest strolled in front and studied us. He pointed at Nathan. "This one shall be first."

I jerked against my bonds. "No, you can't! Kill me first."

He leaned down and stared into my eyes. "And why should I?"

I internally kicked myself. Subtly wasn't my strong suit. "I—" My eyes met his. "—I don't want to watch him die."

He considered my request for a moment, then rose. "Maybe I should kill you first. I am not cruel."

Nathan raised his head. "No! Kill me first!"

"Nathan!" I cast narrow eyes toward him, hoping he would realize my plan.

The priest smiled. "Yes, I think the boy is right. I should execute him first." He motioned to the man standing next to Nathan.

The muscular arms drew back, raising the brilliant axe into the deep blue sky.

"Wait!" I shoved myself over and the block rocked under me. "Don't we at least get a last request?"

The priest held up his hand as the axe-handler started to surge forth but held back. The priest stood before Nathan. "We are not unjust. You are granted one last request before we execute your sentence."

Nathan ground his teeth together, but managed to say, "Where did the caravan take Crystal? Where did they go?"

The priest chuckled. "A strange request for one about to die. But very well. The caravan said their next stop was Morgoth." He bent down to stare into my eyes. "And you, young lady. What is your final request?"

I could think of nothing I needed except a way to get out of this. If I should die today, I would soon be in Paradise with Dad. What else did I need? I bit my lip, stretching this out in hopes an idea would come to me. But what? How could I use the ring to help these people? What did they need? If I could—

"Nothing?" The priest motioned to Nathan's executor. "Then continue to carry out the sentence."

"Father, wait! I know what I want." An idea finally did arrive. "I have a bracelet hanging from my neck. It's special to me. I would like to die with it on my arm, if you don't mind."

"Fair enough." He motioned and a man pulled the chain from under my tunic, took the bracelet off and snapped it onto my arm.

I heard Nathan mumble, "Upwards," and a bright light blasted from him, sending those around him onto their backs. Nathan the brilliant white, winged horse stood before them. He even outshone his surroundings. Real Paradise!

Everyone froze in shock. Nathan banged his hoof upon the latch holding my neck down, shattering it open. I scrambled to my feet and leaped toward his back, but with my hands tied behind my back, my legs lost their grip, and I landed back onto the ground, knocking the air from me.

Someone in the crowd broke the silence. "He's brighter than Paradise!"

"No!" The priest waved his hands toward the crowd. "It's a trick of magic. You saw him change yourselves! A wizard he is!"

Hold on, Sis. This won't be easy. Nathan gathered the ropes binding my hands into his mouth and launched himself into the air.

I heard the priest yell, "Shoot them down!"

Nathan gained altitude and speed, but I could tell the unnatural angle he flew in order to maintain balance would wear him out quickly. Seconds passed, then I heard arrows whizzing past us. The city wall passed underneath us.

Ouch!

"What happened?"

I've been hit, in my right thigh.

His wings beat harder and soon the arrows failed to reach us.

"How are you holding up?"

My rear's on fire with pain, and I don't know how much longer I can hold you.

I choked. "Don't drop me!"

Sis, I'm hurt that you think I would.

"I don't think you would. But where the spirit is willing, the flesh may be weak."

Okay, okay. We're going down.

He flapped down toward the road, which I deduced led to Morgoth since no other road left Paradise other than it and the one we'd entered on. Nathan attempted a spot landing and flapped his wings hard as we neared the ground.

Argh! He said as his feet touched down. He dropped me into a heap on the ground. I gritted my teeth from the effort of rising; my shoulders burned with searing pain from the odd angle Nathan had carried me.

We may not have much time. No telling whether they will come after us or not. We can't stay here long.

I twisted my mouth. "I don't think they can bear to set foot in this corrupt world outside their city walls. But you never know." I spun around. "See if you can chew these ropes off my hands."

He lowered his head behind me and gnawed at my binds. Within a couple minutes, the ropes loosened.

"Whew. Glad to get that off."

Mind dealing with my wound now? It's burning like a fire. He shifted his right rear until it faced me.

I examined the wound. Dried blood caked the opening, but a slow ooze still dripped from it. "Did I ever tell you, Brother, that you have a nice rear."

Shut up and heal me, will ya?

"For a horse." I laughed.

He turned his head around and I could swear I saw a frown on his mouth. "Okay, okay. Hold still." I laid my hand by his wound, the arrow jiggling slightly with the beating of his heart.

"Lord, heal Nathan's wound."

The swelling shrank, the skin pushed the arrow out until it plopped upon the ground. The scar dwindled until it vanished into the smooth hairs covering his thigh. "There, all better."

He bounced on his foot tentatively, then with more force. *Great! Good job, Sis.*

"You hungry?" I reached into my pack.

Yeah, but we need to gain some distance from Paradise, and it will be night soon. I'm eager to make good time. Hopefully we can catch up to the caravan at Morgoth.

"Oh no!" I banged my forehead with my palm.

What?

"My sword! It's still in Paradise."

So's mine, but I'm not going back to get it.

I struggled to not think about it, but it intruded on my mind nonetheless. "But it is my...I mean, I've used it to..."

It's your security blanket.

I nodded. "I feel unprotected without it."

But you have the ring, isn't that enough?

I breathed deep. "It should be, you're right." I swallowed, hoping I could swallow down the sense of doom creeping up my spine. "I'll just have to deal with it. Let's get going."

I climbed on his back, and he jumped into the air. Catching the wind upon his pure white wings, we rose into the evening sky.

Gabrielle waited as two teen girls entered the steam house. She stepped inside with a firm resolve to face whatever she would discover within its walls, good or bad. She had little to lose and everything to gain.

Sisko's stories flowed back to her as she settled down on a bench that ran the circumference of the octagonal building. A muscular man who became flabby. A promiscuous man who turned into a tree. Another depressed man who melted into a shadow. Would one of those be her fate? Or would she discover what to spend the rest of her life doing?

A low fire licked a pile of rocks in the center. She watched as a lady poured water over the rocks and steam sizzled into the air.

She glanced at the women around the building, and couldn't see anything particularly interesting happening to them. From all appearances, she sat in an average, small-town steam house.

"You're Gabrielle, Sisko's wife, aren't you?"

Gabrielle turned to see a portly woman sitting next to her. Her eyes shown with expectation. "Yes, I am. And you are?"

"Sarah's my name." She reached out a hand. "Sure is an honor to sit next to you. Who knows, maybe you'll be able to do miracles. That's why you're here, isn't it?"

Gabrielle stared at the woman as she shook her hand. "No, why would I be here for that?"

"Why would you?" She wrinkled her brow. "Ever since Sisko gained the ability to do miracles from the steam house, everyone who enters wonders whether they will be the next to receive such a gift. Many have come here from afar in hopes of getting a ring like his."

"And has anyone?"

A frown spread across her face. "Well, no. But it's bound to happen again."

Gabrielle shook her head. "That's just it. If it ever did happen again, it wouldn't happen to someone looking for it. Sisko didn't come in here seeking a miracle ring. And most of these people don't know the dangers and pitfalls of being a miracle worker either. If they did, they would thank God every day that He didn't give them such a 'gift.'"

Sarah stared at the ground as if having never considered such before. Then she met Gabrielle's eyes. "If so, you're a prime candidate for getting such a ring."

Gabrielle stared at the woman. She doubted such a gift would ever be duplicated. Father Jonah had said God granted according to one's character, and she wasn't Sisko. It wouldn't be the same. But now she wondered whether something similar might be her fate.

Sarah contented herself with sitting in silence. Mumbled chatter floated with the steam through the building. Gabrielle's eyes focused on the fire lapping at the water, vaporizing it into the air. As she stared, the fire grew brighter.

She glanced around to see if anyone else had noticed it. No one paid any attention. "Sarah, does the fire look normal to you?"

She checked it out. "Yes. Don't see anything odd about it."

Gabrielle stared at the fire again, and it grew bigger. She couldn't believe no one else could see this. Then the fire's brightness blossomed forth until it filled the room, blotting out everything else.

As the pure whiteness flooded her vision, she felt air rushing across her cheeks and buoyancy within her body, yet she still felt the bench under her. She gripped its edge with her hands, the only solid object she could feel. The blinding light dimmed to reveal hills and trees thousands of feet down. A river wound through the valley, and small lakes dotted the countryside. Her whole body tensed as shock froze her in the face of death.

She breathed hard as the scene dropped toward treetops upon a large hill, then swooped upwards, creating a feeling of leaving her stomach behind. She gulped air trying to control the desire to scream. She couldn't tell whether she succeeded or not.

A winged horse and a girl riding atop it slid into her view.

Kaylee and Nathan!

Behind them, a darkness dank with evil sped toward them. Gabrielle knew death rode upon its wings as clearly as she saw Nathan flying.

Nathan, Kaylee! Watch out!

The darkness overtook them. She watched in helplessness as it knocked Kaylee off Nathan's back, and Nathan spun out of control. They both fell from the sky.

Gabrielle willed herself to shoot toward them. *I'm coming, Kaylee! Hold on, Nathan!* She ignored the fear and reached out her shaking hand as she approached Kaylee flailing through the air. The treetops approached fast, but Gabrielle felt she would make it. Kaylee's outstretched hand dropped inches away. Gabrielle forced herself to grab her arm as the trees rushed to meet them.

The scene vanished; another landscape filled the void. Relatively flat land raced under her at speeds she felt would certainly kill most people. Low trees dotted the ground and she passed over a wide marsh as a river branched out to empty into a sea to her right.

Her pulse raced as she sank until she flew a few feet over the ground. Trees flashed by before she could get a good view of them. Travelers on the road flinched as she blazed past them.

A vast body of water appeared as she approached the edge of a cliff. She tensed as the drop raced toward her, but she still jumped and screamed when she flew over it and dropped over a city. She didn't have enough time to soak in any details, but instead swooped down until a few feet over the water, leaving the city behind her.

An island appeared in the sea. The scene slowed as she rose above the trees. She judged one could cross the land mass on foot in one day. As her pulse beat in her ears, she crested a group of trees and a clearing emerged. A thin, armored demon with sword in hand, stood before a black and leafless tree. A unfamiliar man held Kaylee bound and shoved her toward the demon.

The demon plunged his sword into her.

"No! No! No! Kaylee!"

Kaylee sank to the ground; blood spread from her limp body.

How could this happen? Wouldn't the ring have protected her? Gabrielle wailed, "Don't tell me this is my fate, to lose my children and be left totally alone!"

The scene faded into brilliance, and a man approached dressed in pure white. Sorrow gazed into her eyes. "Speak the truth, and you will uncover reality even as the steam house does."

She couldn't stop crying, but his peace and calm did have an effect. "Is Kaylee to die, then?"

"We all must die in this life sometime."

"But she's too young. She's not even twenty yet." Gabrielle wiped the tears from her eyes.

"What you saw is what could be if you fail to act. Kaylee will need you. Seek her out. For if what you see comes to pass, many more will suffer."

"What do you mean?"

The brilliance fractured. "Just speak the truth."

"Who are you? How can I know this is real and true?"

He grinned. "My name is Joel."

Sounds of women's chatter broke into her mind, and the vision vaporized like steam into a bright sky.

"Honey, are you okay?" Sarah waved a fan over her. A group of women stared down at her, mouths open. She lay outside the steam house on the dirt road.

Gabrielle blinked her eyes and wiped more wetness from them. She sat up. A few seconds passed before she could think to respond. "I don't know. How did I get out here?"

"You were hallucinating, dear. Screaming and all. Bad news in there, so we hauled you out. We were afraid you'd lost it."

Gabrielle stared at them. "Thanks." She stood up and wondered how to go about finding Nathan and Kaylee. "Josh!" She shot down the road toward his house, leaving a group of bewildered women.

How could she make a difference? How could she prevent Kaylee from dying? She didn't know, but she would do everything in her power to change it.

She breathed hard as she raced to Josh's house in the country. After several long minutes, she burst into the clearing and sped to the front door. Gabrielle flung it open and jumped in.

Josh glanced up from a book he was reading by the fireplace. "Ah, you're back. How did the steam house go?"

"We have to find Nathan and Kaylee. Now!"

Josh set his book down. "Find Kaylee and Nathan? Why?"

"They're in danger. Kaylee will die if I don't find her. That's what the

31

steam house revealed."

Josh scratched his head. "How did it reveal this to you? I've never heard of it doing anything like that before."

Gabrielle paced the floor and took a deep breath. "I saw a vision, a vision of Kaylee dying."

"A vision you say? How long did you see Kaylee dying? Maybe the ring heals her?"

"No, no. He said she would die."

Josh shook his head. "He? He who?"

Gabrielle stopped pacing and faced Josh. "Someone in my vision. Said his name was Joel."

Josh's eyes widened and he sat up straighter. "Joel, huh?"

"What? You know him?"

Josh sighed. "Yes. He provides me with tea."

"Tea? Look, this is serious. Kaylee will die." She realized her breathing sounded like a fast-turning windmill.

Josh nodded. "If he said it, it's true. But I don't see what difference you can make. You're just a..."

Gabrielle's mouth dropped open, and she placed her hands on her hips. "What? Just a woman?"

"No." Josh scratched his head. "It was stupid. I was going to say you're just a powerless woman. What could you do to stop her from being killed? I might have a chance to stop it. But you? Still, I know heroes aren't always the ones with special abilities."

He voiced her own thoughts in the steam house. She couldn't fault him for that. "Joel said if I didn't find Kaylee, she would die and countless others would suffer." She sat beside Josh and held his arm. "I have to go. I'll go crazy otherwise. Won't you please come with me? I'll need help. There's no way I could catch up to them on my own."

"Well, I did promise your husband and kids that I would watch over you." He sighed. "I didn't start out this day planning to take a long trip, but given the circumstances—"

"And it was your idea I enter the steam house."

He twisted his mouth. "That it was." He sat up straighter. "You know, it's been boring around here lately anyway. A trip would be just the thing."

She squeezed his hand. "Oh, thank you so much. You're the one good friend I have left on this earth."

32

"But I do have to say," he paused. "People already talk because we spend so much time together. This will only inflame the rumors."

Gabrielle waved her hands. "Let them talk. We know the truth."

A gleam came to his eyes. "And that truth is…"

"You don't know?" She smiled. "That you're my personal genie, of course."

His eyebrows raised. "Oh, really? I don't recall you rubbing any bottles to get me to come out."

She waved an arm at his walls. "Didn't I just get you to agree to take a trip from your little 'bottle' here?"

He rolled his eyes before he rose and walked to the fireplace. "I have a few things to take care of before we can leave. Spells to lock up the place from prying eyes, for one. Meanwhile, have some of Joel's tea. Should help clear your mind." He poured a cup and sat it before her.

Gabrielle took a sip and a warmth spread over her, followed by a calm resolve. "Wow, this is…is…"

"Heavenly," Josh said as he rummaged through some books.

"Yes, exactly. Heavenly." She took another long gulp. Who was this Joel character anyway?

Flying at night took my breath away. Nathan beat his wings occasionally as we glided across a nearly cloudless sky. The stars peppered the black canvas in intoxicating patterns. I wished Nathan could fly high enough to visit them. But there were so many. How would I choose?

Scanning the ground, I traced the outlines of lakes reflecting the moonlight against a dark background. Lights from scattered houses or camp fires dotted the darkness. Ahead, mountains loomed into the night sky, silhouetted by starlight.

I'm getting tired. I think we had better land for the night and make camp.

"I'm with you." I rubbed his neck.

We sank toward the road. *I know now why you and horses get along so well.*

"Oh? Why?"

You're always patting, rubbing, and making contact. He shook his head and neighed. *I can't tell you what a bond you develop doing that. I already see you in a new light.*

I felt embarrassed. "I'm not being inappropriate, am I? It's just habit."

Oh no. You're fine. As a human, it would be wrong. But for some reason as a horse, it's expected and right. I can't say why, it just is.

I smiled. "To tell you the truth, if someone had told me four months ago that I would be rubbing your thighs and neck, I would have challenged them with my sword." My smile faded, recalling my sword in the hands of the Paradisians.

Nathan appeared to realize my thoughts, and didn't respond. We glided down to the road as the wind whipped around us. Once on the

34

ground, I took my bracelet off. He reverted to human form, and we set up camp.

While Nathan finished, I nurtured a fire to life and brewed some tea. We settled down to some dried meat, cheese, and flat bread.

As I munched, my mind drifted back to a couple months ago, when my dad had led us on a trip from our home in Belenor to his home town of Reol. "Nathan, remember our trip to Reol and how Beltrid and Rodan kept throwing everything at us?"

He swallowed. "How could I forget? He's the reason I met Crystal and am searching for her now."

"Remember what Beltrid wanted? He wanted the ring. This trip is so much different. I don't feel like I have to constantly glance over my shoulder to see what will hit us next. Instead, we're on this quest to find Crystal. Once done, we'll go about helping people, wherever God leads us."

Nathan paused from his chewing and stared into the starry sky. "I can't believe that Beltrid acted alone. It certainly doesn't feel like anyone is after us, but I wouldn't let my guard down if I were you. I doubt the enemy is through with us. Eventually, the demon who replaces Beltrid will reveal his hand."

I smiled. "And when he does, we'll be ready for 'im!" I watched Nathan's face silhouetted by the campfire. "I'm glad you're my brother."

He turned to face me and winked. "I have to say, we make a good team."

I chuckled. "So you're glad I'm your sister?"

He raised an eyebrow. "You could say that."

I feigned a frown, then shook my head as a smile broke out.

We finished our meal, rolled out our bedding by the fire, and I drifted into a deep sleep.

The sound of distant thunder interrupted my dreams. I saw the first rays of sunlight piercing the darkness in the east. Nathan busied himself with rolling up his bedding and dousing the smoldering embers with dirt.

"Is it going to rain?" I sat up and rubbed my eyes.

"It's off in the distance. If we hurry, we might make it to Morgoth before it hits, or at least fly above it if I can."

We carried few supplies, so within minutes we packed, changed Nathan back into a horse, and lifted off into the air.

If I recall the maps correctly, Morgoth is at the base of those mountains ahead. We should be there before nightfall.

He beat his wings a steady rhythm instead of the easier glide he had used before. He wanted to keep ahead of the storm if possible.

I glanced over my shoulder and saw the tall, dark clouds. Lightning flashed among them and the tops billowed like erupting volcanoes. "You sure you can out-fly the storm?"

If I keep up a steady beat, yes.

"You can't keep up this pace all day. You'll have to rest and get some water."

I know. We'll drop to a river or lake as need be. We'll be okay.

I detected a note of doubt in his thoughts—hard to hide with a mental link. But I didn't want to press the issue. Maybe his confidence would prove true.

The ground slithered by mile after mile. I kept a watch on the clouds behind us. They had drawn closer, but I couldn't tell whether they would overtake us before reaching Morgoth. Judging the distance to the mountain proved difficult, and the hours oozed by one after another while the storm grew louder.

I'm landing at that lake over there for a rest. Afterward we'll see if I can climb above the clouds.

"I don't know, Nathan. Those clouds are pretty high, as high or higher than the sky island we fell from. I doubt there's enough air to go high enough. Our time would be better spent flying straight to Morgoth. Then if we have to, we can ride the rest of the way on the ground."

I'll think about it and decide what to do after we rest for a while.

He banked toward the lake. As we sank, my heart fired off warnings. I glanced around, searching for the problem.

What's wrong?

"I don't know. I sense a growing evil, headed our way, but—" I scanned the sky behind us. "Nathan, hold on!" I gripped his mane tightly.

A blackness swept over us, and I felt as if someone had taken a tree and smashed it into my gut. I felt Nathan's hair slip through my fingers as I flew off him and spun through the sky. Briefly, I caught a glance of Nathan twirling end over end as he too plummeted to the earth.

36

My spinning slowed until I fell facing the sky. I knew I needed to get my feet under me if I hoped to have a chance of survival. The ring would protect and heal me, but would it prevent my brain from being smashed flat? Could it heal that?

A sound echoed faintly in the air. Someone called to me. I scanned the sky to see the dark evil pass by and reveal a blue sky once again. Then the faint outline of something appeared above me. It grew nearer and stronger.

It was a hand! Reaching out to me. I stretched toward it. Maybe as death approached, I hallucinated, but what did I have to lose? I knew the ground must be getting close, but the hand drew within a foot of my fingers. The closer it inched toward me, the more of a solid flesh color that revealed itself, as if emerging from a veil. Then a face etched its way faintly into the sky.

"Amma!"

She reached out to clasp my arm. I felt a firm, bony wrist fill my hand, and I clamped onto it with all my strength. My fall jerked to a halt and pulled me sideways. Treetops slapped against me and I closed my eyes to keep from getting them poked out. The slapping stopped and I opened my eyes to discover that I had gained altitude.

Hold on, Sis. We'll set down soon.

I stared upwards—my fingers had wrapped around Nathan's leg. Had I hallucinated Amma? She felt real. Nathan flapped his wings frantically as my weight pulled him off balance. He headed for the lake.

I can't land with you under my feet. I'll fly over the lake and you'll drop off into the water and swim to shore. I'll meet you there.

"All right," I yelled to him as loud as I could, but I couldn't tell if he heard me over the pounding of his wings.

The lake grew until its edge approached. Nathan adjusted his beating to lower us closer to the ground.

See where the water turns bluer opposite the white rock on the shore? Drop in there. It's not a far swim.

The spot approached and Nathan flew a few feet above the water. My toes broke the surface, and I released his foot. White cascades of water showered over me as I tumbled around, then sank under the water before breaking the surface. Treading water, I regained my sense of direction. When I saw Nathan landing on the shore, I swam toward him. My arms and legs felt like jelly, but I forced them to keep going, until I felt the sandy shore hitting my knees and my hands digging through sand.

My arms gave way when I attempted to stand. I took the bracelet off so Nathan could pull me to shore. Soon, strong hands lifted and carried me. He laid me against the white rock.

He plopped down beside me. "What was that?"

I shook my head and said between breaths, "I'm not sure. But it felt very evil. Yet, I didn't detect that it sought us out specifically. It flew to some destination, and we happened to be in its way."

I turned to face Nathan. "And I had the strangest experience as I fell. For a brief few seconds, I thought Amma hovered above me and reached out to grab me. But when I grabbed her hand, your leg filled my palm instead. I must be losing it."

"I barely caught you in time. I swung my leg into your outstretched hand, hoping you would catch it."

"Whatever happened, thanks."

Thunder cracked close by. I turned to see the storm clouds rolling toward us. "Looks like we'd better stick to the road now. We aren't out-flying this storm."

He grimaced. "You're right. As soon as you can stand, change me back and we'll get underway. Maybe we can still make Morgoth before it gets too late."

I nodded as I forced myself to calm my breathing and rubbed my legs to work out the nerves. I hoped the dark evil didn't foretell things to come. The need to stay on watch returned with renewed force. As long as I wore the ring, I could never relax.

6

Josh laid a carpet on the ground.

Gabrielle pointed at it. "Are you preparing a picnic?"

Josh wrinkled his brow. "A picnic? No, we're going to fly. How else can we catch up with a flying horse?"

"Fly? On that?"

"Haven't you ever heard of a flying carpet?"

She frowned. "Yeah, but I'm not too comfortable flying way up in the air on a thin, limp, piece of cloth."

"It'll feel good and solid. Trust me."

She pointed at the sky. "Have you ever done this?"

Josh mumbled something under his breath before spitting out, "No. But I know the spell works. I've seen it done."

Gabrielle bit her lip. "I don't know."

Josh held out his hands. "You have a better suggestion? I'm all ears."

She huffed. "No, I guess we'll fly on your carpet. But how are you going to know where they went?"

He held a finger up. "I did have to research a little, but I found an old spell that enables me to see the auras people leave in their wake, but only fifty yards out. It is a little used spell because a person's aura can stay intact for months. On the ground, the mass of auras creates an intricate web of colors that makes it nearly impossible to follow any one person. But in the sky there are few, if any, we would find up there other than Kaylee and Nathan's."

Gabrielle nodded. "I'm sorry I'm being stubborn. It's just that...well, I'm afraid of heights."

Josh's face fell.

Gabrielle added quickly, "But I'll deal with it. I have to. I have no choice. If flying is the fastest way, then flying it will be."

"I have everything we'll need, so step aboard, Ma'am, and we'll get this trip underway." Josh stood on the edge of the carpet and waved her on.

"Everything?" Gabrielle examined the carpet and Josh. "But the carpet is empty. What are we going to eat? And what will we sleep in?"

He reached into his cloak and pulled out a small ball. "I have everything I need in my cloak, and everything else I can provide with a flick of my wrist. There's little room on the carpet for baggage."

She stepped toward the carpet but stopped at the edge. "You're not going to take off until I'm ready. Right?"

"Wouldn't think of it."

Gabrielle hopped onto the carpet, dropped onto her back, and shut her eyes. "All right. I'm ready."

Josh chuckled. "I have a couple more items to take care of and then we'll be off." He recited a spell and waved his right hand toward the house. Gabrielle peered out to see the house vanish as if nothing existed in the clearing.

Then Josh stared at his palm before reciting another spell. "Ah yes, there are two trails leaving here into the sky. One is obviously when they left to return to Belenor to move you to Reol. The other one I see branches to the west, toward the towns in the forest."

He glanced down at Gabrielle lying on the carpet. "Ready?"

She nodded and shut her eyes. Josh mumbled another spell and the carpet rose from the ground.

Gabrielle gritted her teeth and released a series of muffled cries.

"We're only a couple inches off the ground. See."

She cracked her eyes open and relaxed a little.

"Look, I can jump up and down and it's fine." He bounded into the air and landed on the carpet. It held his weight without a budge.

She pushed on it with her hand and nodded with approval. She felt silly being so afraid of flying, but she couldn't help it. "I guess the anticipation is getting to me."

"What anticipation? We're up."

"Huh?" She glanced over the side and jerked her eyes toward the carpet. "I can see...see treetops. We're above the trees!"

"Yes, and see, it's not that bad."

She felt shivers race across her body. "I'll pretend I'm in bed, getting some rest. I'm not several feet in the air. I'm not on a flying carpet." Whimpers erupted knowing just saying it wasn't so wouldn't convince her brain. "I am on a flying carpet, way up in the sky!"

Josh sat next to her. "You'll get used to it. This is faster than a flying horse. So we should be able to catch up to them eventually."

"If eventually isn't too late." She reminded herself that Kaylee's fate depended on her, and nothing would keep her from saving her. Even fear of heights. She should consider herself lucky to have Josh's help. Not everyone's friend is a powerful wizard. *But I'm so high up!* She shivered again and let her tears drip onto the firm carpet.

A few hours passed, and Gabrielle could lie on her back, staring at the sky and imagine she rested in a meadow. As evening marched across the blue background, stars popped out from hiding, one after another. She imagined Sisko out there on one of them far, far away. She wondered if he still watched her. Certainly not. There must be plenty to keep one busy in Paradise. He wouldn't have time for watching her boring, daily activities through some window.

Then again, the tension in her joints as she lay on a carpet, who knows how high in the air, didn't strike her as boring. As her thoughts returned to the carpet ride, so did the conviction that at any minute she would fall through to her death. Yet after several hours on the carpet, not falling through, and being aware of Josh walking around on it, the fear had diminished some.

Josh touched her shoulder, causing her to flinch. "We'll be landing soon. You've not eaten anything since we left, and we need to set up camp."

Despite the warning, when treetops appeared in her peripheral vision, she tensed and closed her eyes. She couldn't feel anything different once Josh announced, "We're down."

Gabrielle turned her head to see solid earth resting under the carpet. She rolled off the carpet and onto the welcoming ground. Relief flooded her body as hours of tension vaporized into the night air.

Josh stood over her shaking his head. "See, you made it just fine. There's nothing to worry about."

"Nothing to worry about, he says. I can't even get up I'm so shaken, and he says I made it fine!" She glared at him.

"Don't look at me. You're the one who demanded to go on this trip."

Gabrielle sighed. "I know. I wish there were a better way. Can't you simply transport us to them?"

Josh rummaged around in his cloak. "Not if I don't have a clear picture of where they are. If I had a link like I did with Sisko, that would be possible."

Gabrielle jerked up. "You had a link with Sisko? When? How long?"

Josh pulled a coin-sized ball from his cloak and held it out. "Tough thing about reduced sized supplies, hard to find in your pockets." He threw it into the opening and yelled, "Expand to a tent!" Before it hit the ground, a colorful tent bloomed to the size of a small house. From the raised center, a hole allowed smoke from a fire inside to escape. Each corner held a small flag flapping in the wind, with Josh's wizard emblem embossed upon it against a red, green, blue, or yellow background.

Gabrielle's jaw hung open. "Wow, Josh. I didn't expect to be living in luxury on the road."

"I can put it back and we can sleep on the ground if you like."

"Oh, no, no. This is...fine."

He swooped his hand toward the opening. "Even comes with a full kitchen, dining room, and separate rooms with beds."

Gabrielle blinked a couple times and shook her head. Nothing could compare to traveling with a wizard. She held her hand up. "I think my legs have stopped shaking. Help me up."

Josh grabbed her hand and lifted her to her feet, then guided her into the tent, showing her the rooms. The place even contained a toilet where waste would magically disappear from the hole. No flies or disease.

He led her into the kitchen. A fire danced in the center of the room with a pot suspended from three poles tied at the top. Josh opened a cupboard and pulled out some spices and dried meats. "These should make a good stew."

"Allow me. You've already done so much work." She grabbed the pouches from his hand, pulled out a bowl, and proceeded to mix them together.

She glanced at Josh as he sat a pot of water over the fire and threw in some tea leaves. "Now, about that link."

Josh paused his work and sighed. "I hoped you would forget that. But I suppose it's all history now, and it no longer matters if you know."

She held onto the edge of the counter for support as the truth sunk in. Sisko had hidden something from her? What else did she not know? What did Josh know?

Josh stirred the tea leaves around the pot. "Back when Sisko first left Reol at nineteen years old to fulfill the calling of the ring, I had learned a spell from Milnore that linked two people together, allowing them to communicate mentally over great distances. I established the link with Sisko before he left, being he was my best friend. I could keep him up to date on happenings with his family."

Gabrielle pushed out her bottom lip. "He never told me about that. I can't believe it. I didn't think we kept secrets from each other."

Josh stepped beside her. "Gabrielle, you have to remember, when you and he were married, stories of his miracles already filled taverns and homes alike. They took on a life of their own, exaggerated beyond the reality, despite that being astounding enough. If anyone had discovered that he knew about events in Reol, his family would have been put at greater risk from those who sought to control him. And several did attempt that, but they rarely bothered his family because he stayed far away from them and everyone assumed he had no clue what happened in Reol." Josh frowned. "Except for Beltrid. He discovered our link and though I prevented him from killing Sisko's parents, their sickness sped up their deaths."

Gabrielle sighed. "We did have a constant stream of visitors seeking him out, wanting him to heal them when he couldn't. That is true."

"He did it out of love for you. If you didn't know, there was less risk that you would reveal it, and less danger to his parents."

"I know. He did the right thing." She dumped the bowl's contents into the hanging pot of water and watched as the bubbles churned the meat and spices around. "It still hurts, though."

They finished preparing the meal in silence until they sat at the table to eat.

Josh slurped some soup into his mouth. "Excellent. My compliments to the chef."

Gabrielle smiled. "Thanks." She swallowed a piece of meat and washed it down with a gulp of tea. "One question."

He glanced up from his bowl. "Yes?"

"Sisko told stories about you and him before he left Reol. It didn't sound like you were all that accomplished of a wizard. Yet now, I've heard

43

that you're the most powerful wizard of all."

He raised an eyebrow. "Who said that?"

"Jake."

Josh frowned. "I told him not to be spreading that around. Last thing I need is for every two-bit wizard to come challenging me to a duel."

"So it's true?"

He nodded. "And it has nothing to do with conceit. It's a matter of fact. Milnore gave me what I needed to become the most powerful wizard possible."

Gabrielle wiped her mouth before scooping another spoonful of soup from her bowl. "So, tell me about it."

Josh slurped more soup as he stared at the ceiling. "It's a long story."

She shrugged. "We've plenty of time for a long story. What else are we going to do before sleeping?"

The corner of Josh's mouth twitched up, as if he ran through a list of retorts she had left herself open to. But instead he said, "The *Harrower*."

7

Gabrielle wrinkled her brow. "The *Harrower?* What's that?"

"That's when my life as a wizard changed in a big way." He leaned over the table and said in a more whispered tone. "I don't ever tell anyone about this, because I don't want it passed around. If you promise not to ever breathe a word about this, at least until my time in this life is up, I'll tell you."

Gabrielle nodded and drew her fingers across her lips. "My lips are sealed."

He sat back in his chair, dipped a piece of flat bread in his bowl, and ate it before continuing. "Like I said, it began on the day Milnore gave me the *Harrower...*"

At twenty-one years of age, I studied at the table in Milnore's house while he read a book by the fireplace. He laid his book down and said out of the blue, "I have the ultimate power in my possession."

I swung my head around and stared deep into the eyes of the old wizard. "You have what?"

A smile crept out from under his white beard. "The ultimate source of power a wizard can have."

"Why haven't you told me about it before?" I couldn't believe that after seven years together he now brought this up.

"You were not ready for it, my young apprentice."

"And you think I am now?"

His lips turned down. "Josh, you may be close. I do not know if you are ready or not. However, I am old. I do not have long to live in this land. So I tell you now. Hoping, perhaps, that whatever you may lack, this knowledge will encourage you to seek after it."

"What is it then?"

He bowed his head as if thinking. His white hair hung over his head, hiding his eyes from view. I suspected he debated revealing it to me. But why?

He pushed his chair from the table, grabbed his cane, and arose.

I jumped from my seat. "Master, do you need help?"

He waved me off. "No, stay there." He stepped toward the mantle over the fireplace. It ran high and wide over the hearth, decorated with carved vines and grapes along its edges. A small fire barely crackled, keeping warm tonight's broth.

He stopped before the hearth and paused. I watched intently as he raised a hand. He mumbled something I couldn't make out. The hearth wavered like ripples of water. When the distortion ended, several drawers now lined the mantle where before wood and plain rock had been.

My master's secret hiding place! The importance of the moment overwhelmed me. He had never revealed these drawers in all the years we'd been together. I forced myself to suck in air.

He opened one drawer, then muttered another spell. A vial rose into his open palm.

He motioned for me to draw near as he eased himself into a chair. "This is the *Harrower*. Outside a body, it remains inactive for as long as need be. Once in a body, it blossoms with life and unites with the host."

"Unites? What do you mean?"

"You swallow it, and it enters your body to live. It establishes a connection between heart and brain to open one to the power behind all creation."

I hesitated to ask, but I had to. "If you have this, why have you not taken it yourself?"

He sighed. "I never felt I could risk the consequences."

Of course there was a catch. "What consequences?"

"If you're not ready, it will destroy you. Uniting with such raw power is like..." He pointed at the mantle. "Like building a fireplace out of wood. If you're made of the wrong stuff, you will learn what Hell is like. That's why I've never used it."

He held it out, but I paused. The ultimate temptation flirted with me while the ultimate risk dared me. I reached out to take it and noticed my hand shook. I breathed deep, trying to control myself.

The bottle felt cool. I examined the blue, translucent liquid and wondered how it could be so dangerous. Yet, I knew my master and trusted his judgment on such matters.

"I'll take special care of this and won't use it lightly, if at all."

He nodded his approval. A sigh escaped his lips, and he relaxed. "Maybe now, we should eat?"

"I'll get the bowls right after I store this in my hiding place." He raised an eyebrow and I grinned at him. "You've taught me well, Master."

The next day started normal enough. Milnore left for town while I attended to my chores. The morning gave way to noon. I swung my ax down and split a log in two. I sucked in a deep breath of air before reaching for the next one.

Yes, I could have split these a lot faster with magic, but labor is good for my health. Besides, my master had drilled into me that a good wizard doesn't waste his magic-strength on frivolous tasks. A wizard never knows when he will need all he has.

"Anyone here?" A voice sang from the front of the house. It sounded like an older woman.

I buried the ax into the cutting block and rounded the corner of the house as I wiped sweat from my brow.

"Yes, can I be of assistance?"

Aged skin sagged on her face, but bright eyes shown just below the gray hair tucked under a flat hat. Her brown-green dress blew stiffly in the breeze.

"Ah, my boy. Is this where the wizard Milnore lives?"

"It is, but he is buying supplies in town right now. He should be back soon."

"And are you his apprentice?"

"Yes, I am. Are you a friend of Milnore?"

A smile cracked her wrinkled lips. "You could say that."

"What is your name?"

"He knows me as Joline."

"My name's Josh." I pointed to a seat on the porch. "You can wait there if you like."

A flash of energy tickled my mind as she passed close by; she wore a disguise spell! Who was this and why the disguise?

Her smile died off suddenly, and I wondered if she realized I knew. But I decided to keep playing along for the moment.

"Joline, could I get you a drink of water while you wait?"

"Water would be very nice. Thank you." She sat in the chair.

"I'll be right back." I stepped into the house and grabbed the water bucket, then glanced at the window—she couldn't see in. After detecting no attempt to watch me by spell, I opened a drawer and pulled out my wand, stuffing it inside my inner vest pocket. Can't be too careful.

I exited the back door and drew water from the well. But upon returning to the front of the house, she no longer sat in the chair. I scanned the area. "Hello?"

I felt a rumbling under my feet. Bars thrust through the ground all around me. I lost my footing as the ground shook, and I crashed onto the grass, the water spilling into the dirt. The bars shot upwards until they bent in and met above my head.

I regained my footing. A form materialized; the old woman stood there again. She grinned at me. "Yes, you are an apprentice, and not a very smart one. Of course, your powers are no match for mine, but I didn't think you would sense my disguise spell."

I slipped out my wand and attempted several spells; none of them so much as nudged a bar out of place. My vision grew blurry from the effort, so I stopped. Who knew what magic prevented my wand from working in this cage?

She laughed at my attempts. "Be happy. I've given you a ring-side seat to the demise of Wizard Milnore." She sat on the porch again.

"Demise? Why?" I grabbed the bars and attempted to physically move them. They didn't budge.

"For meddling one too many times in my affairs. Now don't you start, or you'll be next in line."

My stomach felt sick. I didn't know the power this witch wielded, but I didn't want to see my master tested by this deceiver. I slumped onto the grass, my back resting against the edge of the cage.

Now what could I do? I scanned the cage, hoping to see some sign of weakness in the magical field surrounding me. I stared at the ground, and realized the obvious. She had not protected the dirt beneath me.

I could dig out, but did I have enough time? She would notice long before I finished. But I didn't need to dig out! I only needed to place my wand below the magic-inhibiting field.

With my back to her, I pulled the grass up where the spilled water had softened it and tossed it aside. Then I dug my fingers in the moist dirt. As the top soil gave way beneath my efforts, it revealed a tighter packed earth. Yet, it continued to loosen. A hole grew with each rake of my hands.

The sound of a whistling tune broke my concentration. My master strolled toward the house. He'd arrived! I clawed at the ground with a quicker pace, knowing the witch would be focused on Milnore.

The whistling stopped. I glanced about and now saw my master approaching from a new direction, whistling again as he drew near. Then the whistling blew from yet another direction, and he now arrived from the side of the house.

The witch rose from her chair. "Why do you persist with these parlor tricks, Milnore?"

He appeared behind her. "Parlor tricks? From my one student who failed the transport spells five times before getting them right?" My master raised a bushy, white eyebrow. "And what's with the old woman getup?"

She flung her hands down her body and transformed into a he. A salt and peppered beard hung from the chin of a bald head. Greedy eyes flashed his anticipation of fulfilling his plan.

My master stared at his former student. "So Darak, what do you want from me?"

He cracked a sly smile. "Your life."

My master's jaw set. He backed away, but kept his face focused on Darak. Darak likewise slid to the side and into the yard. They circled each other for a moment, staring eye to eye.

I pushed my hands as deep into the dirt as possible, and yanked out clods. The hole looked big enough. I grabbed my wand and shoved it below the cage. I recited a spell to burrow through the ground. The hole spread, the edges crumbling inwards as a deep crevice cracked open in the earth.

Once big enough, I jumped in and pointed my wand upwards. A ray of light flashed from the wand and cut into the ground, boring a hole toward the outside of the cage. In seconds, I crawled out.

The two wizards stood ten feet apart, facing each other down. My master pulled back a flap of his robe to reveal a wand peeking out of a leather sheath. His fingers twitched over it.

Darak reshuffled his clothing to provide easy access to the wand in his belt. His eyes narrowed as he stretched his fingers toward the wand's handle.

Bushy-eyebrowed lids stayed focused on gray-blue pupils. Older wrinkles bearing experience contrasted with younger skin flashing with fire.

I had to help my master. Maybe I could distract Darak. I flipped the wand into my hand and shot it straight at the wizard, but he sensed it. In a blur he whipped his wand out and met my energy with a blast of his own. I felt a force shove me back for several feet until my body crashed into a tree trunk. I collapsed onto the ground; shards of pain shot through me, causing me to cry out.

My master latched onto his wand and pulled it out. In a wink, a flash of energy flew from Darak's wand, and landed on my master's. The bolts of energy hovered for a moment as in an eternal push-of-war. Then Darak's beam shoved my master's back. My master pushed back, but he gritted his teeth from the effort.

I felt so helpless. I didn't stand a chance against this powerful wizard. But I couldn't stand here and watch either. I needed more power. Power? The *Harrower*. Should I? What if it destroyed me? Darak's beam now pushed past the midway point. My master couldn't hold on much longer.

Unlike Darak, I had learned my transport spells well. I lifted myself from the ground, despite the aches cursing my movement, and focused on the vial in my drawer. Upon uttering the words of the spell, the bottle materialized in my hand.

I snapped the top off and put it to my mouth, but I couldn't bring myself to swallow it. This would either make me the most powerful wizard around or kill me. I hovered in indecision as my hand shook.

Darak shoved his wand toward my master, and he stumbled backwards before regaining his footing. His hand trembled and Darak's energy shoved in closer to his wand.

The old wizard's face gained a measure of calm in the struggle, as if accepting that this wouldn't end for his benefit. He turned his face toward me and I heard his voice in my head, *Remember all I've given you. Use it well for you're the Wizard.*

In a blazing flash of glory, Darak's beam smashed into my master's wand. It exploded in his hand; the force of the blast threw him back onto the ground—he didn't move.

"Master!" I cradled the vial to my stomach and fled to his side. I fell to my knees as tears laced my eyes. "Master, are you alive?"

No answer returned, only a chest that didn't move with life. I stared at him in shock. How could it end like this? Why did he deserve such treatment?

I turned my head toward Darak. His lips barely turned up on the ends; his eyes gleamed with victory. "He was like a father to me. If only he..." Darak's voice trailed off, as if what he would say might convict him.

"Why? Why did you kill him?" No answer would satisfy me, but the churning in my stomach demanded the question be asked anyway.

He checked me over. "You can be my apprentice now. I will train you in ways he would not have. Milnore had no stomach for wielding his power for practical purposes."

I felt a cold wind flow through me. "And what do you call unpractical purposes?"

He waved his hand. "Helping people without pay. Unwilling to use it to gain power or wealth. Why else would one want such a power? Not to pretend you're a benevolent god."

This wizard had killed my master for being kind and generous! What perverted reasoning could justify such an action? None, none at all.

Darak narrowed his eyes. "You have no chance against me, boy. Either become my apprentice or I will destroy you."

I stared at my lifeless master. He had given me so much, including the *Harrower*. He had known I would use it. He must have believed I could handle it. He had said I was "The Wizard," the one who would serve in his stead to protect and help those who could not. The cool vial hummed against my skin in anticipation.

Strength bubbled to life in my will. I could face Hell's gates if it would avenge my master.

Darak cocked his head to the side. "What do you have hidden in your gut?" He raised his wand in anticipation.

I stared him in the eye. "Water, a vial of the water I went to get. See?" Before he could notice the blue color, I drained it into my mouth.

A fiery glow grew in my belly. But the glow built into a burning sensation, and then into a flaming inferno. I knew I would die; I would live in hell. I wasn't pure enough to take it!

A fire enveloped me and I writhed on the ground in agony. Shards of energy ate at my soul and body. I screamed but couldn't hear it; cried but couldn't feel the tears in my eyes.

Then the pain shrank. The fire turned from a burning heat to a glowing radiance within me. The energy still encompassed me, but the agony gave way to a blissful reality.

What had changed? I thought about it and realized my desire for vengeance no longer burned in me. My soul, purified by the Fire.

I reached out and energy flowed toward me. Divine power sparked on my fingertips. The *Harrower* and I were one!

Darak stared at me with interest. "That must have been bad water, it looked discolored. But you haven't answered my question. What will it be? A quick death or a life of abundance?"

I stood and squared my shoulders. "Neither. I would rather die than kill my soul with your abundances."

A growl formed in his throat. "Then death you shall have." He flipped his wand at me and fire poured from it.

I held my hand out and it blasted harmlessly upon an invisible shield.

Darak frowned, then swirled his wand while reciting an incantation. From his wand the head of a dragon formed and raced toward me. I stretched forth my hand and it grew until I could wrap my fingers around the dragon's neck. In my tightening grip, the dragon choked, and Darak did too as if connected to its experiences.

I smiled. He deserved this for killing my master. I gripped tighter and Darak fell to the ground, clutching his neck with his free hand. His face turned blue from lack of air.

He would pay for his insolence. I was his judge now; I had the power to deal him a final blow, and he knew it.

A flash blinded me for a moment, and I fell upon the ground. My hand returned to normal size. The dragon coughed but gained its breath back as did Darak.

The wizard struggled to his feet, and the dragon-head reached out and gathered my body into its teeth. I tried a spell, but couldn't focus long enough to get the words out due to the pain striking upon every nerve in my body, rolling as waves upon the shore of misery.

The energy retreated from my will. The reality of what I had done struck me like a slap across the face. I, of all people, should know the dangers of unbridled desire fed by power, and I had let it control me.

"Forgive me, Father," I managed to whisper through the pain.

As if a hand pushed its jaws apart, the fiery teeth left my body and soul. The dragon's energy evaporated into a whiff of smoke, knocking Darak upon his back.

I rose to my feet and gazed upon my fallen master. His mind touched mine for a brief moment, whether from his body or not, I couldn't tell. He said, "Harrowing is for repentance, not destruction."

The words rang in my ears, and I knew my error had been to take vengeance, to use the power for my own will. But it could not be bent to my will. I would have to bend to the *Harrower's* will to use it.

I stood over Darak. Fear etched its way along his face and eyes, as he watched me. I lifted a finger; energy blew through it into a gale. Darak's body lifted from the ground until his face hovered inches from my own.

His eyes stared at me wide with fear. "Where did you get this power?" His eyes relaxed. "Can you teach me?"

I shook my head. "Real power isn't a possession. It's a gift to be given." I searched deep into his blue eyes. I needed to provide for his possible repentance, not destruction. But what would that be?

An idea flashed into my mind. "I do have a lesson for you to learn, however." I reached out and placed my hand on his sweating forehead. A glow of energy rushed through me and into him. His eyes grew wide and his mouth gaped open. A burst of light shot his head back.

He blinked a couple times. "What...what did you do to me?"

I set him back on the ground. I couldn't help but grin. "Just putting into reality a saying a special man once said: do unto others as you would have them do unto you."

He frowned. "What do you mean?"

"Well, I did change it a little. Any spell you cast on another will affect you in the same manner and degree as you intended for your target. Now, go and learn to do good."

I turned away but heard grumbling and then the words of a spell. I spun around.

With his wand pointed at me, a blue streak of flame erupted from it. But it circled me and sped back toward him. He barely blocked the fiery ball of flame in time.

I chuckled as he rushed down the road, screaming and yelling obscenities. He promised to be back.

I fell upon the body of my master. I could finally grieve for him—celebrate his life and the one he would continue to have with God.

I dug his grave, said prayers over him, and threw dirt over his pine-box casket. When I finished, nothing more needed to be said. I would attack life with repentance and love as he had, and no doubt still did from Heaven's gate.

Gabrielle stared at Josh for a few moments as he swallowed the last of the soup and bread. "That's quite a story. Did Darak ever return?"

Josh twisted his mouth. "Come to think of it, no, he never has. Hopefully he learned his lesson."

"Why do I feel that is unlikely?"

Josh chuckled. "For a woman with no powers, you are very perceptive."

"Comes with the experience of caring for a crazed father and brother, and an unusual husband." She sat her empty soup bowl down as her thoughts returned to Sisko. The hole his death had left in her life still gaped wide open. She hoped it would heal someday, but she doubted it would be anytime soon.

8

"I expect more from you. Do you know the plan?" The bright demon tapped on the edge of the water stand.

"Yes, master. You can count on me."

"I have in the past. Don't fail me this time. Make sure you don't rush her. Lead her along. Be patient."

"Yes, master."

"And what is your goal?"

"To bring the ring to you."

He smiled and leaned back. "Yes. Bring me the ring, and He can never trouble us again."

The pouring rain soaked me to the bone. Nathan had trotted along the road to Morgoth at a brisk pace, but didn't want to go any faster for fear of slipping in the mud. Shanty houses appeared here and there as he splashed through puddles. At least I didn't have to wade through the mud.

I think I'd better change back. The traffic on the road is getting more frequent and there are too many houses ahead. There may not be any good places to change unnoticed after this.

So much for not sloshing my feet through the mud. I patted his neck. "I think you're right. At least the city wall isn't too much further." I slid off his back, and my feet sank into the squishing ground. I unlatched the bracelet and hung it from the chain around my neck, tucking it into my tunic. I barely noticed the flash of light when Nathan changed, highlighting the trees bending in the gusts of wind.

Lightning lit up the sky and thunder vibrated my bones. I instinctively winced as if it would hit me.

Nathan brushed his soggy hair back. "Not exactly good traveling weather. Let's get to the city. Hopefully we can find a place to dry off there."

We struggled through the mud as the city gate grew and the wall towered above us. Wooden beams extended as high as the treetops in intricately layered patterns, no doubt several feet thick. The length of the gate tunnel indicated an inner wall, creating enough space for shops and dwellings.

Though the storm cast a darkness over the city, the city itself felt dark. Buildings rarely showed any vibrant colors. Browns and blacks ruled the landscape. Old wood, aged to dark stains, plastered the buildings as if designed for that purpose.

People filled the streets even in this downpour. Many of them appeared to live in the alleys. Pieces of wood leaning against a wall served as the only shelter for several, while others sat in the mud and rain as if half-dead.

I whispered to Nathan, "This place feels evil."

He nodded. "Not a place I would like to live, for sure. Visiting is enough."

"But I'm talking about my heart. The ring, it's communicating evil here."

"Then there should be many here you could help. No?"

I nodded. "That's just it, there are so many suffering here I can't pull out just one or two. That's why it feels so bad."

He pointed down the street. "I see two taverns on opposite sides of the street. You up to going into one? I'll take the other to see what we can find out about Crystal, and where room and board might be found."

I stared at the dim glow of light emanating from the windows. I would have felt better if my sword still hung by my side.

He patted my back. "I'll be right across the street. Remember, I can sense your emotional state. If anyone so much as lays a hand on you, I'll know and come running."

I smiled and breathed deep. "Thanks. I'm sure I'll be all right."

He headed toward the *Stalwart Tavern's* doors. I sloshed through the mud until I reached the entrance of the *Spinning Duck Tavern* and stepped inside.

Like the city, the room bustled with bodies and chatter. At one table, a group of guys told jokes as they shared ales together. At another, a couple of men entertained ladies who I sensed sought the men's money. At yet another, a group played cards. Several sat alone, and those eyes followed me as I strolled into the tavern.

The barkeep finished with an order and bustled over to me. "What'd ya have, Miss?"

"An ale and some information."

He threw a towel over his left shoulder. "The ale'll cost you a couple shillings. The information—that depends."

I pulled out two shillings and slapped them onto the counter. He pulled out a mug and drew from a keg a dark-amber liquid with a full head. He sat it in front of me and scooped up the money.

I clamped onto the handle and downed the mug in one, long, drink. When I finished I snapped the cup onto the wooden bar. The barkeep stared at me; his eyes darted between me and the empty mug.

"I was thirsty," I explained. However, the truth was I hoped it would calm my nerves.

He shrugged. "And the information ya need?"

"One, where's a good place in this town to get a night's sleep? Two, I'm looking for a woman, goes by the name of Crystal...," I described her to the man. "Do you know anything about her? She was supposed to have come with a caravan."

"Haven't heard of the woman. There was a caravan that left three days ago. And there's an inn one block that way." He pointed out the window. "About a block, and another block to the right."

I nodded. "Thank you, sir."

A hand landed on my rear. I spun around and backhanded the man behind me. His head twisted from the hit, emitting a loud crack. He stumbled backwards, and a chorus of laughter erupted from a table against a wall. The man re-joined his friends as they pointed at him and stole glances at me.

I shook my head. Idiots. Yet, I felt a little better now. I didn't need my sword to take control.

I scanned the room, searching for someone I thought might be safe to approach and ask about Crystal. As I glanced from one face to another, a man caught my attention. A spark flittered across my soul and I knew this man needed my help.

I shuffled between tables and stares until I stood before him. He sat at a table, drinking an ale in measured gulps. His clothing, like many here, appeared dark and worn. A scraggly beard surrounded a frowning mouth.

He glanced up at me. "What do you want?"

"You're sick, are you not?"

"And if I am, what business is it of yours?" His eyes returned to watching the bubbles on his ale-head disappear.

I couldn't place it, but I felt odd. Out of place. "I'm a healer. I can mend whatever ails you. I felt you needed my help."

He grunted. "You felt wrong. Go help someone who cares."

I would have loved to do that, but the pull of my heart wouldn't let go. I sat on a chair opposite him. "It's not my decision who to help. I'm directed to you. So, if you could tell me what's wrong, and let me—"

"Look, Miss. It was a woman who did this to me, and it is a woman—"

"Who can heal it."

He scowled. "It is a woman who is breaking my oath to have nothing to do with them again by sitting at my table. Now get up and leave!" He pounded his fist causing his ale to spill over the mug's lip. Chatter in the immediate vicinity died momentarily as heads turned our direction.

I sighed. He wouldn't cooperate, and I couldn't figure out how to get him to do so. Why the feeling in my heart persisted with this man didn't make sense. I rose from the chair.

"Gregory, Gregory." A deep voice echoed from behind me. "You've had that bad leg for years now. Why don't you let the young lady heal it if she can?"

I spun around to find a gentle pair of coal-black eyes peering into mine. His well-trimmed beard and dark hair hung obediently from his head. I couldn't place it, but this man felt different. Disarming, yeah, that's what I felt. Confidence and trust exuded from him.

Gregory grimaced. "But Michelle—"

The man pointed at me. "Gregory, she's not Michelle. She didn't do this to you, but she wants to fix it. Why not let her?"

Gregory huffed and grumbled as he swallowed a gulp of ale.

The man knelt on one knee beside Gregory and wrapped an arm around his shoulder. "You know me, I'm rarely wrong. I sense this lady's good. She'll take care of you. If she doesn't, I'll deal with her myself." He turned his head toward me and winked. I cracked a smile.

Gregory sat up. "All right, because you say so." He pulled his leg out from under the table and rolled his pants up, revealing a rotting mess.

I swallowed a sick feeling back down as I knelt beside him, laid my hand above the wound, and said, "Lord, heal this man both physically and spiritually." I didn't know why I added in the spiritual, but I sensed his hurt ran deeper than merely physical.

He jerked for a moment, then the rot shrank, color returned to his skin, the holes sealed, and a light sprang into his eyes. He stood to his feet and bounced on the leg. A grin spread underneath his beard.

"This lady healed me!" he shouted to the room. He wrapped me in his arms and hugged hard. "I'm sorry for the way I treated ya. Thank ya so much for puttin' up with an old stubborn man like me."

Relief flooded my mind. "You're most welcome."

He bounced from table to table, pointing at me and telling his story. Soon he shot out the door.

"This will be all over town by morning," the man said.

I stared at him. "Is that a bad thing?"

He grinned. "Depends whether you like eating and sleeping on occasion or not. There's a huge mass of people in this town. You could spend weeks healing them all."

"I've sensed as much."

He sighed. "How rude of me. My name's Cole." He thrust a hand forward.

"Mine's Kaylee." I put my palm in his, and I jerked. An image flew into my mind of him wrapping his arms around me. The expression on my face clearly spoke of love and joy. I pulled my hand from his.

I stared at the ground to hide the shock in my eyes. I wanted to run away, but I didn't want to be rude. "I'm...I thank you for...for helping me heal him." My pulse beat rapidly. What was happening to me? I met his eyes and felt a calm rush over me.

He nodded. "No problem. Always happy to help a damsel in distress."

He didn't act like he had experienced anything unusual himself. But the scene in my mind remained vivid. Did it indicate his intentions? Or did it show his eventual or current love for me? Memories surfaced of Dad first touching Amma. He had seen them embraced in a kiss, and they eventually married. Was this my future husband? I glanced at the ring on my finger as I sat at the table.

I wiped my forehead. "I think I need another ale."

Cole waved to the barkeep. "Two ales over here. I'll pay." He sat in a chair next to me. "You seem a little shaken. Is everything all right?"

I hid behind a smile. "I'll be all right. I experienced an unexpected...very unexpected vision."

"What is it? Maybe I can help."

I shook my head. "I don't think I'm ready for that."

He sat back. "No problem."

The barkeep sat two mugs in front of us as Nathan rushed through the tavern's doors, taking less than a second to zero in on my location. He pushed through the hive of activity to where I sat.

He approached as I downed another mug of ale in a series of gulps. I sat the glass down, but the battle between confusion and fright lingered with the image. "Do they have anything stronger in this place? Whiskey maybe?"

Nathan sat next to me. "Kaylee, you don't drink whiskey."

"I do now." I waved my arm. "Bartender, a whiskey for me and my brother."

Cole scratched his head. "Is she often like this?"

Nathan eyed Cole before returning his gaze to me. "Kaylee, what happened. I felt you were in some kind of distress, but I didn't expect this."

I pointed at him. "You didn't come when someone laid a hand on me. Ha!"

"I started to, but could tell you dealt with it well enough."

The barkeep placed two shot glasses of whiskey on the table. I grabbed one and downed it. Fire raced down my throat and exploded through my nasal passages and mouth. I shook my head. "Wow, that hit the spot."

I placed my hand on Nathan's shoulder. "Those men over there laughed at me. One of them hit me in the rear, and they laughed like it was some game. You should have been here to defend my honor!"

Cole cleared his throat. "I'll offer my place for you two to stay the night if you wish."

Nathan met Cole's eyes. "And you are?"

"Cole's my name. Long time resident here."

I slapped Cole on the back. "He's a good man, Nathan. He helped me. A good man." I gazed at the other shot glass. "If you ain't takin' that one, I will." I scooped it up and tossed the liquid-fire down my throat.

Nathan winced and held his hand out to Cole. "My name's Nathan, and under the circumstances, I thank you for your hospitality and will take you up on your offer." He grabbed me under my arms and lifted me to my feet. "We need to get you out of here before you spend all our money on your sorrows, whatever they are."

Cole reached under my other arm and helped Nathan pull me from the tavern. I tried to move my feet, but couldn't keep up for some reason. Time felt warped. I finally gave up and let them pull me along. I barely noticed as we entered a house, and they laid me in a bed. Reality shifted into dreams and sleep.

Moonlight filtered over streets clouded in fog. I worked my way along damp dirt, past buildings. Few people walked about, content to rest in well-lit homes.

Why did Nathan leave a twelve-year-old girl like me in town alone? My brother couldn't be counted on for anything. He was more interested in playing with his friends. No doubt he'd forgotten all about me.

Somewhere in the confines of my young mind, I paused with a realization of reliving an event I thought I'd dealt with. I didn't want to go down this path, I didn't want to relive this experience when I was twelve. But the scene continued.

I strolled by an alley, decided it would be a good shortcut. Not far, I could see the gate of the city, and I could maybe catch a ride with someone. I gathered my skirt around me to fend off the chill of the fog and entered the alley.

A dread fell over me. The darkness, the trash, the stench, all combined to make me wish I'd gone around instead. But the end of the alley wasn't too far off. "Just keep moving," I told myself.

A hand clamped around my arm and I screamed. It threw me into a pile of dirty rags and the form of a man moved over me.

"Leave me alone!" I crawled to run away.

But he fell over me. The smell of alcohol hung heavy on him, pinning back my will even as his hands pinned my arms against the trash.

I started to scream, but he crammed one of the rags in my mouth. The putrid smell sent my stomach into convulsions; my limbs stopped struggling as his overwhelming power couldn't be defeated. I lay helpless, unable to defend myself. Unable to stop the evil this man desired. Unable to do anything other than to shed tears and cry in my mind to God, "Please! Make him stop!"

His calloused hand brushed up my legs and under my skirt. I vainly pulled my hips away as he hooked his grimy fingers around my undergarments and started to pull down.

"Hey, you. What are you doing over there?"

His pawing stopped as he froze. I tried to scream through the rag, but sucking in air caused my head to spin instead. I turned to see a tall man at the end of the alley. He stepped toward us.

The attacker jumped off me and fled down the alley in the opposite direction. The man approached and leaned over me.

I jerked the rag from my mouth and curled up into a ball, daring not to look at the new man. Maybe he'd go away.

"You're only a young girl. Are you all right?"

I didn't answer. I pushed against the rags, burying myself in their smell, closing myself off to this new attacker. But my view pulled back, and I saw myself lying in the alley with the man leaning over me. For the first time I saw something I'd never realized either that day or up until now. The man radiated, and his facial features resembled Joel's. Even then he watched over me.

The man, or Joel, stepped to the end of the alley and glanced around. He waved a hand. "You there? Are you looking for a young girl? She's over here."

A few moments another set of footsteps fell through the alley. A hand rested on my shoulder and I flinched.

"Kaylee, it's me, Nathan."

I turned my head to see, then I leaped onto him and clung for all the strength I could muster. Fresh tears cascaded down my cheeks.

"Sis? What happened. You don't look harmed."

Joel's voice stabbed through the fog and darkness. "I found a drunk in the process of raping her. Luckily he didn't get far. But I'd take her home if I were you." He turned and walked out of the alley and then down the street.

Nathan pulled me to him. "Oh Kaylee, I'm so sorry. I'll never forgive myself for leaving you." He lifted me in his arms and carried me the mile outside the city to our house. I was an armful at twelve, and more so for a fourteen-year-old boy. But Nathan's muscles and guilt must have driven him.

As I clung to him, and he worked his way home, I couldn't stop reliving the experience. But I didn't dare talk about it. It would go away if I didn't talk about it. I didn't want to talk at all for fear of mentioning it, being all I could think about. The intruding scenes replaying over and over instilled fear into my brain. I could trust no men other than Nathan and Dad. I would never put myself in that situation again. I would never allow a man to get that close. Somehow, I would get this out of my mind and act as if it never happened. I could run away from it. I must escape this horror.

As my consciousness returned to current reality, the vivid memories of the event cut through me. I thought I'd dealt with this. I thought Joel had helped me get over my fear. Why did it return to haunt me now?

I jerked awake. My head swam in the darkness of the room. Tears whetted my pillow. "Oh, God, help me!"

The darkness answered, "He is. Now sleep." An arm rested on my shoulder. The voice, I recognized it. But before I could place it, my eyes rested, and I sank back into a dreamless sleep. The horror sank into its depths to be muffled into a distant impression.

Gabrielle could now glance past the side of the carpet and watch the horizon off in the distance without shaking from fear and gritting her teeth. Even though she felt uncomfortable flying hundreds of feet in the air on a little piece of cloth, the longer she didn't fall through it, the more she felt it wouldn't happen. Still, she couldn't bring herself to sit up or even glance downward. The constant tension of feeling that at any moment the whole carpet would collapse and send them plummeting toward the earth never abated.

"We're almost to Spinard. Kaylee and Nathan's auras are heading toward the ground. They must have landed about a mile outside of town," Josh announced.

She nodded with relief; another leg of this flying would soon end. How far did they have to go to catch up with them, and how many more hours of flying on this thing would she have to endure? However many, she knew she would endure as many of them as need be to get to Kaylee.

The carpet slowed to a crawl before resting in a knoll a few feet off the main road. Gabrielle sat up and rubbed her legs and arms, trying to work the tension out.

Josh hopped off. "I could roll you up in the carpet and carry you into the city, if you'd like."

She squinted an eye at him. "Not funny."

He smiled. "Or the carpet could take off without me and there would be no telling where it would take you."

She leaped off from a sitting position, then pointed at Josh. "That's definitely not funny!"

He grinned as he rolled the carpet up and shrank it down to size, sliding it into a pocket in his cloak.

Gabrielle straightened out her dress. "Can't we find where their auras head back into the sky?"

"We could, but it could take a while circling the city to locate where they took off at, and it's possible they are in the city and haven't left. Best to go in and check. Besides, we could use the chance to stretch our legs. And more information is always a good thing."

Gabrielle cracked a smile. "What you really mean is you want some ale to drink."

"Now that you mention it, there is a place in town known for its ale. Decent food too. Can't pass that up."

She smirked. "Yeah. Sure."

They strolled through the city gate. The double-layered wall enclosed a good sized city—Gabrielle guessed around five thousand or so. By outward appearances, the city appeared normal enough. Steep roofs built from the forest trees indicated that they received snow on occasion. Aside from the browns and woody colors one usually saw, some greens, reds, and yellows peppered the storefronts with creative letterings.

As they reached the center of the town, buildings crowded together creating dark alleys and nooks, even in the middle of the day. Gabrielle could sense, though she knew not how, that the day-life appeared normal enough, but the night-life hid a dark side.

Josh pointed to the lone cross rising above the other buildings. "Let's check with the priest first."

She nodded and they worked their way along the streets until they knocked on the priest's door. He hadn't heard of or seen Kaylee, Nathan, or Crystal.

Gabrielle shook her head. "I thought I brought that girl up better than to ignore the Church in a strange city."

"Teenagers, what can you do with them?"

Gabrielle stared sideways from her eyes at Josh. "You don't have any teenagers or children. Where did that come from?"

He stuck his tongue in his cheek and stared around. "I'm good at putting myself in other people's shoes."

"Yeah, right." Gabrielle rolled her eyes.

"In any event, next we should check the taverns."

She twisted one corner of her mouth into a frown. "Right. If they skipped the Church, they must have gone to the tavern."

Josh led Gabrielle into the *Wagon Wheel Tavern*. The few people who occupied the building chatted and minded their own business, except for five who glanced to check them out as they entered.

Josh pointed at the bar. "Order us some drinks and find out what the barkeep knows. I'm going to see if I can discover anything among the crowds."

"Anything particular you want?"

"Just an ale." He headed among the tables and sat at one, his eyes half-closed as if searching out the minds around him.

Gabrielle sat at the counter and caught the barkeep's attention, which didn't prove difficult.

"Yes, Ma'am? What'll it be for you?" He planted his hands on the bar to prop up his body. She figured him to be in his mid-twenties.

"A couple of ales, please. And also, you wouldn't recall having met a young girl a few days ago. Her name's Kaylee. Shoulder-length, sandy-blonde hair, blue eyes, carries a sword, or if not her—"

"Oh yes!" His eyes lit up. "How could I forget her. If I hadn't been on duty I would have loved to take her home with me."

Gabrielle bit her tongue but wanted to slap the young man. As long as she could get info, however... "Did she say where they were headed?"

"She was looking for some girl..." He scratched his head for a moment.

"Crystal."

"Yeah, that's it. Told her a girl matching her description had passed through here with a man. I think the other gent said they had headed to Paradise a few days before."

"Paradise?"

"A town about fifty miles south from here as the crow flies. But some odd folk live there. People go in and never come out."

Gabrielle couldn't help but wonder at such a name for a town when everyone who did go into the real Paradise never came out. That is, except for Sisko. "Was anyone with her?"

"Nope, came in and left alone."

Gabrielle sighed. First Kaylee fails to make contact with the priest, then she goes into the tavern alone. A seventeen-year-old girl! That's just asking for trouble.

A grin spread across the barkeep's face. "She looked sizzling good, but you know? You're pretty tasty looking yourself."

Gabrielle stood up. "For your information, young man, you're talking about my daughter, and I'm old enough to be your mother." She felt her jaw quivering.

His eyes sparkled with anticipation. "I prefer the more experienced women myself. I'm getting off work in a few minutes. How about if you come home with me? I'll make it worth your while."

She couldn't contain herself any longer. "You're nothing but a jackass!"

He laughed at the insult as if it were a game. But his laughter morphed into a *he*, then a *haw*. His head dropped lower and fine hair spread across his face as it lengthened out.

Gabrielle blinked a couple times, but the barkeep could only *he-haw* as his hooves clicked against the hardwood floor. She stepped back from the bar and glanced at Josh who stared wide-eyed at Gabrielle. She pointed at the animal behind the counter and mouthed, "Did you do that?"

He shrugged and shook his head.

The jackass barkeep kicked, and bottles shook on their shelves. A couple tipped over and crashed upon the floor. He continued to smash his hooves into the cabinets, sending bottles to their deaths and blasting glass mugs into fragments upon the counters and floor. A couple of women screamed, and several people dashed for the door.

The owner burst from the backroom. "Who let this animal in my tavern!"

One of the patrons pointed at Gabrielle. "She turned your barkeep into a jackass. Said he was one, and then he became one."

"Get that witch out of here! I don't need your kind of business!"

Josh grabbed her by the arm and pulled her outside before she could utter another word. But as he guided her along the road, she said, "A witch! Me! He's just a—"

Josh slapped a hand over her mouth. "Don't say anything."

She jerked her face out from under his palm. "You don't think I did that, do you?"

He stopped and faced her. "I know you did. Now tell me, did anything else happen in the steam house you didn't tell me about?"

She bit her lip. "Well, Joel did say something else, but I don't recall specifics."

Josh ran his fingers through his hair. "Don't recall? You're in the steam house! You have to pay close attention! What do you mean you don't recall!"

She stared at the ground. "He had just shown me that Kaylee would die. Played the scene of her death right in front of me! Sort of hard to pay attention to anything else when that's been thrown at you."

Josh paced back and forth. "I know, but don't you see? You have some ability the steam house gave you, and you don't know how to use it. You changed a man into a jackass, simply by speaking the word."

"Speak." She thought a second. "Truth. Speak the truth. That's what he said."

Josh scratched his chin. "Speak the truth. Hum, did he say anything else?"

She stared at the people passing by. "Maybe. I think so. Yeah, perhaps." She frowned. "I don't know. Seems he said something."

A passing man, his head covered by a hood, stopped before them. "Speak the truth, and like the steam house, the reality will be uncovered."

Gabrielle jumped back. Josh stared into the hood. "Joel, is that you?"

He pulled the hood back. "Yes. I'm not good at changing my voice. But that's what I told her."

Gabrielle rubbed the cloak covering his arms between her fingers. "You looked much brighter and angelic in the steam house."

"It's the steam."

Josh glanced sideways at Joel.

Joel pulled the hood over his head. "But that's what I said." He stepped away and headed down the road.

Gabrielle leaped after him. "Wait, I want to ask you something!" She laid a hand on his shoulder.

He turned around and pulled the hood back. A bald man, old and wrinkled, stared back at her. "Yes Ma'am, is there something I can do for you?"

Gabrielle jerked her hand back. "Oh, sorry. I thought you were...someone else."

He shrugged, replaced the hood and proceeded on his way.

Josh shook his head and resumed his march toward the city gate. "Come on, we can't stay here. There's a reason wizards keep a low profile in a city like this. People either fear you or want to use you. Either way, it makes them do strange things. Now that they've seen you turn someone into a jackass, no one will want you around."

Gabrielle scurried to catch up. "I didn't want any special abilities. Why would the steam house give me such a power?"

"You'll need it. Apparently God wants you to force people, maybe someone specifically, to deal with their hidden character flaws and unfulfilled purposes. You're like a steam house on feet."

"Terrific. Now I've got to worry about what I say."

Josh chuckled as they exited the city gate. "Welcome to my world."

I opened my eyes, but the pounding in my head yelled to shut them tight. Sunlight poured in from a window. I felt a soft bed under me.

As my eyes adjusted, I sat up and rubbed my head. "Kaylee, you're such a fool!" Thoughts slogged through my mind.

Where am I? Vague memories flashed through my mind of Nathan and Cole pulling me along.

The room contained a plain bed, a mirror of polished metal, a place to store clothing, and a bulky chair in one corner.

A series of raps echoed from the door. "Kaylee, you up?"

"Yeah. Come on in."

Nathan peeked his head in and entered the room. "How do you feel?"

"Like a horse bucked me off and I fell on my head."

"But you didn't drink much whiskey."

I frowned. "I downed two mugs of ale before that. Besides, I've never drank whiskey before, not until last night. My body wasn't ready for it."

"Apparently." He pulled a chair to the bed and sat in it. "So what happened?"

"I healed a man after Cole helped me convince him to let me do it. Cole introduced himself and when I shook his hand, I saw a vision of him hugging me, and me enjoying it. Like Dad saw Amma kissing him first time they touched."

He sat up. "Really? That doesn't make any sense."

"Why? I know I hardly know him, and while the idea of him and me together did cause me to lose it, he seems like a nice guy."

Nathan shook his head. "No, that's not it. What doesn't make sense is that this guy is not a Christian."

I shrugged. "Maybe he'll convert."

"Kaylee..." Nathan drew closer. "He's a priest in a different religion."

"A priest?" That didn't make sense. Why would the ring...why would God, want to unite me to a priest of another religion? And why didn't it bother me that it didn't make sense?

I shrugged. "Priests can convert too."

Nathan stared hard at me. "Why are you defending him? I thought the idea caused you to lose it?"

Why did I? "I don't know. All I know is what the ring showed me. Can it be wrong?"

Nathan hung his head, then bobbed back up. "Remember when Beltrid used Crystal to seduce me? I knew I loved her and would marry her. None of the warnings from Father or you would cause me to see the truth. I thought you were all wrong. Now I'm telling you, I think this guy is evil. Let's leave and get on down the road."

"Evil?" I shook my head. "I would have felt that from the ring if it were true."

Nathan sighed. "Kaylee, think for a moment. All your life until recently, you've kept men away from you. You've never experienced a real romantic relationship. You know what that makes you?"

"Uh..." I shrugged. "Single?"

He shook his head. "Inexperienced. You don't know the power of infatuation. How easy it is to ignore the negatives, only see the good, and see everything about him through that filter."

I flapped my hand at him. "Come on, brother. I'm not like that. I have the ring. I would know. And though I'm surprised by it, the ring is pointing me to him."

He threw his hands up in the air. "I'm telling you, avoid him. Let's thank him for his hospitality and hit the road." He moved to the door. "Besides, I found out last night that Crystal's caravan left three days ago. The longer we sit here, the longer it will be before we can catch up to her."

I nodded. "All right. I'll get my stuff together and we'll leave." If God intended for Cole and me to unite, He would bring it about whether we stayed or not.

"Right after breakfast. Cole's cooked up something." Nathan stepped out the door and closed it behind him.

I rubbed my head again. "A priest?"

After freshening up and strapping my vest and belt on, I found my way to the dining room and seated myself as Cole and Nathan already ate.

Nathan swallowed a bite of apple. "So, Cole, what did you say the name of your god was again?"

Cole kept his focus on the food he tossed in his mouth. "Morgenstern."

"And, what kind of rituals do you have? Like, maybe a marriage ceremony?"

I kicked Nathan's leg under the table. He didn't flinch.

Cole nodded. "Yes, we have a marriage ceremony."

"Anything in your books about human sacrifices?"

Cole stared at Nathan.

I kicked him again, harder. "I'm sorry, Cole. My brother has a strange sense of humor sometimes."

Cole cracked a slight smile. "Oh yeah. We sacrifice people all the time." He pointed at me. "If she hadn't got drunk on me, she was next." He winked.

Nathan's eyes widened and nodded toward me as Cole focused on picking up some grapes. I kicked him again.

Cole lifted his head. "There's no question that you're brother and sister."

I figured we'd better change the subject. "We'll have to leave soon. We're tracking a girl named Crystal who Nathan thinks is in trouble, and we believe she left in a caravan three days ago."

Cole nodded. "I remember them calling a girl by that name. Dark hair and eyes. An odd girl, near lifeless."

Nathan nodded. "Sounds like her all right, except for the lifeless part. Maybe she was tired?"

"The caravan is headed to Octum across the arid plains on the other side of this mountain range. Then it'll continue to a town on the sea, Shore Cliffs. If you hurry, you might catch up with them before they reach Shore Cliffs."

"We'll get there way before that," I said. "Nathan can fly."

Nathan kicked me under the table and he stared at me through narrow eyes.

"Fly, eh? I've heard of stranger things. But may I ask, do you have enough money to buy her back?"

Nathan stopped chewing. I glanced at him and his eyes met mine.

Cole slurped some coffee. "I see you hadn't thought of that. Well, you'd better. Cause they'll see her as their property and won't release her without payment."

Nathan ran fingers through his hair. "We've some money, but not enough to buy a slave. And if we wait until we can work for more, we might lose the caravan."

Cole sat his flat bread down. "Tell you what I'll do. I'll go with you and negotiate for her price. Traders know me because I've been around here for a while, and I'm the priest. And I have some money I'll donate to the cause."

I glanced at Nathan with a smile and nodded.

Nathan twisted his mouth. "I'm pretty good at negotiating. You're very generous, but if you're not uncomfortable with the idea, give us however much you think we'll need to buy her and we'll take care of it. I'd hate for you to leave your duties here."

He rose from the table. "You're very kind to consider my convenience. But I'm overdue for a vacation. I have an assistant priest who can fill in. I would very much enjoy a little trip."

Nathan bit his lip. "I don't—"

"Don't want to deny you the joy of our company," I tossed in. "I for one would be glad to have you along."

"But—"

"Great!" Cole said. "What a wonderful opportunity to make new friends. I'll get my supplies together—"

"But!" Nathan slapped his palm on the table. We both stared at him. He continued, "But I don't know how well I'll be able to carry two people."

Cole wrinkled his brow. "Carry? Him?"

"Nathan turns into a winged horse when I put my bracelet on and he says 'Upwards,'" I explained.

Nathan kicked me hard under the table. "Sis, watch your mouth!"

Cole sat back in his chair. "Interesting. A winged horse. That should be fun."

Nathan sighed. "Yes, but the extra weight will tire me faster. We'll have to make more stops, it'll slow us down."

I placed my hand on Nathan's. "But we'll get there all the same. And we'll need his help to get Crystal from them." I smiled at Cole. "That's a very loving and generous offer."

Nathan sank into his chair and crossed his arms. "All right. I'll carry him too."

Cole smiled. "I also noticed that neither of you have swords, though you have the sheaths to carry them. I have some extras."

Nathan's eyes widened and he sat up. "Uh, sure. That would be great. What do we owe you?"

"Nothing, they are gifts."

I perked up at the idea, but my heart squished my excitement flat. "Cole, I appreciate the offer..." I sighed. "But I think I'll pass on a sword."

Nathan's jaw dropped.

Cole nodded. "Very well." He headed down a hall to a room.

Nathan stood up and called after Cole. "Think light, don't bring much. Just what you can carry on your back."

I smiled. I shouldn't be. Why should I want some stranger to ride with me on Nathan's back? Why did I trust him? The ring's vision? Or a spell of Cole's? But the ring gave me the ability to sense a person's character. I didn't read evil or deception in him. Instead, he engendered trust.

And the ring had indicated we loved each other. Did I? Could I? I couldn't tell. Yet, my actions said maybe I did. Maybe.

"Sis, what gives? Why don't you want a sword? I would think you most of all would love to hold one again."

"Yes, I would. But the ring has other ideas, and maybe it's for the best. Security blankets eventually must be laid down to build trust in the Lord instead." My mind wandered to past times. "Dad did it, and so can I."

I rose and stepped toward the front door. "I think I need some fresh air." I flung the door open, then leaped back. I peered out the door again.

A mass of people moved toward me. "There she is! Heal me!"

I leaned against the door-post. Tears welled up as I gazed upon the throng of pained faces. Their sorrow overwhelmed me. I stepped forward.

11

Nathan and Kaylee's auras landed around a mile outside of Paradise. Gabrielle squinted as they entered the city's gates. "This brightness is painful."

Josh nodded. "This is the first time I've visited this city. The stories I've heard don't do it justice." He held a hand over his eyes and scanned the streets. "Better be careful. If what I've heard is true, this isn't a safe place."

Gabrielle glanced at him. "It's a little late to be telling me that now."

"Would you have changed your mind about coming here if I had told you earlier?"

She shielded her eyes from the light. "I suppose not."

"I didn't think so."

Gabrielle watched the people, as painfully bright as the rest of the city, scurried by, but they took no notice of Josh or her. "How do you suppose this place came to be like this?"

Josh pointed to the cross protruding over the skyline. "Stories say that the founder, ironically named Jesus, wanted to establish Paradise in this life. So he and his followers set up this colony to bring about his vision. A year after Jesus' death, one of the city's leaders discovered the 'light of glory' and turned all of Paradise into a shining city on a hill."

She frowned. "Sounds like a bunch of hocus pocus to me."

"That's what most people think."

They entered the center of town and saw four wooden blocks topped with latches resting in the grassy open area. She laid her hand on Josh's arm. "Are those what I think those are?"

He sighed. "Yes. Execution blocks."

"In Paradise?" This certainly could not be Paradise.

Josh shrugged. "But look, two of the block's latches are broken." The corners of Josh's mouth fell. "And I can see Kaylee and Nathan's auras heading into the sky from there, headed to the north-west. They left in a hurry. Not a good sign."

She shivered. These people tried to execute them? But why? At least they escaped, but in what condition? "Then I suggest we head that way and leave this place."

He nodded. "I'm with you. Just don't draw attention to yourself."

She chuckled. "I think it's too late for that. Our dullness stands out among this brightness like fireflies on a moonless night."

"Halt!"

Josh and Gabrielle turned to find a priest with several men behind him.

Gabrielle hoped a priest would be safe. "Oh, Father. I'm glad we found you. Have you seen a nineteen-year-old boy and a seventeen-year-old girl in town the last few days?"

"Only the pure may enter the Holy of Holies in Paradise. Are you pure?"

Gabrielle glanced at Josh who bit his lip. She returned the priest's gaze. "Please tell us about the boy and girl if you know anything. Then I'll answer your question."

He furrowed his eyebrows. "Yes, two such humans passed through here recently. They left on the road to Morgoth. Now, answer my question."

She bowed to the priest. "Though I am a sinner, by God's grace He will grant me mercy and forgiveness."

The priest frowned and narrowed his eyes. "So you admit to being imperfect?"

Gabrielle noticed Josh sliding into place beside her. A crowd gathered around them. Gabrielle nodded. "No one is perfect, save one."

The priest turned around. "From her own mouth, you heard it! Not only does she admit to being imperfect, but she denies the possibility of perfection except to one." He swung his finger toward Josh. "I suppose he is the one exception?"

Gabrielle's jaw dropped open. "You are a priest! Haven't you read the Scriptures?"

"How dare a woman try to teach a man of God! Arrest them!"

The men moved forward to grab them, but Josh put forth his hand and the men froze in mid-step. "You have no need to arrest us. We will be on our way to Morgoth."

The priest's face turned red. "He's a wizard too! Stone them!"

Before they could react, people all through the crowd lifted their hands into the air and flung rocks at them. Gabrielle could see a group of men handing them out among the crowd.

She ducked as she wondered about the sanity of these people.

Josh cast his hand out and blocked several rocks headed toward Gabrielle, but two stones smashed against his head from behind, and he collapsed like a house in a tornado.

Gabrielle dropped to his side. "Josh!" He didn't respond. She felt her stomach churning both afraid for Josh and disgust at the stupidity of these people.

The rocks no longer fell around her. The priest pointed a finger at Gabrielle. "Now arrest them."

The men moved forward again. Gabrielle watched as they approached. A burning in her soul grew until she could no longer contain it.

She stood and faced the priest and his men. "This isn't Paradise." She drew inches away from the priest's face. "This is dazzling lights hiding rotting souls!"

A gust swept the street and the ground shook. Then the sky dimmed and the air grew still. Toward her left, the bright colors and shiny sparkles vanished as if someone rolled up a carpet. As the wave of change crashed over them with a whipping gust of wind, Gabrielle nearly fell to the ground. In its wake, it left rotting wood, broken hinges, collapsed walls. And upon the people hung worn cloth, dingy and gray.

The people screamed and some called out, "The end of all things has come!" Only Gabrielle and Josh now displayed any color and health at all.

She stared around, amazed at the vast change. She hadn't expected such a drastic reaction to her words. She did have the ability to reveal the truth simply by speaking it, just as Joel had said.

The priest stared at Gabrielle from a wrinkled and disease-ridden face. His eye sockets barely held in his eyes, and rot ate away at his nose and cheeks. He held out a bony hand. "Leave us! Leave us and maybe this will all go away!"

Gabrielle shook her head. "No, this will not go away. This is the world you have created and lived in. Instead of fixing it, you hid it behind fake beauty to avoid dealing with it. But it sat there, rotting away your souls nonetheless."

The priest fell to his knees. "No, don't speak. Just go!"

She stared at the man and the people. Some in shock, others wailing and screaming. She shook her head. "You can live in this hell you've created, or you can repent. It's your only way out."

The priest pointed at a horse tied up on the other side of the street. "Take the horse. Take it and go! I cannot abide your presence!"

She sighed, then put her hands under Josh's armpits and dragged him to the horse. She struggled to lift him onto its back, but Josh's weight fought against her. Yet, she couldn't give up, and who in this town would offer any help?

"Ma'am?"

Gabrielle swung around to see a teen boy dressed in brown pants and a white shirt. His face shown a healthy pink and his eyes sparkled with life.

He bowed to her. "Ma'am, could you use some help?"

She nodded slowly. "How come you're not like the others?"

He gazed upon the mass of disease-ridden people huddled over the city streets before meeting her eyes. "I did what you said. I repented."

Gabrielle smiled. There would be hope in Paradise after all. "Yes, I could use a hand. Thank you."

He helped her pull Josh onto the horse's back and secure him. She grabbed the horse's reins, put her foot in the stirrup, and swung her leg onto its back. She stared at the sea of pain and despair churning through the streets of Paradise. Then her eyes drifted to the young man who stood in such stark contrast.

She patted the front of the horse as she studied the boy. "Not sure if this is the best place for you. You can come with me if you wish."

He sighed. "That's very nice of you, ma'am. I'm tempted." His eyes turned to the people in the streets. "But I believe my place is here, to show them the path."

Gabrielle stared at the young man, amazed at his courage and maturity. "What's your name?"

He focused on her again. "Moses."

Tension she didn't realize she held ebbed from her. She smiled at him. "Moses, a fine name. I believe you'll find success in your endeavors. Don't give up, for many are stubborn and refuse to hear the truth. But you'll be rewarded by those who do listen, even as you've rewarded me by hearing my words and acting upon them."

"Thank you for your prayers, ma'am." He bowed once more.

She squeezed her feet and jiggled the reins. "Come on, horse. It's about time we leave Paradise, such as it is." She swore the horse perked up as they rode past the gate.

After more than three hours on the road, Gabrielle pulled the horse to a stop and dismounted. She examined her previous attempt to reduce Josh's swelling. The ball-sized bump appeared to have stabilized, but he still lay unconsciousness. What if he never did wake up? If she possessed a ring like Kaylee's... She shook her head. No, she couldn't worry about what isn't or may never be. Focus on what is and deal with that.

She pulled Josh off the horse and leaned him against a fallen log. She slumped down beside him to rest. She considered her options. One, she could wait for Josh to wake up so he could retrieve their supplies with his magic. Two, starve until she could reach the next town. Going back to Paradise wasn't an option. Three, try to make do with supplies around her. Could she construct a bow and arrow to hunt something? Or maybe she could find some edible plants in the forest?

She sighed. If Josh didn't wake up soon, she'd have to figure out something. Meanwhile, Kaylee and Nathan flew further away.

Groans sounded from behind her as if answering her thoughts. She turned to see Josh's eyes open and jerking around.

Tension escaped from her body as she settled next to him. His eyes fixed on her and they widened. "Are...you an angel? Am I dead?"

He joked; that was a good sign. "I'm not an angel, and you're not dead, though I feared as much."

"I believe the second, but I don't believe the first." He grimaced. "My head, it's pounding!"

"I'm not surprised. I don't have anything to help the swelling. I've cleaned the wound and applied what herbs I could find. But if you have anything to heal it in your cloak, you'd better get it out."

He reached a hand over, opened his cloak, and peered in. "In here? Why would anything be in here?"

Gabrielle put her hands on her hips. "Josh, you can quit playing games. After what I've been though, I don't have much humor left for your jokes."

"My name's Josh?" He stared around. "If I'm not dead, where am I?"

Her stomach twisted. The scared way he glanced around appeared real—not a joke. "Are you telling me you don't recall who you are, or me, or why we're out here?"

He stared up at the sky. "I don't recall anything before I woke up here. I know there must be more, but I honestly don't remember it." He turned his head and stared at me. "Are we...married?"

Gabrielle shook her head. "No. You were my former husband's best friend."

He frowned. "That's too bad. You're beauty is stunning."

Gabrielle sat back, not sure what to think of his comment. "You must be hallucinating."

"But you did say your husband is 'former,' correct?"

Is this what Josh really thought but never felt comfortable saying? Or did the knock to his head do more damage than she realized? "Former in the sense he's no longer in this life. He departed into Paradise about three months ago."

A smile cracked across his lips. "Great, that means I still have a chance."

Great? Did he say great? "A chance for what?"

"For you."

Gabrielle bit her tongue to prevent a hasty remark from escaping. "Josh, you're my husband's best friend. You swore to protect me."

His eyes sagged. "What better way to protect you than to marry you?"

She sighed. "You don't understand. He is waiting for me in Paradise. I'm not marrying anyone else. You would never have asked this before."

He sat up and rubbed the back of his head. "Maybe I'm not me anymore."

Gabrielle forked her fingers through her hair. If he couldn't remember who he was... "Do you remember that you're a wizard? Do you remember your spells?"

"I'm a wizard? Spells?" He stared at the ground and rubbed his head.

Gabrielle sunk onto a rock. Josh's magic supplied them with nearly everything on this trip. How would they feed themselves, and where would the money come from? She stared at the tree leaves waving in the breeze. They would starve!

Josh leaned his head forward. "Are you sure we're not married?"

Gabrielle dropped her head between her knees. This couldn't be happening! How would she ever catch up to Nathan and Kaylee now?

12

I laid my hand on her arm. "Lord, heal her wound and restore her strength." The open sore shrank, leaving pink, healthy skin behind.

"Oh, thank you so much!" She reached out her arms and hugged me. "You are a gift from God."

Another lifted her child into the air. "Please, my child is dying!"

I felt a tap on my shoulder. Nathan stood over me. "Kaylee, we need to leave. You've been at this for four hours and the crowd has grown bigger than when you started. Crystal gets further away every minute."

I rubbed my forehead. "How do I say no?" But he was right. I could spend days healing them and not finish, and we didn't have days. I would have to cut it off at some point. "Just one more."

He scanned the crowd. "She will do one more healing, but I'm afraid we'll have to go after that. Sorry, but we have to quit sometime."

A cry rose from the crowd. I held my hands out to the lady with the child. "Let me see him."

Thoughts blew through my mind like the wind blowing through my hair as Nathan flapped his wings. Cole directed us to a pass over the mountains, but Nathan trotted along the ground for a while because of the thinning air and Cole's added weight. When we arrived at the other side, a cliff dropped onto the plains below. Nathan leaped over the edge, and we fell for several yards before he caught the wind and leveled out. It reminded me of our leap off the sky island.

Which reminded me of Joel. I hadn't seen him for over two months, and I wondered what poor soul he helped now. I cracked a smile. At one point I had thought he might marry me. Still possible, but not likely. That's how it is with men like him and Dad. He might settle down someday, but as long as God sent him to a person he should help, marriage and a long term relationship would have to wait.

Yet now Cole filled that gap. Funny that I thought of him that way. I hadn't said anything to him, but he appealed to me. Unlike other men, being around him put me at ease. Besides, his name rhymed with Joel—that should seal it! I giggled under my breath.

But despite my thoughts about Joel and Cole, my mind couldn't escape the faces in Morgoth. Hurt, pain, and suffering stared back at me. Faces crying for help—help from me. Standing up and leaving them ripped me apart. But I vowed to return when I could. The thought provided some consolation.

Leaving them was hard, I know.

I stroked Nathan's neck. "Yes, it was. But I know we had to."

"Yes, what?" Cole said from behind me.

"Oh, I was talking to Nathan."

He sighed. "That's hard to get used to, hearing only one side of the conversation."

I smiled. "I suppose it would be." The crowd's faces appeared in my mind again. "Cole, I have a question."

"Go ahead."

"Your god, Morgenstern, why do so many in his city suffer? Does he not care for them?"

His arms, wrapped around my stomach, squeezed slightly. "Of course he does, but pain and suffering are not always bad. They can teach humility."

I nodded. "True, but when it is overwhelming, it no longer has such benefit."

He whispered in my ear. "And who am I to draw the line between beneficial and overwhelming for any one person?"

I sighed. "I don't know. All I know is I couldn't look in their faces and do nothing. I don't see how Morgenstern can."

He remained silent; I feared the worst. "I'm sorry. I didn't mean to insult your religion or god. But their faces keep staring at me, crying for me to help. I'm having a hard time reconciling their anguish with a loving god."

"You've not been around suffering much, have you?"

I shook my head. "No. Not the kind I felt in Morgoth."

"There are more places in the world than Morgoth where you'll find no god has acted. Including your own."

I turned my head as far around as I could, to catch his eye. "It's not the god who acts, it's his people acting in his behalf. Who is working to heal their bodies and soul in behalf of Morgenstern?"

His eyes jumped to the horizon in the distance. "There is a monk."

"A monk of Morgenstern's?"

He cleared his throat. "No. A Christian monk."

Do you believe me yet?

"Quiet!" I snapped the back of Nathan's head.

Cole stiffened. "What?"

"No, not you. I was—"

"Talking to Nathan. Right."

My heart tugged at my mind. I scanned the ground ahead. "Nathan, down by that oasis, I sense someone needs me."

He banked toward it. *I need a rest anyway. Crossing the mountains took a lot out of me.*

As we drew near, a body lay on the ground. No dust responded when Nathan's hooves hit the parched dirt. I slid off as he pulled to a stop. I reached down and felt the man's pulse. It barely pushed against my fingers.

I caught Cole's eyes. "It looks like some thieves took everything and left him here for dead."

"Can you do anything for him?"

I laid my hand on his forehead. "I believe should. Yes." I cleared my throat. "Lord, heal this man of his wounds and disease." His body jerked, then relaxed.

His eyes blinked open and he fixed them on me. "Who are you? What did you do?"

"I healed you."

"How?" The man sat up and gained his bearings.

I sat on the ground. "It's a gift God gave me."

He checked out Cole, and then his eyes did a double-take with Nathan. "Your...your horse has...wings? I must have died, but is this heaven?"

I laughed. "This isn't heaven, and yes, my horse does have wings. He's my brother."

He cracked a weak smile. "Your brother?" He blinked. "Yes, either I'm having a vivid dream, or I'm in heaven."

Cole knelt beside us. "Things aren't always what they seem, my good man. I can assure you that you neither dream nor sit in heaven."

The man's shoulder's slumped. "They took everything but the clothes on my back. Now what will I do?"

Cole pulled out some bills from his tunic. "Head back to Morgoth, it is the closest city. This will help you until then, but see my assistant, Simeon, and tell him that the Priest Cole said to help you obtain a horse and necessary supplies."

The man's eyes teared up as Cole shoved the money in his hand.

Cole patted his shoulder. "We'll stay with you until you get your strength back."

He nodded. "Thank you so much! You are most generous and kind."

Cole smiled. "You're welcome." He leaned over to my ear. "Did you see Morgenstern help someone's suffering?"

"Yes, I did." I stared into his eyes. "I'll go see what we have to help him back on his feet." I drew toward Nathan as I slid my pack off. I leaned into his ear. "Do you believe me yet?"

We sat around a camp fire, eating food Nathan had caught. The cool night air sent shivers down my arms and legs, but the warmth of the fire fought back valiantly. I scooted a little closer.

The day riding on Nathan with Cole at my back certainly changed things. Nathan and I talked less, and talking with Cole, while doable, proved difficult because I couldn't face him. So the time before heading to bed provided a chance to chat without fighting the wind-noise and a stiff neck.

Nathan put his plate down. "Despite Cole's added weight, we traveled far in one day. But you know what I could use?"

I finished swallowing the last bite of my food. "What?"

"I miss our sparring. It's been months since we've practiced with each other."

I chuckled. "A few things have happened since then! But I have no sword."

Cole rose and drew one from his pack. "Here, use mine."

I grasped its handle. The balance felt great, as if my arm had grown a few more feet longer and sharper. Wrapping my fingers around it caused me to wish I had taken one of Cole's swords after all. "Thanks."

I placed my feet and established my posture. "I'm ready."

Nathan took his stance, and immediately lunged an offensive thrust toward me. My arm moved without thinking about it, as if the sword moved of its own accord. It wove around Nathan's sword and parried it. The force flung his sword wide, leaving him open.

I thrust and the sword plunged into his rib cage.

A breath escaped Nathan's throat and his eyes widened. His left hand clasped his side as his sword dropped into the dirt with a thud.

I froze in horror before I pulled the sword from his body. He collapsed onto the ground and his face turned pale. I immediately fell upon him and place my hand over the wound soaking his tunic in blood.

"Lord, heal my brother!" I couldn't bear the thought if this time God decided He wouldn't answer my prayer. Not when my arm had killed him. I gritted my teeth and faced the sky. "Please!"

I felt the blood stop pumping. I cast my head down. Color returned to his face, and the flow of red blood dried up. The tension bottled up within me demanded relief; I collapsed upon him as tears wet my eyes.

Nathan blinked and stared at my head resting on his chest. "You could've said no."

I shook my head, trying to shake off the guilt. "I don't know what happened. I nearly killed you." The thought caused my chest to heave erratically as I fought to regain control.

He sat up and cradled me in his arms. "You did kill me. If you didn't have the ability to heal, I would be dead."

Cole knelt beside us. "I'm sorry. I feel partly to blame since you used my sword."

I lifted my head and wiped my eyes. "It's not your fault. I slipped is all."

Nathan's eyes locked onto Cole's while he addressed me. "In all the hours of practice we've put in together, you've never come anywhere close to killing me before. Yet your thrust went deep and straight for my heart, as if you intended to slay me."

"Nathan!" My teeth clinched. "How could you insinuate such a thing?"

"I'm simply stating the facts." He turned to face me. "You're drawing your own conclusions."

"I...I..." I leaped to my feet and stomped to the other side of the fire, facing the darkness. *First I'm feeling guilty and now I'm angry at him! Why? Because he forced me to confront my inner fear? That Cole caused it to happen? Surely the ring wouldn't lead us to someone intending to destroy us.*

I felt a hand on my shoulder. Cole's face slid into view. "He's right, it does look suspicious. He has every right to question me. And perhaps I should have warned you, but I didn't think it would get away from you like it did."

I met his eyes. "Warned me?"

"Yes, I balanced the sword using magic from a friend of mine. It's so well balanced that it can feel as if it acts on its own. It takes mental disciple to use it well."

"I noticed."

Cole bent his head. "I'm sorry."

Nathan's voice sounded from behind me. "I'm going to sleep. I've had enough excitement for one day."

I heard him shuffle around until he settled into his blankets.

I breathed deep and relaxed my muscles. "You couldn't have known I'd lose control. Probably due to months without practice. It turned out all right in the end, thank goodness."

"Yes." His eyes searched into mine. "I have to admit, you've captivated me. You're an amazing woman."

His words slid through my brain and out the other side before I could process what he had said. Then I drew them back in. He indicated interest in me! Was this the beginning of the ring's prediction?

I ran a hand through my hair and brushed it back. "I don't feel very amazing right now."

"You are." He placed a hand behind my head. His lips gently kissed my forehead. An image imprinted itself into my mind of him kissing me on the lips. I could smell his confidence, could taste his gentleness, feel his love. The vision vanished when his lips parted from my skin, though the wetness created a cool spot as the arid winds blew upon me.

He headed toward his bed. I stared into the night as if somehow, the vast range of emotions and how to make sense of them all would find an answer there. Somewhere out there, the answer did hide. When I would discover it would be another matter.

But one question kept rattling around in my brain: Am I in love?

13

Gabrielle held the pebble-sized ball from Josh's coat's pocket in her hands. Now, if they could expand it into their supplies, one problem would be solved.

She held one up between her fingers. "I believe you threw it into the open area and said..." She tossed the ball toward the center of the clearing. "Expand to a tent!"

The ball plopped in the dirt but no tent appeared. She retrieved the ball and handed it to Josh. "Why don't you give it a try."

He shrugged his shoulders and received the ball from her. "So, there's a whole kitchen in this?"

"With food."

"I am hungry." Josh tossed the ball toward the center of the dirt. "Expand to a tent."

The ball blossomed into the full-sized tent that Gabrielle recalled seeing before. She smiled. "Appears it has to be your voice. Let's go eat."

They entered and Gabrielle prepared the meal while directing Josh where he could help. Soon they sat at a table holding flat bread, venison stew, and a lovely red wine, fruity with flavor but smooth as silk.

She held the glass up. "I hope you weren't saving this bottle for a special occasion." She refilled his cup.

He cracked a smile. "I guess what I don't know won't hurt me. Right?"

She held the glass up as if to toast. "Remember those words if you gain your memory back."

He sat his glass down after a swallow. "So, let's see if I have this right. You have two kids. The girl wears a ring that enables her to heal people. The other can turn into a winged horse. You're chasing them because you had a vision that the girl would die if you didn't go after her."

She nodded. "That about sums it up. You agreed to come with me, and we've been traveling on a flying carpet through your magic." She sighed. "While I'm relieved at not flying on it again, it does make catching up with a flying horse near impossible without it. In the last town, they threw rocks at us and a couple hit the back of your head. Apparently your brain's been affected."

"Did you hear me speak the spell to make the carpet fly?"

"No, the one to expand the tent is the only one I ever heard you say loud enough to hear. Usually you mumbled the spells, I guess to keep others within hearing range from listening in."

He leaned back in his chair. "Maybe one of those small balls can be expanded into something, like, another winged horse?"

She bobbed her head to the side. "Maybe. I don't know enough about them to say. But it won't hurt to try. At least, I hope it won't hurt. You did say that winged horses were a creation of magic."

"So, what's our plan?"

Gabrielle frowned. "I have to find some way to get to her. I wouldn't have been told to go if I can't do it. If creating a winged horse is out, then we'll have to make do with the horse we have and hope they are delayed long enough to give us a chance."

He lifted his glass. "Tomorrow we ride for glory and your daughter's life. Tonight, we feast!"

She lifted hers and clinked with his. "May God guide us."

Josh threw a coin-sized ball. "Expand to a winged horse."

It flew through the air and flashed with light. When it landed, a horse appeared.

Gabrielle gasped. "Josh, what's this?"

"A winged horse."

"With wings on its neck?"

He shrugged. "Where else would they be?"

"It's all wrong. It can't fly like that. We'd slide off its back."

He scratched his head. "You have to remember, I have no memory what one looks like."

She hadn't thought of that. "Let me draw you a picture." She grabbed a stick from the ground and drew a crude likeness in the dirt. "See, the wings attach here on its body."

"Oh, I see. Let me try again." He extended his hand toward the horse. "Contract from a winged horse." A light flashed around the horse and the ball returned to his hand. Then he tossed it again. "Expand to a winged horse."

Another horse appeared, this time with wings on its body.

Gabrielle grinned. "Great!" But her excitement died with the thought of sitting on the back of a horse hundreds of feet in the air. Laying on a carpet sounded so much better in comparison. Images of Kaylee falling off Nathan, plummeting to her death, assaulted her.

She swallowed. She would have to do it. She would do it. Kaylee's life depended on it.

Josh contracted the tent back into a ball. He held it in his hand. "You know, I find it strange that I could recreate the tent perfectly, but not a winged horse. Surely I knew what one looked like before. So how did I do it?"

"Winged horses are not common, and it is unlikely you would have seen very many pictures. But you used your tent frequently. Perhaps the image is embedded in your mind deep enough the magic could draw on it."

He nodded. "It did have a familiar feel about it. Like I was home."

"Help me up." Gabrielle pulled herself upon the horse while Josh gave her a boost up. She held out a hand for him to climb aboard. Once he sat behind her, she flipped the reins.

"Giddy up."

The horse broke into a light trot. Gabrielle wondered what one did to get a winged horse to fly. It came with no instructions. She yanked up on the reins. The horse whinnied and reared back on its hind legs, pawing at the air with its front ones. Its wings flapped, but they didn't fly into the air.

Instead, Gabrielle clawed at its neck as her and Josh slid off its back and landed with painful crash to the ground.

Josh groaned as he sat up, and rubbed his back. Gabrielle felt a bruise developing on her calf from hitting a rock.

She rubbed her leg. "Do you have any idea how to get a winged horse to fly?"

He shook his head. "Don't have a clue. Sorry." He rose to his feet. "Let me take the reins. It's possible something will instinctively come to me."

She grabbed Josh's outstretched hand and stood up. "I guess that's what we're left with."

They remounted the horse, and broke it into a trot again. Josh did nothing at first. Then he jumped up a little. Nothing happened. Then he commanded, "Fly!" The horse ignored him. He tried several more variations as they rode down the road. The last one landed them back onto the ground, with more bruises.

Josh massaged his forehead. "If we keep this up, we'll be lying on the side of the road with broken legs."

We have a winged horse and we can't get it to fly! She hit the ground with her fist. "It's no use. We'll have to use it like a regular horse. At least until someone can tell us how to get it to fly."

He stood up. "Let's at least go back and get the other horse. We'll go faster with two horses than tiring out one with more weight."

"Agreed." She reached out for his hand again.

The trip from Paradise to Morgoth would take three days on horseback. They'd gone half a day's journey the day before and hoped for minimal stops. If the horses could keep up a good pace, they could cut it down to two days.

Gabrielle examined Josh as they rode in silence. She wondered whether Josh's desire for her flowed from his own hidden desires or from the bump on his head. "Josh, did you mean it when you said you wanted to marry me?" Gabrielle watched his face for a reaction.

His left eyebrow rose. "Yes I meant it. Are you reconsidering?"

"What about your angel comment? Did it rise with the bump on your head?"

He leaned forward and craned his neck to examine her. "While I did wonder if I had died and gone to Paradise—"

"You did go to Paradise and almost died!" She giggled.

He smiled. "You're as angelic to me now as when I first opened my eyes. You are the first memory I have, and I would be amiss if I didn't say that I hope you'll be my last memory on this earth."

Gabrielle didn't know what to say. She felt her face flushing. Memories of Sisko flooded back to her. He had said similar words to her once. She glanced at Josh. Maybe when his memory came back, he would confirm it, but what if the link he had established with Sisko still resided in some manner inside him? What if he was experiencing her as Sisko did due to his damaged head releasing the link's subconscious connection?

She held her breath as a new thought settled into her mind. What if Sisko, through the link, could be with them? Could such a thing happen, even be possible? The Scriptures do say all things are possible with God.

She stared at him, and he kept glancing at her. His brow wrinkled. "You're staring at me very oddly. Is everything all right?"

She remembered what Joel had said in the steam house. She could reveal the truth. Did she dare? If it wasn't true, nothing should happen.

"Sisko, reveal yourself."

A glow emanated from Josh, and he morphed. His form gelled for a second before reforming into Sisko's body.

"Sisko!"

He blinked and jerked his head around. "Gabrielle? Where are we?" Then his eyes widened. "Gabrielle!"

He leaped off his horse, and she fell into his arms. She hugged him as tight as she could, and he squeezed back. She felt tears trickling down her cheeks. "I can't believe it's you!"

He pressed his lips onto hers. She smelled the familiar scent of his hair, and the brush of whiskers against her skin. She could have stayed like this forever.

He broke the kiss and stared into her eyes. "I feel like I've been waiting for an eternity to kiss and hold you again." He glanced around. "But where are we and how did I get here? Last I recall, I was chatting with St. Timothy about events in the future of this world. You wouldn't believe..." He frowned. "I probably shouldn't say anything."

"About me?"

He shook his head. "No, not your future. The world's, many years from now. They don't let me in on what will happen to you. They say I'm too close to the subject." He nodded. "And they're probably right."

She squeezed him tightly against her. "I'm so glad you're here. I felt abandoned when Nathan and Kaylee freed me from the crystal prison, and I discovered you had already died."

He winked. "And you specifically told me to stay dead, as I recall."

She frowned. "Oh, you heard me? But I didn't say it like that!"

"But you did say it."

"Well, yes. But it's my fault you're back, so I'm not blaming you." She thrust her lips back onto his before he could respond.

They parted, and he gazed into her eyes. "I'm sorry I left as I did. It couldn't be helped. I did feel bad about it. But perhaps that's why God has allowed this to happen. Yet I have to ask, how did you cause this?"

She sighed. "That's a long story. Much has happened since you left for Paradise. Perhaps it's best if we rode while we talked. Kaylee's in danger and I've got to reach her before she's killed. We're losing time."

He helped her back onto her horse. He started to mount his and froze. "This horse has wings."

She smiled weakly. "Yes, but we couldn't figure out how to make it fly. Do you know how?"

"No, but who is 'we'?"

"Oh, Josh was with me."

He scanned the area. "Josh is here? Where?"

She brushed her hair behind her back. "Like I said, it's a long story. He's not here now."

He climbed onto the horse, and they headed down the road as Gabrielle told him the events that occurred since he had left the steam house for Paradise.

14

Did I love Cole? The question haunted me as Nathan carried us among the clouds. The only man I could say I loved was Joel. Even then, I felt unsure I truly loved him. It could have been my reaction for him helping me through a tough time and watching over me. Like my love for Dad.

And I couldn't keep from thinking about Dad, about how he met Amma and the vision he saw when they touched. It took him five years before the ring released him to marry her. Yet he knew before he left her house that he loved her.

So far, I couldn't say the same about Cole. But I'd never fallen in love before. What would it feel like? Maybe if I had to ask the question, it hadn't happened yet. Or maybe it had, and I was so ignorant about love, messed up from my near-rape experience as a twelve-year-old, that I wouldn't know if I'd fallen in love until it abandoned me.

"Why does life have to be so complicated?"

What? Nathan responded.

"What?" Cole asked.

"Sorry. Thinking out loud." I sighed.

You're in love with him, aren't you?

"I don't know."

Yep, you are. This isn't good.

I leaned forward. "What do you mean this isn't good?"

Cole cleared his throat from behind me. "Sounds like an interesting discussion. Mind if I join in?"

My face flushed. We'd been talking about him, literally in front of him.

"I'm sorry. Nathan, we'll have to finish this later."

That's for sure. Look ahead.

A mass of horses and wagons circled an oasis a mile away.

They came into view after we crested that last rise. I'd better set down before they see us.

"Too late." People pointed up at us and a scurry of activity broke out.

Nathan sank behind a small dune. We jumped off, and I unsnapped the bracelet. Nathan returned to his human form. We left the hill for the caravan. By the time we reached the trees at the water's edge, a group of them approached us. One heavy-set man, black-bearded and on the tall side, appeared to be their leader.

The man stepped forward from the group. "What happened to your horse? Why did you leave 'im behind the hill? Certainly he needs water like the rest of us."

One of Nathan's eyebrows raised. "A horse? Certainly you must be mistaken. We've walked here."

The man placed his hands on his hips. "Come now. I know what I saw." He scratched his head. "Though I could have sworn I saw only two of you on it."

Cole cast his palm out to the man. "You see? The desert often gets people to seeing things that aren't there."

"But we all saw it," another man cried out.

The leader strolled around me and stared. "This one's very promising. I'm sure she'll have to be broken in." He wagged a finger at Nathan. "That'll lower the price."

My comfort level rose to a screaming cry. But Nathan and Cole wouldn't let anything happen to me.

Nathan stepped toward the man. "Sir, we're not here to sell her to you. She's my sister."

The leader's smile turned into a frown. "Oh. Too bad. I would have liked this one myself."

Nathan's face turned red. Though I couldn't show it at the moment, a joy sprung forth at his anger in my behalf.

The man held his hands up. "I'm sorry. I didn't mean to insult you." He cleared his throat. "So, why have you approached us? Need protection to the next town? I'm certain we can arrange a mutually beneficial payment." He glanced my way. "I could even give a discount for certain, eh, privileges."

I refrained from hitting him. We didn't need distractions. "Look, mister. We're here to buy a person off your hands. Her name is Crystal. You bought her from the people at Paradise."

He bit his lip and stared thoughtfully into the sky. "Oh yeah. I remember her. I'm afraid you're too late. We sold her to the Burrowers."

Nathan shrugged. "The Burrowers? Who are they?"

Cole broke in. "They're a race of creatures who live under the mountains, over that direction." He pointed to a range in the distance. "Their dwellings are about a day from here."

"Yes, yes," the leader said. "We sold her to them about a day ago, at an oasis a ways back."

A realization rose along with a churning fear. The man at the oasis—were these the thieves who had left him for dead? If so, our fate might not be much better.

I leaned over and whispered in Nathan's ear. "We need to leave—now! We're in danger."

He nodded and addressed the leader. "Thank you for the information. We're desperate to find her, so we'll be on our way."

I noticed a couple of men headed for the hill we had emerged from.

The leader smiled. "Oh, no need to rush off. Even if you don't have a horse, certainly you could use some food and drink. On the house! Why don't you all come on into camp and enjoy our company before we part ways, eh?" His eyes spoke of an eager anticipation.

"We'd love to," Nathan responded. "But our time is short and we can't afford to waste any of it. May you have a profitable trip."

All three of us turned and headed toward the Burrower's mountain range. I moved three steps when a rope fell over me and pinned my arms to my side in its tightening grip.

Nathan turned around and drew his sword in one motion, slicing through the thick, taut threads. I almost fell when the tension released me, but I kept my feet under me and cast the limp rope off as we broke into a hard run.

"After them!" the cry went up, and a whole group of them surged after us, lassos in hand.

I knew we'd never get away by running. I grabbed my bracelet and unlatched it from my necklace. My foot caught a rock and I stumbled. The bracelet fumbled from my hand and hit the dirt. I skidded to a halt and leaped back to grab it.

A lasso fell toward me. I snatched the bracelet off the ground, and rolled to the side and back upon my feet as the lasso fell beside me. I scampered away, and clicked the bracelet around my wrist. "Now, Nathan!"

I didn't hear him, but a blinding light grew around him and a brilliant, white horse arose from its wake. The people chasing us paused for a second before one of them called out, "The horse was the boy! Catch him!" They surged toward us again.

I hurried to Nathan's side, grabbed his mane, and with a hop and a bounce off the ground, I landed onto his back and held on. Nathan galloped beside Cole. I grabbed Cole's outstretched hand and swung him onto Nathan's back as he bounced up.

Nathan started to leap into the air when a lasso fell over his neck and tightened.

Argh! Do something, Kaylee!

I pulled at the rope, but couldn't squeeze my fingers under enough to loosen it.

Another rope fell onto his neck, and then another. Nathan reared back and the people skidded in the dirt as they held firmly to their ends. Then more ropes slipped around his neck.

Before I could think what to do, Cole's hand thrust itself around me and I heard him mutter something. The ropes all snapped apart as if someone sliced through them with a sword in one swift motion.

Nathan jerked away and leaped into the air. His wings beat firmly with quickened pace. Lassos fell short as he gained altitude. I relaxed as the cries below us subsided.

"Talk about a creepy group of people." I cast a glance behind me to catch Cole's eyes. "Did you use magic back there?"

Cole paused. "Yes. I've picked up a few minor spells from a friend."

I'd say it was the tip of the iceberg. He's dangerous, Kaylee.

I didn't respond. How could I? But I pinched Nathan's neck to let him know how I felt.

Ouch! He neighed and thrust his head upwards. *I guess the truth really does hurt.*

I craned my neck toward Cole. "I'm glad you know magic. I doubt we would have escaped otherwise."

"All in a day's work for your local priest."

I knew he smiled behind me. I rested my back upon his torso and his arms squeezed around my stomach. Why did I do that? No, the real question was why did I feel comfortable doing that? No sense of fear, no sense he would take advantage of me, I simply wanted to show my gratitude for his help. Like when I pat a horse's neck, I didn't fear he'd take it the wrong way. But why?

It dawned on me—because how he would take it is how I felt. Nathan was right; I did love him. Why else would I experience no fear?

I rested my hand on his arm at my stomach and squeezed.

Nathan yawned. "I've had a long day of fighting and flying. I think I'll get some sleep." He rolled out his bedroll, settled in, and soon steady breaths of sleep rolled from him as the fire crackled in the still night air.

Cole shifted until he sat next to me. "I've always loved the desert night air. So fresh, clean, and free."

"Yes, it is." For the first time, I detected a touch of discomfort from him. I sensed he wanted to tell me something. I suspected what lay on his mind to say, but I wanted to hear him say it. At least, I found myself hoping it was on his mind.

He turned and faced me. "And that's what you are, fresh, clean, and free."

I caught a glance of him rolling his eyes before he turned his face away from me. I giggled under my breath. "Thank you. That's a very...uh, original compliment."

He turned his face back to me. A half-laugh creased his lips. "A lame attempt to say what I said earlier. I meant it. You are an amazing woman." He stared deep into my eyes. "I'm afraid I've fallen hopelessly in love with you."

He said it! I stared out into the night air. Now I felt uncomfortable. If I said it, there was no turning back. It would solidify what I felt churning in my heart, what the ring had been pointing to. Fears that I would never love anyone as a true soul-mate would vanish with the words. This is what Joel had prepared me for. Everything pointed to the fact that I loved him.

His eyes searched my face. I could tell he waited for an answer. His lips drooped on the ends as if I might not return the sentiment. I breathed deep and locked onto his eyes.

"I...well, you see...it's hard—"

"I know, I know." His head sank. "This would never work. We aren't the same religion. We barely know each other. Your brother sees me in a bad light."

"No, no. It's not that."

He met my eyes. "Then what?"

"You see...I...when I was twelve..." I wrapped my hands over my head. "Oh, bother!" I shot my lips to his and enveloped him in a hug. His eyes widened and then closed. His soft lips pressed tighter against mine as the cool desert air played with our hair. My vision returned. I felt like I watched us kissing from a distance while also being kissed. Energy sparked through me and I thought maybe, just maybe, time had froze, and we could stay this way forever.

But we parted lips. A sweetness coated them and I couldn't refrain from licking them with my tongue. A new excitement flowed through me. My fears gave way, and I found that the waters of love were fine after all. Actually, they were more than fine, they were great!

He gazed at me. "Does that mean you feel the same way about me?"

I nodded as a smile broke out on my lips. "I love you too."

There, I had said it. Relief flooded over me and a joy bubbled up inside. I could love a man after all.

We kissed again and again and again. When we parted to sleep, I couldn't recall. But I woke up the next morning feeling different inside. New, like spring flowers blooming against a barren winter landscape.

I rose to roll my bedding and prepare to eat and leave. I realized as I packed, that one of those goofy smiles graced my face and wouldn't disappear. And the odd thing was, I didn't care either. I caught Cole's eyes as he sipped some coffee. He winked and smiled back.

Gabrielle watched Sisko staring into the forest as the horses trotted down the road.

Sisko rode with an ease and naturalness she couldn't recall before. Paradise had been good for him. A lot better than the town several miles behind them now. She sighed and wondered if she dreamed all this and would wake up along the road somewhere to find Josh sleeping close by.

Sisko turned to her. "If I took Josh's place, that means he must have taken my place in Paradise." He shook his head. "With his memory gone, he'll be one confused but changed wizard when he gets back."

"I still find it hard to believe you're here."

"I know. Me too." He rubbed his chin. "But I'll have to go back. I'm dead to this life. I'm not supposed to be here."

Her heart sank. "Do we have to talk about that now? You don't have to go back right this minute."

He smiled. "I suppose not. But I will have to go back, and you're the only one who can send me back. You'll never feel like it's a good time."

She nodded and bowed her head. "I know."

"But like you said, no need to think about that now. Surely I can spend one day with you without consequence. Let's enjoy it while we can."

Gabrielle didn't look forward to his departure yet a third time. But she could worry about that tomorrow. She smiled. "Yes, we have tonight. As a matter of fact, the sun is setting and we've made good time today. We should arrive at Morgoth late tomorrow morning. Why not set up camp soon?"

He pointed to a clearing a stone's throw off the road. "How about over there?"

Excitement pumped through her heart along with the blood. She so looked forward to spending an evening with him instead of being stuck on these horses, apart from each other.

They slid off their mounts and led them through the trees to the clearing. Sisko must have had the same desire as she did, for no sooner did they leave the horses to munch on a patch of grass, than he wrapped her in his arms to hug and kiss her. The sun may have been setting behind the mountains, but it rose in her soul and swept her away to an isolated world of her own. Just her and Sisko enveloped in an eternal love marinated in Paradise.

After an hour, or maybe four, Sisko said, "I'm getting hungry." He grinned. "You know how long it has been since I've felt hunger?" He caressed her face. "Much less, your touch and love."

Gabrielle felt a tear rolling down her cheek. "You don't know how much I've missed you!" She buried her head in his neck and squeezed. Maybe if she never let go, they could stay this way for a long, long, long time.

"I really am hungry."

She pulled back. "You still know how to spoil a mood."

He shrugged. "It had to be spoiled sometime. We've been in that mood for hours."

"Still, couldn't you have found a more romantic way to stop?"

He ran his fingers through her hair. "You do realize it has been over three months since I've had a good meal...by your time."

She laughed. "All right, we'll eat!" She pointed at his pockets. "There are small pebble-sized balls in those pockets that Josh can expand into things by saying, 'Expand to a...' and he inserts what he wants it to expand to. He has a great tent he gets out of those. But it only works for him. I don't know whether it will for you or not, but you do have Josh's link."

He fished in the pocket. "We can give it a try. Though once we toss this, we might not be able to find it if it doesn't expand. It's a dark night in the forest." He pulled out a ball. Gabrielle could barely make it out in the pale starlight. Sisko threw it out and said, "Expand to a tent."

A light flashed as it soared through the air and a tent big enough for two popped into place upon the ground.

Gabrielle shook her head. "That's pathetic."

Sisko twisted his mouth. "It's a tent, isn't it?"

"Sure, but Josh's tent is the size of a house, complete with kitchen, food, places to sit..." She tilted her head down and trained her eyes on him. "And a very soft and comfortable bed."

He stretched. "Yes, a soft bed would do wonders for sore bones after riding on a horse all day."

She smacked him on the back of the head. "You know that's not what I had in mind."

He wrapped his right arm around her waist and pulled her to him, then circled his index finger over her forehead. "How well I know what goes on in that little head of yours. Even when you'd known me barely a couple days, you tried to get me to kiss you."

She frowned. "You know how few men ever climbed up that mountain to our house? My father and Seth would run them away first time they flew into a rage. I was desperate."

Sisko narrowed his eyes. "So, you wanted me out of desperation?"

She allowed a grin to spread across her face. "And because you were cute, but truth be told, something about your character, your soul, drew me to you. I couldn't let you get away."

She gazed into his eyes. The joy and love she always experienced shown in them. "And I don't want to let you get away now."

Sisko stared into the stars for a moment. "I really, really, am hungry."

Gabrielle rolled her eyes. "All right! Truly I have to go through your stomach to get to your heart!" She reached down to gather firewood. "See if you can imagine a decent meal you could turn one of those balls into. I'll get the fire going."

He saluted. "Yes, ma'am."

When she returned, Sisko stirred some spices into a pot. The smell of tender meats and vegetables as she stoked a fire under it, moved her thoughts from Sisko to food. How long had it been since she last ate? She didn't want to admit it, but was glad Sisko had pushed for dinner.

Once satisfied, her attention returned to him. She snuggled next to him on the log as the fire crackled in the crisp, night air.

He pulled her closer with a hand on her shoulder, and rubbed it. "Remember when Kaylee was three, and she tried to ride that dog?"

Gabrielle smiled. "Tried? She did ride the dog. Funniest thing I'd ever seen."

"That's when I knew she wouldn't be your average woman."

Kaylee. Did she draw near to the black tree? Would Gabrielle arrive too late to save her? "And I hope she lives to fulfill that reality."

Sisko chuckled. "I know what you're saying, but from my side of death, I wouldn't mind her being there with me."

She rubbed his back. "You always did enjoy the children."

He nodded. "Those were the best days of my life. Living in relative peace with you, Nathan, and Kaylee. We were a family."

She met his eyes. "We still are."

"Of course, but you know what I mean. We were together."

Gabrielle patted him on his chest. "And someday, we'll be eternally together with you in Paradise."

"And those," he said placing his hand over hers. "Those will certainly be the best days of any life."

She grinned, then swung her leg over his lap and landed in it, facing him. "Meanwhile, we have tonight. And though we don't have a big, soft bed, I intend to make good use of the stars before they disappear with the morning sun."

His hands slid across her back and pulled her closer. She shivered feeling his rough cheek caress hers. It felt insane thinking she held him in her arms again, but it was him. She sensed it. She basked in the reality as he ran his fingers through her hair.

Then she pulled back enough to face him. "Are you sure...I mean, you're dead."

He raised an eyebrow. "Yes. So?"

"Well, you're not going to get in trouble for this, are you? If it's a choice of having you for one night or for all of eternity, I'll choose eternity."

He laughed. "And you would have chosen well too. But God didn't allow me to return with a physical body for nothing. He's giving us a chance to say the goodbyes we missed out on when Beltrid took you from me, and I died before Nathan and Kaylee freed you."

She sighed. "Good. Because it would be a miserable night otherwise." She leaned over and poured her love into his mouth as she loosened his tunic.

I pointed to an overhang. "I think I saw something over there."

Nathan banked toward it. We'd been flying around the mountains for three hours, scanning them for an entrance. The Burrowers didn't make it easy to find. But as we approached the overhang, a welcome sight slid into view.

A narrow trail traced its way up the mountain and sank under the overhang onto a flat area. Once we flew lower than the overhang, I could see the path crawling up to a small door at the base of the outcropping of rocks.

Nathan navigated the winds racing across the mountain face with ease until he touched down upon the flat area. We hopped off and I removed my bracelet.

I scanned the plains below. "You can see for miles from here." It felt like the whole world lay before my feet.

Cole stepped up beside me and draped his arm over my shoulders. "Gives one a feeling of power, doesn't it?"

I nodded and wondered why he put it that way. Then again, isn't that what I had thought in so many words? "It's a beautiful perspective on life up here. Stunning!"

He smiled. "True, but next to you it doesn't appear as beautiful."

I felt heat rising to my face. Despite the overused compliment, I felt his love, and the thought radiated honesty.

Nathan cleared his throat. "Excuse me, but Crystal is trapped somewhere in this mountain. Can we go get her?"

I spun around and flung my hair back as I approached him. "I'm sorry, Nathan. I guess I'm a little distracted."

"I'll say." He pointed to the door. "We have two problems now. One, how to open this door and two, what to use for light once we're in."

Cole raised a finger. "I learned a simple spell for providing light. I've used it a time or two."

Nathan nodded. "Great. Any idea on this door?"

I approached the door. Intricate lines threaded around the door in web-like patterns. The doors themselves glistened in the bits of sunlight finding their way under the overhand, revealing the beauty of gold overlaid on wood.

Cole shook his head. "I've studied them some, but not enough to learn their secrets." He wrapped his fingers around the silver handle and pulled. It didn't budge. He released it after five good pulls.

I reached out and grasped the handle, and pulled. Dust and dirt fell as it creaked open. A musty smell filled the air.

Cole stared at me. "How did you do that?"

I realized I had used the hand with the ring on it to open the door. I held it up. "Perhaps this has something to do with it?"

He wrinkled his brow. "What? The ring?"

Of course! I'd never told him about how I could heal people. He'd seen me do it, but didn't know that the ring funneled God's healing energy through me.

"Yes, the ring. Long story, but my dad received it from a steam house in his hometown. It charged him to help others with it. Then three months ago, he gave it to me, so now I fulfill that same call."

"Can I see it?"

I grabbed the ring and pulled hard a couple times. "It doesn't come off." Then I held my hand up to his eyes for a closer inspection.

As he peered at it, his face sank.

"What's wrong?" I attempted to meet his eyes.

His gaze jerked up to mine. "Oh, nothing really. It reminded me of someone."

I wondered if he referred to a previous wife or other important person in his life. I glanced to see Nathan frowning at me. "I'm sorry, Nathan—"

"I know, you were distracted. Can we fire up the light so we can get going?"

Cole picked up a stick lying by the entrance. He sucked in a large amount of air and then blew it out in an explosive burst. The top of the stick ignited with radiant fire. And though no cloth or fuel kept it lit, it didn't burn out.

I breathed deep. "Ready?"

Nathan stepped through the door. "Let's do this."

The path through the caves ran broad in some places, and narrowly across precipices in others. We watched our steps, as veins of crumbled rocks left holes that could surprise our feet and send us falling to our deaths.

It was weird seeing no more than a few feet in front of us. I reached out and held Cole's hand tight. He squeezed back and smiled. It felt good knowing that I could finally let my feelings show without fear of being taken advantage of.

We arrived at a split in the path. Nathan turned to me. "Can you see if the ring tells us which way to go?"

I shut my eyes and focused into my heart. It didn't require as much concentration as it used to. I pointed toward the left fork. "That way."

We shuffled along the path, keeping a close eye on our feet. I glanced around in the darkness. "I feel like we're being watched."

Cole nodded. "I'm sure we have been ever since we arrived. Eventually they'll reveal themselves. Their first hope, however, is that we will take a wrong path and spend the rest of our lives trying to get out of the mountain's maze."

Spending my remaining days wandering in a mountain maze didn't rank high on my list of things I wanted to do with my life. I closed my eyes for a moment and allowed Cole's hand to guide me. I sank into my heart, and I could "see" with my mind's eye the creatures slinking around us. Their long bodies appeared very flexible, while their stubby legs and arms worked to keep up. Big heads on a spiny neck swiveled to and fro, and large eyes sucked in the darkness to watch us as we worked our way down the trail.

I opened my eyes. "I'd say there are about a dozen of them around us now." I squeezed Cole's hand. "What if we're captured, what's likely to happen to us?"

He bobbed his head to the side. "They like slaves."

Nathan halted. "And we're going to find out real quick whether you're right about that, Cole."

Several of them appeared at the edge of our light and pointed long sticks at us. I didn't know what the sticks could do, nor did I want to find out. I held up my hands along with Nathan and Cole as they drew near.

"Dim your light," one of the creatures said in a low, rumbling voice.

Cole complied and the darkness crept in closer.

"Follow me." The leader turned and headed down the tunnel.

I stumbled as a set of hands shoved me. They led us through several turns and twists. Finding our way back out would be near impossible. The myriad of tunnels and trails through this mountain created an intricate maze. An ideal defense.

After what felt to be at least an hour—time lost its bearings in the darkness—we broke into an open area.

My mind recalled the Shadow Creatures who lived in the mountains not far from Uncle Seth's house. Hopefully we could reason with these Burrowers.

Low, red lights emanated from poles placed at strategic locations around the cave. The leader directed us to a room enclosed with bars. One of them opened the door and pointed into the cell.

I paused at the door and met the leader's huge eyes. I decided to venture a conversation. "My name is Kaylee. This is Cole and Nathan." I pointed at them. "We're not here to harm you, but we would like to talk to the one in charge."

He flipped his hand to wave us on in. I stepped in behind Cole and Nathan. The gate slammed shut and the lock clicked into place.

He leaned his head toward me and his eyes blinked once. "My name is Zerial to humans. I will take your request to the Benglu."

"The Benglu?"

"Our ruler."

I nodded. "I see. Thank you."

Two of them remained while the rest left. Nathan and Cole sat on a bench carved from the walls. I settled next to Cole and leaned on his shoulder.

Nathan huffed. "How do I keep ending up in prisons?"

"You have that guilty look about you, Brother." I winked at him.

Cole shuffled his feet. "This could lead us to Crystal."

"That was my hope," I added.

Nathan nodded. "Sure, but finding her is only one step. The real question is how do we escape this mountain with her?"

He received no answer, because none of us knew one. I hoped the way out would present itself.

Not much to go on, but what else did we have? Either that or consign ourselves to serve the Burrowers for the rest of our lives.

Gabrielle couldn't bear riding separate from Sisko for the rest of the trip to Morgoth. So she rode behind him on the wingless horse and let the winged horse follow behind, its reins slipped around her arm.

The trees parted in the crisp morning air, fresh with dew from the night's humidity. The massive gates of Morgoth loomed before them several hundred feet away. Shanty houses dotted open fields around it.

Sikso pulled up on the reins and the horse halted. He sighed, and his eyes swung back to meet hers. "I'm getting a very strong feeling that I should go now. I can't enter this city."

Gabrielle sunk her head onto the back of his neck and squeezed tightly. "Can't you stay at least one more night?"

He shook his head. "I wish I could. I really do." He slid off the horse and helped her down. "I would love nothing more than to spend eternity with you. And, that will happen, I believe. But I can't enter this city. I don't know why, but my heart is telling me I can't."

"Maybe we don't have to go in there. Maybe someone outside the city can tell us when Crystal's caravan left and where it headed. Wherever she went, Kaylee and Nathan would follow."

He bowed his head and leaned against a tree. "It's not the city itself. I think you do need to go in. It has something to do with you needing Josh before you enter."

"Josh? But he can't recall hardly anything. What would he have that you couldn't provide?"

He shrugged. "I don't know."

Gabrielle buried her head into his chest. Tears forced their way onto her cheeks, wetting his tunic.

He rubbed her back and kissed her forehead. "I know this is hard. But think of it as an opportunity we wouldn't have had otherwise. It's a gift from God. And someday, maybe soon, you'll be with me again."

She nodded and sniffed. "I know. I should be grateful for the time instead of angry that it's ending. But this is the third time I've watched you disappear into Paradise, and the other two weren't this hard because this time I'm the one sending you back." She wiped her nose. "And I don't want to."

Sisko breathed deeply and let the words slip from his lips, "I don't want you to either. But we have no choice. Every minute Kaylee gets further away, and you might miss getting to her in time. And I can go no further."

He squeezed her tightly. His lips caressed hers in a sweet kiss—a kiss of promise, a kiss of eternal love bathed in Paradise's joy. Then he pulled himself from her and stepped back.

"Go ahead. Long goodbyes won't serve us now," he said.

She tried to restrain the tears flowing down her cheeks, but they wouldn't obey. She'd let them fall, for they spoke of her true feelings for him. She'd send him off though every fiber of her being demanded otherwise. How does one argue with God and win?

"I love you, Sisko. Thank you for all the joy you've brought me over the years in this life, and I eagerly await the chance to share eternal bliss with you as well, where there will be no further sorrowful partings like this."

He smiled. "I look forward to that as well. Thank you for making me who I am, and for your unselfish love for me. I love you too." He nodded that she should go ahead with it.

Gabrielle swallowed, then hoping the winds might take the words away where they couldn't work, she mumbled under her breath, "Josh, reveal yourself."

The glow of light grew over his form and when it died, Josh's eyes blinked back at her.

He scanned the area. "Whoa, what a trip! Where are we?"

Gabrielle fell to the ground and buried her head in her hands. Her chest heaved as salty liquid wet her hands and face.

Josh knelt beside her and placed a hand on her shoulder. "What's wrong? Did...did I do anything?"

Gabrielle glanced at him. She felt her eyes swelling. "You're not Sisko!"

He wrinkled his brow. "Am I supposed to be?"

She answered with more sobs. She didn't understand—Sisko leaving again did hurt, very much. It came much earlier than she had expected. Still, she rarely displayed her feelings like this; they appeared out of proportion. Her emotions bucked within her like a wild, uncontrolled horse, and she attempted to tame them in vain.

Josh pointed to the city walls. "Are those the walls of Morgoth?"

She nodded.

"Then I've missed nearly a day. It seemed like a few minutes."

Her curiosity broke through her sorrow. She wiped her eyes and sat up. "Where were you?"

He stared into the sky. "I can't do it justice, but I sat in a room, vibrant with life is all I can say about it. And a man full of inner light introduced himself as Timothy, the disciple of St. Paul the Apostle.

"I didn't believe him and didn't pay him much attention at first. But as we talked, I sensed that he was St. Timothy."

She pulled her knees up and wrapped her arms around them. "Sisko said he had been talking to St. Timothy when I forced him here. Apparently you both switched places."

"Sisko? Here?" Realization spread across his face. "You mean, I was in Paradise?"

"Where else would you find the real St. Timothy?"

"And Sisko was here, with you? No wonder you're so sad."

She pushed herself to her feet and wiped her eyes. "We're wasting time. Let's get into the city and see what we can find out about Kaylee and Nathan."

"Oh yes!" He jumped to his feet. "St. Timothy did tell me a person we must search for in this city."

She widened her eyes. This must be why Josh needed to return. "Who?" They started heading toward the city gate.

"A monk by the name of Zosimas."

"Zosimas? That's an odd name."

Josh nodded. "That's what I said, and St. Timothy said like a Zosimas before him, he finds his best spiritual growth in a desert. In this monk's case, a spiritual desert."

She gazed at the towering city walls. "Yes. I can feel the lack of spiritual life here. Must be what the steam house would see. But this is dark. Real dark."

"All the more reason to find this monk and get his help."

She glanced at Josh walking beside her, the horses in tow. "If you were in Paradise, did it help your memory any?"

He shrugged. "While there, everything was back, even better than back. Upon returning, though, the only new memories I have are what seemed barely five minutes with St. Timothy, the joy I felt, and what he told me to tell you. Like, I wasn't supposed to be there, and so it remained hidden to some degree from me."

A sharp pain hit Gabrielle's stomach. She clutched it and bent over.

Josh laid a hand on her shoulder. "What's wrong?"

"I don't know." She grimaced. "Maybe I'm getting hungry. Can we get something to eat inside the town?" Hunger pains? Not likely. She must be sick.

"Could be the monk has something."

Another pain caused her to squeeze her eyes shut and groan.

"Those are some serious pains. We'd better hurry." Josh lifted her onto a horse and led them through the city gate.

After asking a few people where this monk lived, they worked their way through the city streets to his house. Josh knocked upon the door, and it responded by opening.

A frail frame of a man stood before them. Instead of the traditional black robes of a monk, he wore a torn and weathered inner garment. The rips revealed much of his chest and legs. His arms protruded bare from holes on either side. His hair appeared in disarray, and a smell wafted from him that Gabrielle could have done without.

The monk opened the door wider. "Come in. I've been told you would be here."

Gabrielle met Josh's eyes and could tell it surprised him too. She responded, "And we've been told to seek you out. Have you been told of our mission and have the information we need?"

He lifted a scrawny finger into the air. "Indeed I have. I'll bet you're excited." He motioned for them to sit at a table and proceeded to gather some food and drink.

"I don't know if excited is the word I would use." Gabrielle settled into a chair. "Anxious, maybe."

He set cups on the table and poured some tea. "Oh no, you shouldn't worry about it. This is a wonderful occasion. We should celebrate! I'll break out the dried meats I've saved for visitors on special feasts."

She glanced at Josh and he shrugged. She focused on the monk scurrying around with a smile on his face. "Father Zosimas, I don't see why the potential death of my daughter is an occasion to celebrate."

He paused in mid-stride and met her eyes. "I see I've not been told everything, as is sometimes the case. 'Need to know basis' is what he tells me all the time."

Josh sipped the tea and his eyes took on a distant gaze before widening. "Joel!"

Zosimas nodded. "Yes, he's the one."

"This is Joel's tea. I remembered something from my past!" A grin spread across his face.

Gabrielle took a sip. "Indeed, this does taste like the tea you gave me before. Nothing else like it. Can you remember anything more?"

He shook his head. "Just his name and that he always gave me great tea leaves."

Gabrielle sighed. "Father, can you tell us where Kaylee and Nathan are? Or where they are going?"

He cocked his head. "No."

She fell back into chair. "Then why did God want us to come here?"

Zosimas laid plates filled with dried meat, cherries, and apples before them and sat down. He lifted a hand and placed it on her stomach. He held it for a few seconds. "You've been having pains, haven't you?"

"Yes, they started right before coming into the city." Gabrielle bit off a chunk of meat.

He nodded. "It has started."

"What has started?" Her anger flared. She didn't mean it to, but she'd been on such an emotional ride up and down in the last few hours that it didn't take much to send her careening up another peak.

He blinked. "You're pregnant."

Her jaw dropped open and the chewed meat fell out. She stared at the monk for a couple of seconds before responding. "What did you say?"

He patted her belly. "You have a baby in there."

She glanced at Josh. He shook his head. "I didn't do it!"

Gabrielle rubbed her forehead. "But Father, that's impossible. I've not slept with a man—pardon my speaking of this in your presence but I don't know how else to say it—for months. Not until last night."

He smiled and nodded.

She shook her head. "You don't mean to tell me this is Sisko's child?"

He nodded again.

"But...but, that's impossible! How could last night's encounter result in such pains due to a pregnancy?"

He shook his head. "Remember, you're dealing with God here. For reasons I've not been told, the baby's growth rate is highly accelerated. That's why you're experiencing the pains. Your body's struggling to keep up."

She rose from her chair and paced the floor. "I'm pregnant?"

Josh gulped more tea. "It could be worse. I could be pregnant."

"Nathan and Kaylee will have a...what? Brother or sister?"

The monk chewed on a piece of meat. "It's a boy. Are you ready to celebrate now?"

She fell back into her chair and gazed past the walls. "I'm going to have a baby. I've been given a new life to watch over." She rubbed her stomach as another pain hit.

I prayed that God would help us find some way out of this mountain prison. I sat with my head on my knees. Cole rubbed my back while Nathan paced the floor.

Nathan kicked some dirt into a cloud. "I feel like it's been hours. They must have forgotten us."

An image formed in my mind. The door at the mountain's entrance stood before my mind's eye. The lines clearly marked in varied patterns across its face resembled a thick web of twisting and turning threads. Yet, neither did they appear random. The patterns...they reminded me of...of... I jumped up.

"The door!"

The two guards turned their heads our direction.

I whispered to Nathan, "It's a map."

Nathan stopped pacing. "What?"

"All those lines on the door we entered the mountain through, it's a map of the tunnels in this mountain. And it's in my head. Maybe we can get out."

His eyebrows raised. "Maybe. But even knowing how to get out, how can we outrun them? They are used to the dark and we need light, and even then we must travel slowly to keep from falling into some crevice."

I frowned. He was right. The thought of outrunning them in the maze of tunnels bordered on stupidity. I flopped back onto the bench. Cole squeezed my shoulders. "Don't let the image fade. We may need it before we're done here."

I nodded. I didn't see how, but it sure couldn't hurt to keep it focused in my mind's eye.

The sound of padding feet echoed through the tunnels and grew louder. A group of six Burrowers with weapons approached the prison and commanded the guards to open the door. We all stood in anticipation.

Zerial, who led the soldiers, said, "You have been granted an audience with the Benglu. You will follow me. Veer in the slightest from my path, and you will die." He turned and marched back into the tunnel.

We followed him through a series of tunnels. I wondered at how easily he navigated the twists and turns. They grew up playing in these tunnels and knew every nook and cranny without thinking about it. But in my mind, I scanned the map for the series of turns and twist he followed. I smiled. Only one spot on the map matched the turns we'd taken, and the path to get out laid plainly before me.

After several turns, we entered an open chamber. The cave ceiling towered above us. Red lights hung from the side walls, casting a rosy tint over everything. A high-backed throne of rock sat on one end of the vast hall. A straight path ran from it to the edge of a glowing red lava river. It flowed from the wall on my right and disappeared into the wall at my left. The path, by which we approached, picked up on our side, yet no bridge crossed the river. I wondered if a secret tunnel linked the two areas.

Several Burrowers stood along the path leading to his throne. Zerial led us up to the edge of the fiery river and he held out a hand for us to halt.

The Benglu appeared old, yet still retained a glow in his eyes. He stared at us for a moment before speaking. "You desired an audience with me. You may speak your piece before I send you to work in the tunnels."

Cole stepped forward, his feet inches from the lava. He bowed. "O Great One, I have come with these two—"

"Silence!" He glared at Cole. "It is the woman who asked for an audience. Not you."

Cole stepped back and bowed.

I stepped forward and bowed to him. I trusted that Cole knew the proper address for the Benglu. "O Great One, we are searching for a woman, and we believe..." My heart jumped within me, and I knew who I needed to help here. "I mean, I believe that you are not the Benglu and your Benglu is sick. I can heal him."

A murmur rose from the line of Burrowers in the cave. The Burrower on the throne leaned forward as if he might discern the truth better by doing so. "If such a sick person resided here and you can heal him, you must come to me across the river of fire."

I nodded and lifted a foot to cross. A hand grabbed me from behind. I turned around to see Nathan pushing Cole's hand off of me and shaking his head.

I smiled to give him confidence. "I'll be all right." I could see the fear for me dancing in his eyes, and it warmed my soul that he cared so.

I faced the lava river and sunk my right foot into it. Pain shot up my leg, but quickly subsided. I pulled the left one in and strolled through the knee-deep lava. Gasps could be heard echoing through the cave along with an occasional exclamation in their own language as I pushed my way through the scorching liquid without so much as a whimper.

I stepped onto the other side. I raised my pant-legs up enough so he could see my pink skin, untouched by the lava.

His big eyes blinked a couple of times. Then he called toward a room to his right, "Bring in the Benglu."

Six human women, dressed in white robes, carried a bed resting on poles. The procession worked its way along a path winding around a series of stalagmites. One of the women lifted her head. My mouth fell open. Crystal stared at me from under the hood, but I found no hint of recognition in her eyes.

She, along with the women, set the bed onto the ground and backed away. The Benglu wore royal colors, but even I, not used to the Burrowers, could tell that he would die before too many more hours passed.

The current leader on the throne cast a hand toward him. "You may heal him. If you do not, you and your friends will die."

They liked the threat of death a lot. I drew near the Benglu's bed. This would not be a good time for the healing not to work! But it would; my heart had alerted me to him and his need. I lay my hand on the Burrower's head.

"Lord, heal the Benglu of his sickness and restore to him a righteous reign."

A second sped by before his body jerked, his face regained life, his eyes blinked open, and he sat up. He scanned the area, and me, and then focused on the one sitting on his throne. "Tilitar, why do you sit upon my throne?"

Claps erupted within the chamber. Tilitar stepped down from the throne and knelt before the true Benglu. "I have kept the throne from enemy hands while you lay sick, O Great One. Now that you are well, regain your rightful place upon the throne so we may all rejoice in your kingship."

The Benglu smiled. "You have done well, Tilitar." Then he turned to me. "What is your name?"

I bowed. "Kaylee, O Great One."

The Benglu turned to Tilitar. "Did she cross the River of Fire to reach this side?" Tilitar nodded. The Benglu turned to face me again. "You could not have known this, for we do not easily share such secrets with outsiders. But we established a law many kingdoms ago that one who crossed the River of Fire without harm should be released from their bondage."

Really! I wanted to jump for joy, but knew that would be out of place. I bowed to him. "Oh thank you, Great One. My friends and I greatly appreciate your mercy—"

"Your friends, if they wish to be released, must also cross the River of Fire unharmed." He stood, rising at least two feet above my head, and he sat upon his throne.

I glanced at Nathan and Cole. Their mouths hung open and they backed away from the lava. I sank into my heart, asking if I should protect them as they crossed the lava but received no answer. I could heal them after they crossed, but would they make it? Despite being highly painful for them if they did get across without sinking into the heat, it might not be enough if I simply healed them. The Benglu expected them to not be hurt by it.

The Benglu gestured toward Nathan and Cole. "What shall it be? Will you attempt to cross the fire as your companion did or shall I return you to the prison?"

Seconds passed. Nathan stared at me, probably hoping I would motion for him to proceed. I shrugged and shook my head. I couldn't promise any help.

Nathan raised his hand.

"You may speak, sandy-haired one."

Nathan stepped forward and wrung his hands. "O Great One, I beg your mercy, but I cann—"

"He cannot do more than trust in your gratitude, O Great One," I broke in. I realized what the Benglu didn't know. "The gratitude I earned in healing you from near-death so you may regain your rightful place upon the throne."

The Benglu's eyes widened and he turned to Tilitar. "Did she do as she says?"

He nodded. "And more. She perceived I stood in your place and knew you had fallen deathly ill. It is she who asked to heal you when she could not have known, who traversed the burning river, and laid her hand upon your body to heal it."

The Benglu's eyes studied me before he rose from his throne, knelt before me, and bowed his head. "You are a great prophetess. Ask what you will of me, and I will grant it."

I glanced at Nathan and Cole on the other side of the lava. They both stared at me with wide eyes. I turned to face the Benglu. "I do not ask for much, for I would not burden you with needless requests, O Great One. However, I would ask that you release my friends and I, and provide me with a slave of my choosing."

He placed his hands on the sides of his head and shook wildly. "The release of your friends I can grant. The slave I can grant. But you must stay here! We have a great need for one such as you."

I bowed. "You honor me. But you must understand, I've been given to all who roam these lands, not just the Burrowers. I will stay and heal those who need healing, but I cannot remain. It would be selfish of me and of you."

He sighed. "Your words lay bare my soul! So be it. One other condition do I lay upon you if you wish to add one of my slaves to your company."

"What further condition must I fulfill?"

He pointed at a tunnel on the far side. "If you are who you have proven to be, you will enter the tunnels unassisted. If you navigate our maze to reach the outside, you will all be free. If you fail, you will die of hunger and thirst deep in the mountain's bowels."

I bowed down and kissed his bald head. He jerked up and a smile creased his face. I placed a hand on his shoulder. "I will not soon forget you, and you will reign over the ascension of the Burrowers among the mountains with justice and love."

"You honor me," he said.

I turned to the women standing to the side. I pointed at Crystal. "I would like her as my slave."

The Benglu rose to his feet. "But Great Prophetess, your selection is...ill informed. This one is near mindless."

"Do you doubt my wisdom?" I caught Nathan sinking his face into his hands. Perhaps I shouldn't go too far and risk losing it all. "I know her condition. Among them, she needs my help the most. That is why I chose her."

He nodded to the Burrowers around him. "Great Prophetess, your compassion exceeds even your wisdom. She is yours." He swept his palm toward Crystal.

I lifted her into my arms and carried her through the lava river. Nathan stared at me. His wide eyes cast images of shock and awe, while his upturned lips emanated the joy of one who receives a prize long fought for. I arrived on the other side and placed Crystal into his outstretched arms. A blissful smile poured over his face as he squeezed Crystal in a hug.

I turned to face the crowd of Burrowers gathered around us. "Bring me your sick and wounded. Bring me those diseased in body and mind. I will heal them." I sat on an outcropping of rock. The Burrowers moved forward as others filed in upon hearing the news.

Hours passed as the line of sick and needy dwindled. I stretched as the last one approached me. I froze in mid-stretch when I recognized the remaining supplicant.

"Nathan? What are you doing in line?"

He pointed at Crystal next to him. "It's her. The comments of her being lifeless were more than tiredness. She really is lifeless. Blank. She stares past me, and when she does talk, it is often in one or two words at a time. It's as if she's dead inside."

I peered at her, trying to get a sense of what was inside her. I received nothing. No evil as it used to be, but no life either. Emptiness. "What does she say?"

He shivered. "That's the scary part. Most of the time she says 'Beltrid.'"

"Beltrid!" The demon had used her in an attempt to get the ring from Dad a few months ago. "I thought she'd been freed, and Beltrid sent to the abyss?"

Nathan glanced at Crystal. "I thought so too, but it appears we freed her body, not her soul. Beltrid must have it locked away somewhere." He bowed his head. "I hoped you might be able to do something."

This would be a tall order. "I'll see." I closed my eyes and searched my heart. The answer returned: I could not heal her. I shook my head and searched harder. This would be difficult, yes. But couldn't God do anything? Please? The answer returned: I could not and should not try.

I sank my head into my hands. "I'm sorry, Nathan. I can't heal her."

19

Gabrielle sat at a table in the tavern. A few people chatted nearby, but took no notice of them. Josh stood at the counter to obtain some food and question the barkeep for information on Nathan and Kaylee. After some discussion, Josh headed toward Gabrielle.

The door to the tavern opened and two burly men, unshaven and in need of a bath, stepped inside. The one with a big nose pointed at them as Josh returned to the table.

"There they are." The two men weaved among the tables.

Gabrielle motioned to Josh with her eyes as he set the ale and cheese in front of her. "I'm afraid two men bent on mischief are coming our way."

He turned his head and watched them approach. "Stay seated and let me handle this." He rose as the two men stopped before them.

Josh smiled. "May I be of service today?"

The men didn't smile back. The big-nosed one gritted his teeth. "You came from the Christian monk's house, didn't you?"

Josh glanced at Gabrielle. Did these men represent the prevailing opinion? Apparently some didn't care for the monk or Christianity in this town. She understood more why she felt such darkness since entering the city gate.

Josh responded, "Yes we did. Is that a crime?"

Now the man smiled. "In this town, yes. If you're gonna be here, you're gonna worship Morgenstern. Got it?"

Gabrielle scanned the room and noticed several glanced their way but no one jumped to their aid.

Josh raised his eyebrows, then met the man's eyes. "We're not residents here, just passing through. But we are Christians, so naturally we'd visit a Christian monk. Let's not make this an issue. We'll be gone before the day's out."

The man winked at his friend. "Oh, well then, that's different. Come on Jorem, let's leave these folk to eat their 'Christian' meal."

The other man nodded with a silly grin and patted his friend on the back.

Josh started to sit down. The big-nosed man spun around and swung his fist. It connected onto Josh's face with a solid snap. The punch lifted Josh out of his chair, and he crashed onto the floor. Blood dripped from his nose. He shook and rubbed his head.

The man reached toward Gabrielle. "We know how to take care of a woman. You're coming with us."

Gabrielle backed into her chair. The man's hand reached out toward her; a greedy grin lit up his face and eyes. She turned her head at the last minute, but his hand never felt her skin. The man shot away from her and flew through the room, hitting the tavern wall before collapsing unconscious. The chatter of conversation died and all eyes focused on Gabrielle's table.

She turned to where Josh lay and saw him with his hand extended, staring wide-eyed at her. He turned his palm to stare at it in wonder.

The other man, also big and muscular, prepared to kick Josh. Josh jerked his hand sideways, and the man's feet slid out from under him. He landed with a loud thud on his back.

Josh rose to his feet and stood over the groaning man. "I said, leave us in peace. We'll be out of here before the day's over."

The man nodded slightly; his eyes fixed on Josh. He flinched at each of Josh's movements as he rose to his feet, grimacing several times. He left the building, hauling his unconscious friend out the door.

The tavern patrons erupted in cheering and clapping. The men must have been town bullies. But did they work for the local religious leaders? Or did they appoint themselves as guardians of their faith? Either way, it appeared the crowd wouldn't harass Josh or her.

Josh sat in his chair and wiped the blood off with his sleeve. "I have no idea how I did that. It just happened."

Josh's story bubbled to the surface of Gabrielle's mind. "It must be the

Harrower. It's still in you and can operate by thoughts, without reciting a spell."

"The Harrower? What's that?"

Gabrielle sighed. "It's a long story. You told it to me a few days ago. I'll tell you the full story later, but the short answer is it unites you with the power that created all the universe. But you have to use it for the benefit of others, not for their demise. Otherwise, you'll lose it. For a time, maybe forever. You didn't say."

"But I attacked those men. How did that benefit them?"

She thought for a moment. "They almost committed soul-damaging sins. You prevented their error and gave them pause to think about where they're headed. You didn't destroy them, but you may have helped them."

He gazed at his hands. "But how do I control it? I can't recall the first thing about it. And most likely, my previous knowledge helped me know how to deal with it properly."

She nodded. "You did say that the Harrower was dangerous. But only to those with impure souls. You're still in one piece, so I guess you're safe."

His face fell. "I don't know about that. I've had these feelings and desires for you ever since I woke up. I know they can't be fulfilled, especially now. But they are there."

Gabrielle stopped chewing a piece of cheese. "That's because of your link with Sisko. Even though he's in Paradise, the link still exists, and in your mental condition, you're feeling what he feels for me. That's why I could cause you and Sisko to trade places."

Josh stared out a window and gulped a swallow of ale. "But our souls changed places, not our bodies."

She stared at Josh. "Yes, but your body changed into Sisko."

"Right. However, if Sisko's body changed using the same substance as mine, the Harrower still resided in it." He pointed at her stomach. "The baby would have inherited it."

Gabrielle froze. "You're right. I hadn't thought of that." She glanced at her stomach. "Might be why he grows so rapidly."

Josh nodded. "Exactly. And based on what you've told me so far of the Harrower, it could be a dangerous baby."

She shook her head. "But he also has Sisko's blood and a link to Paradise as well. He's the baby of a man who's not alive. Maybe he will have some eternal wisdom in him from the start too."

Josh shook his head. "Who knows what the baby will be like. But one thing's for certain. It will not be—"

"He. The monk said it was a he." She squinted one eye at him.

"Oh, excuse me. He will not be a normal baby."

Josh and Gabrielle ate quietly for a moment before Josh spoke again. "Oh, I discovered where Nathan and Kaylee rode off to. Or flew off to as the case may be."

"Where?"

"A town called Octum, over the mountains and across an arid plain. He said a caravan would leave in a few hours for it. I suggest in your condition, we join them."

She swallowed a bite of cheese. "Sounds good. Hey, can you get me some more cheese? I'm terribly hungry."

He rose, and his chair scraped the floor.

"Oh, and see if they have any pickles too. That'll hit the spot."

Josh raised an eyebrow and stared at her for a moment before proceeding to the barkeep.

"Yes, yes. We'd be happy to have you join us. My name's Silo." He stuck out a hand.

Josh grasped it. "Thank you. She's pregnant and it will be a big help to have others around to help if need be."

His eyes sparkled. "Congratulations! I'll bet you're excited."

Gabrielle thought now would be a good time to say "yes," in case the man harbored any ulterior motives.

Josh chuckled. "Oh no. It's not my baby. Well, not really, though I guess in some small way I had something to do with it."

The man wrinkled his forehead. "Let me guess. She's your sister. The old Abraham traveling scheme."

Josh rolled his eyes. "No, she's not my sister. Just a good friend."

He smiled. "Ah, a new twist! Come now, we all make mistakes. No sense making them worse by telling stories, and I'm not going to kill you for her."

Josh clenched his teeth. "I'm not the baby's father or her husband!"

Silo shrugged. "Have it your way." He leaned over to Gabrielle. "If you would like, Ma'am, you can ride on my wagon. It'll be easier on you."

Josh's eyes widened. "Thanks for your kind offer, but—"

"That would be wonderful. Thank you so much." Gabrielle broke in.

Josh gritted his teeth and stared into the sky.

Silo noticed. "Don't worry. You can ride your horse right beside us. I'd offer you a ride too, but the seat isn't long enough for three."

Josh eyed the man. "You bet I'll be riding beside you. And keeping a constant watch too."

Gabrielle rolled her eyes. "Josh, don't be rude." But she felt safer knowing he would protect her. Or, was he jealous? She couldn't tell. Either way, it would be for her benefit.

Silo grabbed Josh around the shoulders and patted him on the back. "No harm done. Someone who's as protective as you is a very good friend." He winked at Josh. "Certainly not a husband." He pointed at Josh's horse. "By the way, did you know your horse has wings?"

Josh sighed. "Yes. But we don't know how to make it fly."

"I've never seen one before, yet I have a nagging thought sayin' I'm forgetting something. But I don't know how to make a winged horse fly." He released Josh and headed down the line of wagons and horses. "We're moving out in a few minutes. Prepare!"

Gabrielle climbed up the wagon steps and settled onto its bench.

Josh tied the other horse's reins to the back of the wagon and mounted the winged horse. He gazed up into the mountains. "Looks like we'll be going upwards."

The horse jerked its wings out and reared up on its hind legs. Josh pulled down on the reins. "Whoa, boy! Calm down!"

The horse lowered itself down onto all fours, and shook its head. Josh wiped his forehead. "Crazy horse. Can't get it to fly, but it's ready to throw me off at the mere mention of going up into the mountains."

Gabrielle shrugged and settled onto the seat for the long ride ahead of them.

20

Nathan stepped forward. "You can try! At least try and heal her!"

I stood. "You don't understand. I want nothing more than to heal her, but if my heart says no, I'd be cursed to use the ring by my own will."

He flung his hands into the air. "Try! Ask God to do it as you always do. I've seen you do it with many, even today!"

My eyes watered; I so wanted to do this for him. "Nathan, I can't."

He moved into my face. "Ask again." His eyes bore desperation. "Please?"

I closed my eyes and searched deeper, harder, longer. It almost felt as if God held a consultation with someone on the matter. Then finally an answer came.

I opened my eyes. Nathan stared into them, expectation hanging on my next word. I took a deep breath. How do I say this? "Nathan. God says, 'Go to Hell.'"

He jerked back. "What?"

"No, literally, he says to save Crystal's soul and restore it, we must go to Hell to get it."

He blinked his eyes a couple of times. "You...I mean, He can't be serious!"

"That's the answer I received."

He flopped his rear onto a rock and stared past distant cave walls. "If I have to go to Hell and back for her, I will." He sucked in a deep breath. "But I wouldn't have the first clue how to get there." He turned and faced me. "I mean, in a way so as to get back."

Cole, leaning against an outcropping of rock, cleared his throat. "I happen to know the way."

We both jerked our heads his direction.

Nathan narrowed his eyes. "How would you know the way to Hell?"

He smiled, yet a hint of regret hung on his lips and tone. He lifted a hand. "You have to remember, my city is full of evil, as you well know. I've encountered this type of thing before and research revealed the way into Hades, which it is more properly called."

I moved to his side and sat next to him. "So, you can tell us the way there?"

He frowned. "You get there by going through the Dying Tree."

"Dying Tree?" Nathan said. "Why is it called that?"

He shrugged. "We are talking about the land of the dead, you know."

Nathan bobbed his head. "Yeah, I guess. But how do you get there?"

Cole folded his hands and tapped them against his mouth for a moment. "The one who gave me this information made me promise not to tell the route."

Nathan slammed his fist onto the rocks.

"But I can show the way. I can lead you there."

Nathan's eyes perked up.

I wrapped my arms around Cole. "That would be great!" I chuckled at the thought of rejoicing about going to Hades. But it dawned on me why. Cole would have left now that we'd found Crystal. This meant he would stay with us for a while longer.

"Beltrid." Crystal's blank eyes stared at Cole and me.

My fear of the demon returned. Even from the abyss, his shadow haunted me. "Well Brother, looks like we're going to Hell."

Cole put his hand on my shoulder. "Hades, not Hell. Please. I'd rather not contemplate going to Hell."

I glanced at his eyes. They held a fire and fear in them. "Sure. But what's the difference?"

He continued to stare into the distance. "Hades, though bad, is livable. It is a holding place like Paradise. Hell is the final punishment and fate of those...exposed to the...fire."

I nodded. "Then I guess we'd better go to Hades if we want to come back."

"Beltrid," Crystal rang off in a monotone voice.

Later, the Burrowers threw a big feast, and we ate until we could eat no more. While the food bore little resemblance to anything of my normal diet, it still tasted delicious. But I passed on the pickled cave-bat eyes. I knew they wouldn't stay down.

The Burrowers loaded our packs with food and supplies. With much fanfare, they launched us into the caves to find our way out. I could still bring up the map from the doorway in my mind and direct us at each turn. Sometimes when doubt filled my mind, I would seek in my heart to make sure of the way.

I also felt the Burrower's eyes on me. They watched from the darkness to see whether or not I could find the way out. If I turned down the wrong path, I wondered what they would do? Point us the right way or kill us on the spot?

With relief, however, I didn't have to find out. We arrived at the door and stepped into the ledge. The dark-blue sky contained whiffs of clouds. The evening sun barely peeked over the western mountains.

I shut the door and caressed the image of the maze on it, thankful for its guidance. "We made it."

Nathan hugged me. "I never had any doubt, Sis. Not after you led Uncle and me out of the wizard's maze on the sky island."

I cracked a smile. "Sure."

"But," he said, "we do have one problem. There are now three I need to carry."

"Beltrid," Crystal said again.

He frowned. "Maybe four. At any rate, I don't think I can fly well with three people on my back. But I can glide us to the ground. However, once on the ground, we'll have to stay on the ground."

I ran my fingers through the cool breeze. "At least now we're not chasing after Crystal. We don't need to rush."

"True," he said.

Cole pointed at the sinking sun. "But we'd better get down now while there's still light to see our landing spot. You won't be able to maneuver well at the last minute with us all on you either."

We all agreed. Nathan converted into a horse and we all climbed onto his back. After we acknowledged our readiness, Nathan leaped off the edge, and we sank quickly toward the horizon.

Wind sheers hit us, and Nathan struggled to stay upright. Each blast leaned us slightly to the right or left before Nathan could adjust by banking into a turn to regain control.

Kaylee, would you mind not holding onto my neck so tightly?

"Oh, sorry. But in all the time of flying with you, this is the first time I'm scared of falling off."

We'll all fall if you choke me till I'm unconscious!

Once we gained some distance from the mountainside, the winds smoothed out and Nathan continued to sink. The land grew gray in the waning sunlight. Stars peered out from the encroaching darkness above. The air warmed, and my heart did too.

We'd accomplished our task to find Crystal. But Crystal's condition and the journey before us felt unreal and distant. I would rather think about relaxing, getting to know Cole better, and enjoying his time with us, however long that might be. It would be a while before I needed to think about Hades.

I saw a campfire in the distance. My heart leaped within me. "Nathan, someone at that campfire needs me."

I see it. He banked and adjusted his glide.

The ground raced under us as Nathan's hooves settled upon the land and kicked up dust behind us. He slowed down until he trotted to a halt at the camp site.

I jumped off his back and raced toward the fire. A man sat on a log, bent over, hooded. A horse nibbled at grass behind him. I slowed and stepped before him. "Sir, is there something wrong? Something I can help you with?"

He raised his head and pulled the hood back.

I gasped and fell backwards. "Joel! What are you doing here?"

His jaw remained firm; his eyes flashed in the firelight. No smile or welcome came from him. "Kaylee, I must talk with you." He glanced at Cole. "Alone."

21

The sun climbed through the sky and headed toward the western horizon before the caravan crested the mountain valley pass. Silo led the group between two of the highest peaks. Snow covered their tops, but lay a mere inch thick on the lower pass. Still cold enough to chill Gabrielle's bones.

"Josh," Gabrielle called from the wagon. "Can't you create some coats?"

"I don't remember the spell."

"What about the Harrower?"

He shrugged. "I don't know how to control it. So far, I've used it in reacting."

Silo reached back into the wagon and pulled out a blanket. "Here, wrap this around you."

"Thank you!" She cuddled into it.

Silo nodded toward Josh. "So, is your friend there a wizard or something?"

She nodded. "But he's not been himself lately."

Silo raised an eyebrow.

"Long story."

He nodded. "So, why're you headed to Octum?"

"Another long story."

He cast a hand toward the horizon. "You certainly don't have to tell me, but we've plenty of time for long stories. I've a few I could tell."

She smiled. "Of course, you're right. But I don't think you would believe me if I did tell you."

He chuckled. "I doubt you'll believe some of my stories either."

She sighed. "Very well, but don't say I didn't warn you. I suppose I should start back when my husband—"

"I thought you didn't have a husband."

"I do, but he's in Paradise."

He frowned. "Not that 'bright shining city on a hillside' I hope."

She laughed. "No, the real one. He's been dead...well, I guess literally left this life, for about three months now. That is, if you don't count the last time."

He wrinkled his brow. "The last time?"

"The last time he left this life a couple days ago."

He rubbed his forehead. "Lady, you're making no sense."

"Like I said, it's best if I start at the beginning, when my husband first received the ring."

Gabrielle grimaced, covered her stomach with her hands, and bent over.

"What? What's wrong?" Silo wrapped his arms around her shoulders.

"They're pains I get. They come in bunches." She clenched her teeth through another one. A few more hit before they passed.

"I'm sorry," she said.

"What do you have to be sorry about?"

"These pains, they come in a series every once in a while."

He swept his hand through his hair. "That's nothing to be sorry about."

She opened up the blanket and felt her belly.

Silo cocked his head to one side. "Ma'am, looks like you're a month along."

"A day and a half is more like it."

He brushed snow off his boots. "I don't think you're pregnant. I think you're sick and need a doctor."

"No, it's a baby. It grows in spurts and that's why I'm getting the pains. My other pregnancies never caused this much pain."

"Hum, you mean no one's had pains like these before." He paused. "So you do have children?"

"Two. Nathan who's nineteen now, and Kaylee who just turned seventeen. Those are the two we're trying to catch up with, hopefully in Octum."

He chuckled. "Should be easy to catch up with a couple of young 'uns."

"Except Nathan can turn into a winged horse and fly."

Silo's eyes grew big. He leaned over and stared at the winged horse Josh rode.

"No, that's not Nathan. Nathan knows how to fly. We can't figure out this horse."

"I'll tell you, Lady, you can whip up an awfully intricate story. Maybe you'd better start at the top like you said."

She nodded. "When my husband was fourteen years old in Reol..."

When they reached the bottom of the mountain, the sun hid behind the peaks on the western horizon. Clouds reflected a red glow that died slowly away. The arid plains stretched far into the distance. Cracks ran across the ground as if water rarely touched these lands.

The caravan wound itself around until the group formed a huge circle of people, wagons, and animals. Everyone set up camp around their belongings. Silo invited them to his campfire, which Gabrielle gladly accepted, over Josh's objections.

Through the meal, Gabrielle and Silo chatted. Silo told a couple of his own stories. Gabrielle's imagination carried her away into his world, and she found it a delight. Josh remained quiet except for mumbling a couple of times.

Gabrielle laughed. "That's a very good story, Silo."

He waved his hand. "Not near as good as the one you told me today." He shook his head.

She smiled. "I said you wouldn't believe me."

"Well, you were right!" He laughed again. "Though I do recall hearing stories of a man who traveled the countryside healing people many years ago. Nice touch adding a bit of rumor to verify your story."

Gabrielle laughed with him. If nothing else, he helped to pass the time.

Josh coughed and spit upon the ground.

Gabrielle cast her eyes toward him. "You all right?"

He cleared his throat as if finally getting back his air. "Don't worry, just ignore me. I'll be fine."

Gabrielle frowned. He did that on purpose. Jealousy?

Silo rose to his feet. "I think I'll turn in. You're welcome to sleep in my wagon if you wish."

Josh glared at Silo. "And I suppose there's no room for me, eh?"

"Josh!" Gabrielle narrowed her eyes. "That was uncalled for." She turned to Silo. "Thank you so much for your hospitality. But I think we'll be fine out here."

He nodded. "Have it your way. But if you need anything, don't hesitate to ask."

"Thank you."

He stepped into his wagon.

Gabrielle stared at Josh for a moment. "What's gotten into you?"

He kicked the dirt with his boot. "I don't trust him is all. He's after one thing, I tell you. That's you."

She waved a hand. "Don't be silly. I've felt nothing from him in that regard. He's very kind and generous."

"Love blinds a person, you know."

She widened her eyes. "You think I love him?"

"You're certainly acting like it. He'll pick up on that."

She crossed her arms. "And how am I 'acting like it'?"

"You've never told me the whole story before."

She threw her arms down. "Josh, you've lived the whole story! Why would I tell it to you?"

He stared at the ground. "I don't remember any of it."

Gabrielle took a deep breath. "I'm sorry. But really, I'd know if Silo had any bad intentions. Remember, I'm a walking steam house?"

Josh lifted his head and wrinkled his brow. "Walking steam house? I don't see any steam coming from you."

She sighed. "Of course, you said that before you lost your memories. You don't even remember the steam house."

"Maybe you should tell me the story. It might spark my memory."

She nodded. "I tell you what. I'll ride with you tomorrow and tell you the whole story."

He smiled. "I'd like that."

She jerked and bent over. Her arms covered her stomach, she gritted her teeth, and groaned for a couple minutes as wave after wave of pain racked her body. When the last one finished, she flopped onto the ground, face up, trying to catch her breath.

Josh drew near and placed a hand on her face and caressed it. "I wish there was something I could do."

She smiled. "You can, you just forgot how to do it."

Josh felt her stomach. "You're already showing slightly. Feels like it's two or three months along, all in one day."

"You mean a couple days. We found out about it yesterday, but it was the day before that I conceived."

Josh rubbed her stomach as he leaned upon one elbow. "You know, this feels right and natural, me lying here with you."

"Josh."

"Right, sorry." He stood and pulled a ball from his cloak. "I guess it would be too much to bring out the tent."

"Probably. Can you just make a bed?"

He nodded. "I'll try." He threw the ball into the air. "Expand to a bed." It flashed and a huge canopy bed rested upon the ground.

Gabrielle scrambled to her feet. "I think that might be a little too much."

Josh extended his hand.

Gabrielle grabbed his arm and pushed it back down. "But under the circumstances, greatly appreciated. Maybe you could create a little tent to go over it?"

He smiled. "I think that could be arranged." He threw another ball and a small tent enveloped the bed.

She wagged a finger at him. "There'll be nothing going on between us, you understand?"

He sighed and stared up into the starry night. "It's all your fault, Sisko!"

"Yes, you could say that. We could all say that." She entered the tent and eased herself onto the bed. She whispered toward the sky, "I love you, Sisko." She hoped he could hear.

"Hey in there, you'd better get up or the caravan will soon leave you behind!"

Gabrielle's eyes flickered open. Josh's arm lay across her chest. She glanced over, and he appeared to still be asleep. She frowned and pushed it off. He rolled over and mumbled something.

She shook his shoulder. "Josh, wake up."

He jerked himself up and thrust his hands out. The whole tent burst into flames.

"Josh, what are you doing!"

He shook his head, rubbed his eyes, and stared around. "Stupid dream!" He cast out his hands and water burst forth from them, dowsing the flames. A stream of water hit the canopy reflecting it toward the bed, flooding Gabrielle. The frame collapsed, leaving them soaked in the middle of an uncanopied bed. A gathering crowd stared at the dripping pair as murmurings drifted among them.

Silo, his mouth gaping, stared at Josh and Gabrielle lying on the saturated bed as wisps of smoke trailed into the air. "If I didn't like you so much, I'd have half a mind to leave you here. I don't need this kind of excitement." He shook his head. "Dry off and get ready to go." He turned and stomped back to his wagon.

Gabrielle drove her fist into the soggy bed. "I've never been so embarrassed!"

Josh splashed back onto his pillow and mumbled something that Gabrielle knew she didn't want to hear.

22

I watched Joel's hardy facial features move in the moonlight. It created a captivating glow around him. His eyes met mine, but jerked back toward the horizon.

"Kaylee, I've been sent to give you a message."

I frowned. "Aren't you going to say, 'Hi, Kaylee. Missed you, Kaylee. Good to see you again, Kaylee'?"

"I've seen..." His eyes met mine. "I mean, from your perspective, I guess it's been a while."

"From most anyone's perspective, it's been over two months. And I've heard nothing from you!"

He sighed. "That's because you were...I mean, you were becoming..."

"I fell in love with you, that's what happened."

He nodded. "And that's why I had to stay away. I came now because God told me to deliver this message."

I laughed. "You know, you're more afraid of a relationship than I was."

"You don't understand."

"Maybe more than you realize. But it doesn't matter now. I have Cole."

Joel glanced at Cole sitting by the fire with Nathan and Crystal in the distance. "Watch out for..." He bit his lip. "I wish I could say more, but I'm under restrictions, again."

I raised an eyebrow. "God's sent you to me when you didn't want to come in order to say that you would tell me something about Cole, but you're under restrictions?"

His eyes met mine. I expected jealousy, but what I sensed was sadness and pity, much like what I felt from him before entering the steam house. Dread overshadowed me.

He laid a hand on my shoulder. "Kaylee, you remember when I told you about the ring's history?"

I nodded.

"I didn't tell you about the purpose of the ring. There's a reason for that."

"Its purpose is to heal and help people through me."

"Yes, that is a side purpose, but not the main reason God created it."

I realized what he would say next could be life changing. "So, you're here to tell me the ring's true purpose?"

He shook his head. "No, I'm here to guide you to its true purpose. My message is: you are not the ring's final destination."

I rolled my eyes. "Of course I'm not. You didn't need to tell me. Someday I'll pass it onto someone, probably one of mine and Cole's children, like Dad did to me."

He waved his hand back and forth. "No, no no! That's just it. When you pass it on, it will not be to someone you're related to."

I crossed my arms. "I don't suppose you're going to tell me who I should pass it to?"

"No, I'm not. You'll know when the time comes. But for you to know, I needed to tell you that much, but I can tell you no more."

These bits of information doled out to me resulted in frustration. *How am I supposed to operate in the dark?*

"You're in the light, not the dark."

I frowned. Nothing hidden from this man. "You're amazingly powerful for a prophet. Do you and God sit down and chat every day or something?"

He stared upwards. "You could say that."

"I think I believe you. I suppose you already know where we're going."

He nodded. "Hades."

"And will I see you again?"

He bowed his head. "If I could answer that, I'd be God. Maybe, maybe not. I can't promise anything either way."

I stared at Cole for a moment. "Joel, can you tell me anything about

Cole? Should I..." I turned to find empty air. I stomped the hard ground. "Not so much as a goodbye. I hate it when he does that!"

At least I have Cole. At least he doesn't pop in and out of my life randomly. He's here to stay. And he loves me, is willing to say it and act like it.

I strolled back to the camp fire and sat down beside Cole. My arms fell around his waist. I squeezed him and laid my head on his shoulder.

Nathan put his arm around Crystal's waist and squeezed.

She blinked. "Beltrid."

Nathan frowned.

I gazed around the darkness, hoping Joel watched and saw. I think he really was jealous. I'm sure that's what I felt.

We ate dinner and chatted a while about the next day. Cole said Octum was still our next destination, but would say no more. I supposed he should keep true to his word, but it felt like Joel teasing me with bits of information but not telling me the whole story. Why did men do this to me?

Nathan helped Crystal lie on a bedroll by the fire. He lay down beside her and soon fell asleep. Cole also unrolled his bedding and lay down. I watched the fire crackle for a while, thinking about the recent events. The last few days brought images of people in awe of me. A whole race bowed at my feet as if I were a goddess. And the expression on Nathan's face when I crossed the river of lava and laid Crystal in his hands, I'll never forget that. And even my own brother coming to ask a healing from me. Even he viewed me differently now.

I glanced over at Cole. He shuffled around on his blankets, trying to get comfortable.

Cole thought I was amazing. He loved me. I felt I did want to spend my life with him. No, I knew I wanted to spend my life with him. Everything pointed to it, except for one small part.

I arose and pulled my bedroll from the pack and started to lay it down. I paused and turned my eyes toward Cole. He glanced at me. I needed to talk with him in private. I moved beside him and unrolled my bedding. I lay on my side facing him. He turned and gazed into my eyes.

I brushed my hair back. "Cole, I want to know more about your religion. It's the only thing dividing us. And though I love you, I hope we'll eventually worship together too."

He gazed into my eyes for a few seconds. "A noble and good goal. I too would wish that. But which one? We both believe we're right."

"That's why I want you to tell me more. I'm hoping maybe yours isn't any different." Not much of a chance, I knew, but if there, I wanted to find out.

He scratched his head. "I know a little about your religion. After all, it is the dominant one in these parts. And I've chatted with a monk in our city. There are differences, some quite major."

"Well, tell me one then."

He fingered his beard as he thought. "Take morality for instance. Like in a lot of cultures, morality varies a good bit. What's wrong in one place can be quite acceptable in another. In yours, for instance, physical intimacy is reserved for marriage. In ours, it isn't just marriage, it's for whoever you love and wish to show love to. It is opening yourself to a special person, whoever they are and being open to receiving love from them."

His reasons sounded so right. I bit my lip. "You're right. We're instructed that such intimacy is one facet in bonding two people into one reality, and you have to be prepared for the possibility of children, thus marriage is needed."

"In ours, the community takes care of any children."

I raised an eyebrow. "If your city is an example of that, I'm not sure it is a shining one."

He stared into the stars. "True, we do have some kinks to work out, but overall, it works."

I frowned. "What do you call 'working' then?"

He met my eyes. "Well, for one thing, we rarely have rape in our city."

My eyes widened. "No rape? Are you sure?"

"Well, think about it. We teach that everyone has a right to their own body, and to violate that goes against the core of our religion. If you don't limit such intimacy to only those who are married, a person has more to choose from and isn't as likely to violate another person's rights when they know someone else can be found without too much trouble."

He spoke logically but not from experience. Controlling another motivated a rapist more than a desire for pleasure. Did he really know?

After all, if there's no law against it, who's going to report it? "But is this what you think should be happening, or does rape not happen at all?"

He nodded. "Rape does happen. No religion has one hundred percent compliance with its teachings. But I think you'd find the incidents of it extremely low compared to those found in Christian cities."

I let my head fall onto the ground. He spoke the truth. Though the young man in the bar had slapped me on the rear, he intended it as a joke and not an attempt to rape me. But the man who nearly raped me resided in a Christian city.

I sighed. "Guess I can't argue with that."

He smiled. "And to tell you the truth, I would be dishonest if I didn't tell you I hoped we could have such a relationship. I want to respect your religious sensibilities, I'd never force myself on you, but I do long for that."

I felt excited and uncomfortable at the same time. But he'd said the magic words. He wouldn't force himself on me. And I believed him. Even though we lay close together, I felt totally safe.

I wiggled closer and pulled him into my arms. Our lips met and I felt as if heaven opened and showered blessings upon us. I rubbed his broad shoulders, and he pulled me in at the waist. My chest pressed against his, and I could feel his heart beating in sync with my own.

His hand moved down onto my hip and then my rear. I jerked back.

"I'm sorry," he said. "Like I said, I'll not force myself upon you if you're not ready."

I breathed deep to dowse the surge of fear rushing through me. "I'm not ready to unite with you, but that's not such a union." I moved his hand onto my hip. "Those are old reactions I need to get over."

He squeezed and a wave of excitement shot through me. I closed my eyes and pulled his lips back onto mine.

"Beltrid."

I leaped into the air. My blanket shot away and Cole flung himself away from me. I stood panting and peered across the fire to see Crystal sitting up in her bed. I forced deep breaths and sat down again as I tried to regain control of an out-of-control heart.

"Crystal," I said between inhales. "Go to sleep."

She lay back down. Nathan hadn't budged, the heavy sleeper. Cole watched as I pulled my blanket a couple feet away.

I met his eyes. "I think maybe it's best if we get some sleep tonight.

We'll be traveling all day tomorrow. Then we'll be in Octum."

He nodded. "Yes, good idea. Octum." He rolled over in his blanket.

I lay down, and stared into the stars. "Dad," I whispered. "What makes one belief right and one wrong?" What if our belief was wrong? Could God be pointing me to him through the ring because our religion was too restrictive? If a belief caused something as horrible as rape, could it be right? The thoughts battled inside me. For the first time in my life, the morals Cole believed didn't immediately give up the fight.

I sighed. "Then why do I feel so darn guilty at nearly being caught?" My words flowed upon the wisps of the wind blowing across my face. If Cole heard, he didn't react.

But Joel heard. I was sure of that. He must have forced Crystal awake; he was jealous. I knew it. Why else would he return when I fell in love with Cole? His excuse to tell me I'd have to pass on the ring echoed hollow in the halls of reason. Of course I'd have to pass on the ring. He didn't need to tell me that. When the time came, it would be clear, so why arrive to tell me the obvious?

I'd show him. If he wanted me, he'd have to do better than that. Cole was my future now, and Joel would have to get over it or fight for me. But I'd not have him destroying my relationship with Cole and then blink out of my life again.

I rolled over as I prayed for guidance.

23

Gabrielle smoothed her dress out. Bare tidbits of moisture clung to the fabric. She turned to Silo. "Thanks for letting me ride in your wagon again."

He smiled. "No problem."

Josh slowed the horse to ride beside them. "Gabrielle, I'm sorry. Please ride with me. It was an accident, I swear."

She huffed. "Maybe later."

His head dropped, and he allowed the horse to drop back.

"I'm being too hard on him, aren't I?" She turned her head toward Silo. "It's just, he has to be more careful. He can't be throwing flames in his sleep."

"I'm gathering your story is true—he is a wizard. Like, where did your tent and bed come from? You carry no packs or baggage."

She bit her lip. "Yes, he's a wizard all right. It has its ups and downs."

"Well, I'm not one to get involved with marital—"

"We're not married!"

He held up a hand. "Oh yes, I forgot." He winked. "Not married. Right. But as I was saying, I'm not one to get involved with lover's quarrels—"

She leaped from her seat. "We're not lovers!"

"Shush! You're attracting attention to yourself." He waved her to sit down and she did.

"All right, so you're not lovers either." He rolled his eyes. "I'm not one to get involved with..." He shot an eye at her. "With friends fighting among themselves, who apparently care for each other very, very much and sleep in the same bed..."

Gabrielle opened her mouth but he held up a hand. She closed it, crossed her arms, and stared at the horizon in front of her as intently as she could.

"But given he's a wizard who's lost his memory, as you said, I'd give the poor guy a break."

"But he nearly set me on fire and then soaked me with water."

"Has he ever set you on fire while he's awake?"

She sighed. "No."

"And you're still alive, given you're a bit wet and your ego's hurt."

She brushed her hair back and sighed. "I think you've hit the boar in the eye. I'm more concerned about my ego than Josh's condition."

He eyed her with a grin and then acted as if he no longer noticed her.

She took a breath and let it out slowly. Then moved to the edge. "Josh?"

He trotted up beside them. "Yes?"

"I'm ready to ride with you."

His face lit up. He pulled the horse close to the wagon and matched its speed. She slid off the seat and onto the horse's back.

Josh craned his neck. "What's that knot in the small of my back?"

She glanced down. "My stomach. Does it bother you?"

"No, no, not at all. I'm perfectly fine."

She wondered if he feared she'd leave him if he admitted that it bothered him. He really was sweet.

He patted her hand holding on to him. "I'm sorry for what happened this morning. I dreamed wolves attacked, and you know what happened then."

"Forget it. I'm over it, and you're forgiven." She squeezed him for physical confirmation.

He sat taller on the horse's back. "What changed your mind?"

"Silo did." She chuckled. "He thinks we're married and lovers. I don't think there's anything I could say to convince him otherwise."

"Well, if you think about it in a certain way, we are—"

"Josh!"

"Sorry." He sat quietly for a few seconds. "Now, your story..."

She laid her head on the back of his neck. "When Sisko was fourteen..."

144

Josh wiggled a piece of flatbread at Gabrielle as the fire brightened and the sky darkened. "Some of the stories you told, things did sound familiar. The Ball of Desires, Milnore, the link Sisko and I share—they're like memories floating under the surface of a pool, just out of reach. If I could grab one, I would see it clearly then others would follow."

She swallowed a piece of the bread dipped in the broth. "I'm sure it'll come back to you. Be patient."

"It's not easy to be patient when you feel like a whole lifetime of memories could be lost forever."

Gabrielle glanced at Silo. "By the way, very tasty broth you've brewed. Who taught you how to cook?"

He smiled. "Thank you. My mother did, bless her heart and eternal be her memory." Silo crossed himself.

Gabrielle sat up straighter. "Oh, so you're a Christian?"

He nodded. "Been so since I's born. I don't go saying much about it. Figure I'll speak with my actions."

She smiled and glanced at Josh.

He swallowed his bite. "Just like I was telling her, 'Gabrielle, there goes a fine man, a very fine man.'" He bobbed his head.

She pinched Josh on the back and he jumped.

She smiled at Silo. "We'll, you've done good for yourself in more ways than one."

Josh rose. "I think I'll go set up our tent. I guess since everyone knows I'm a wizard now, thanks to this morning, they'll be no hard feelings if I toss up the full tent?"

Silo waved his hand. "Everyone provides as they care to and can do."

Josh put his hands behind his back. "Well, you've been so good to us, if you want, you can sleep in our tent. There's room enough for us all."

Silo smiled. "That's very kind of you. But as caravan leader, I have to stay out here with my wagon. I've got to be prepared if we're attacked or any problems develop. Harder to do so enclosed in a big tent."

Gabrielle broke in. "How about if you have breakfast with us in the morning then?"

Josh nodded. "Yes, that would be great. Please join us."

Silo nodded. "All right, I will. Thank you."

Josh turned and bounded off with a light step in search of a good place to set up the tent.

Gabrielle stared at Silo across the fire. "This has been a wonderful trip. You're such a good leader. You should be proud."

He shook his head. "Nothing to be proud of. Just doing what I'm told to do, is all." He scratched his head. "I do provide myself one small amenity as I travel."

She raised an eyebrow. "Which is?"

"I have a collection of desert snakes I've caught."

Gabrielle jerked her eyes open wider. "Live?"

"No, killed and pressed in a book. Wanta see?"

"Sure." She felt privileged to view his private collection. She sensed he didn't show this to everyone.

He stood up and helped Gabrielle to her feet. He kept hold of her hand, leading her to the back of his wagon and inside.

He pointed to the bed. "Sit there, I'll get it out."

She sat and the bedsprings squeaked. He opened a box and pulled out a thick book.

Gabrielle raised an eyebrow. "That's big. How thick is it?"

"About three inches at least."

Coughing erupted from outside the wagon. Gabrielle thought it sounded like Josh. They paused before continuing. "Check this one out." He opened to a page.

"Wow, it's really long."

"A good foot long."

The voice outside groaned and ended in a near cry. Gabrielle wondered what bothered Josh. Maybe she should go check on him? She focused back to Silo's book. "I've heard these are good for eating. Are they?"

"Oh yes. One method is to open your mouth wide and slide them down your throat. Eat them like a snake would. Very tasty, especially when the juices burst out."

A light flashed in the wagon and Josh materialized before them. In his hand, he held a sword. "I can stand no more of this!" He swung the sword at Silo, who rolled to the side as the blade sank into the bedding.

Gabrielle jumped to her feet and grabbed Josh's arm. "Josh, stop! What on earth do you think you're doing!"

He jerked his arm from her grasp. "Getting rid of filthy vermin who pray on naive women!" He flung the sword at Silo, who spun to the side. Josh's weapon missed Silo by an inch, but cut through the ropes holding Silo's bookshelf in place. A cascade of books rained down upon them along with the wooden slabs. Silo swung his fist and landed a blow to Josh's head as the last book bopped upon Josh's outstretched arm.

Josh fell back onto the bed, gritted his teeth, and lunged at Silo again.

Gabrielle screamed. "Stop it, Josh! You're acting like a love-sick, jealous dog!"

Josh pulled the blade back, but as he pushed his hands forward the weapon dropped onto the floor with a thud. He gazed at his hands transformed into—paws! He stared at Gabrielle. "Oh no, you didn—arf, arf!"

He shrank and morphed until a white dog with black spots sat panting at Gabrielle's feet.

She slapped her hands onto the sides of her head and plopped onto the bed. "Oh no, what have I done?"

Silo, breathing hard, stared at Gabrielle. "You...you were telling the truth in your story, weren't you?" He glanced at Josh and back to her.

She nodded and tears formed in her eyes.

He crossed himself. "Lord have mercy."

"Arf, arf." Josh stood on his hind legs and panted while staring at Gabrielle with big, sad eyes.

"Oh, Josh. I'm so sorry." She scooped him up into her lap and scratched behind his ears. He barked and turned over on his back.

"Josh!"

He whined and his head dropped.

She sighed. "All right." She rubbed his belly and his leg jerked back and forth. "What am I doing!" She thrust him back to the floor. "You tried to kill Silo here for no reason at all."

Josh bared his teeth at Silo and barked. Silo jumped upon his bed.

"Bad dog!" Gabrielle grabbed Josh by the nape of his neck and hauled him outside as he pawed at the wagon's wooden floor and barked at Silo. She plopped him on the ground and focused on his face.

"Josh, I don't know what you thought he would do to me, but you can't blindly kill someone before you know the facts. He was only showing me a book of desert snakes he'd collected."

Josh cocked his head to one side.

"Now, if you'll stand still, I'll see about changing you back." She thought for a moment.

Josh's eyes opened wider and his ears stood up straight.

"I guess I'll say the opposite and see if that does the trick." She stood up. "You're really—"

Josh shot off behind her, barking wildly.

She spun around. "Josh, come back!" She watched as he chased a rabbit into the night's darkness. Her shoulders slumped. "Oh bother. He'll be back by morning." She scanned the area and saw the tent Josh had set up. She cupped her hands and called out to Silo's wagon, "Don't forget. Breakfast in the morning."

He poked his head out. "I wouldn't miss it for the world." His eyes scanned the area. "Where's your, friend?"

She shook her head. "He's out chasing rabbits I'm afraid. I'm going to bed." She mumbled to herself, "But he's one sleeping dog I won't let lie."

The trip from the Burrowers' mountains to Octum took all day. We left the campsite early that morning. Nathan trotted, sometimes galloped, sometimes rested. Since no trail guided our path, we encountered no oases. I thanked the Burrowers for the water in our packs. Nathan slurped it up when we paused for a rest.

Cole said Octum lay at the bottom of a mountain shaped like a tower with ramparts atop it; we used it to guide us across the featureless plains. With Joel's horse, we could split up so Nathan wouldn't have to carry everyone. Cole and Crystal rode on the other horse, and I on Nathan, though I so wished Cole could ride with me. But Crystal couldn't ride by herself, we feared she might fall off.

The day passed quickly until the evening stars twinkled in the sky as the walls of Octum rose on the horizon. The moonlight revealed rock buildings and walls. Flat roofs provided an open floor, and we saw not a few sleeping on them in the cool night breeze.

"I think it's time to switch you back, Brother." I scratched his neck.

Not as long as you keep that up!

He halted. I slid to the ground, took the bracelet off, and he transformed into his lovable self.

He knocked dust off his arms. "One problem. We're running low on money. I think I have enough left to pay for a night at an inn."

Cole pulled up beside us. "I never spent the money I had reserved for buying Crystal from the traders, so I can cover the bill for a night or two. Why don't I let Crystal walk with you two, and I'll ride on ahead and make arrangements?"

I perked up. "Why don't I ride with you into town?"

Nathan put a hand on my shoulder. "Sis, I want to chat with you about a couple things, could you stay with me?"

I let my shoulders sag. "If you need me to."

Cole leaped from his horse and wrapped me in his arms. "Don't worry, we'll be together again real soon."

He kissed me, and the vision returned. But this time the vision changed: Cole wrapped his arms around my back and kissed down my neck.

He pulled away, helped Crystal off, and remounted the horse. "See you soon, my love." He flipped the reins and the horse sped into a gallop toward the city gates, leaving me standing in the dust.

"Kaylee? Is something wrong?"

I turned to meet Nathan's eyes. "Oh, well, no. Not really."

He cocked his head to one side. "Kaylee, you forget. We're linked, I can sense your emotional state. You can't lie to me."

I shook my head. "A vision caught me off guard is all. Every time I kiss him, I see us locked in each others arms, kissing."

"And something changed this time?"

"Yes."

He took Crystal by the hand and we proceeded to the city gate. "You don't have to tell me if you don't want to, but I have a feeling what you saw confirms my own fears. You're getting too involved with a man you know little about. And what we do know isn't good."

I kicked at the dirt. "Nathan, he's kind, generous, respectful, and he loves me. A lot like you. What isn't good?"

"Beltrid," Crystal recited.

Nathan kissed her on the cheek. "I thought the same thing about Crystal when Beltrid possessed her. She could do no wrong in my eyes." He turned to face me. "I do have concerns about his religion, and it isn't good for you to link yourself with someone who isn't spiritually compatible."

I chuckled. "Look who's talking! You'd have married a demon if I hadn't stopped you."

He nodded. "Exactly my point, I'm experienced in being deceived. It isn't just his religion, it's what I'm sensing in you. You're changing, and I don't feel it is for the good."

I frowned. "Everyone changes. Who's to judge what change is good and what is bad? Don't I have control of my own life?"

He stared into the night sky. "Sounds like something I told you a few months ago." He sighed. "I know you can't see it, but the level of involvement with him is going too far. If you're not careful, you'll find yourself in bed with him, doing more—"

I stomped my foot on the ground. "No! He would never do that. He told me as much. He would never force himself on me. I feel safe with him."

Nathan hung his head. "I didn't say that he would force himself on you."

I clenched my teeth together. Did Nathan not trust me? Now I wished I had ridden with Cole to town. The doubts about how far was too far whirled inside me.

I rubbed the back of my neck. "Nathan, to tell you the truth, I'm debating what we believe about morality. I mean, how do we know we're right and other cultures and religions are wrong?"

He glanced at me. "This is what worries me. You above all people should know. Reality is real whether you or I or Cole believes it or not. My belief or non-belief doesn't change the truth. If you hadn't stopped me, I would have married a demon even though I strongly believed at the time that Crystal wasn't one. What I believed didn't change the facts."

My heart confirmed what he said. Yet... "But you didn't address the problem. Belief is belief that something is the truth. It may not change what is the truth, but it is our attempts to discover the truth. We're either right or wrong, but how do I know we're right and Cole's religion is wrong?"

As the gate drew near, Nathan remained silent. The shadows of moonlight cast by the gate's arch slid under our feet; he turned to me and peered deep into my eyes. "Kaylee, you've experienced God's reality more than I have: with Father in the cave, with Love, the power of the ring, the testimony of the Church—what else do you need?"

I bowed my head. He was right. How could I deny the reality I had experienced? "That still doesn't answer one question. Why is the ring pointing me to Cole as my future husband if he's so bad?"

He shrugged. "I don't know. Maybe he is to be your future husband. But there is a right way and a wrong way to go about it. I think you're headed down the wrong way."

I frowned. The doubts still raged, but Nathan's opinion was just that, his opinion. Why continue the discussion? "Thanks, Nathan, you're right. I'll work this out. Don't worry about me, I'll be fine."

He cast a glance my direction. "I wish I could not worry. Promise me one thing."

"What?"

He bit his lip. "If things go badly, don't hesitate to come to me for help. I'll never say I told you so."

I smiled and squeezed his hand. "I will."

My eyes fluttered open. Crickets chirped outside the window of our room. Nathan, Crystal, and I stayed in one room, Cole in another. I wanted to stay in Cole's room, but Nathan wouldn't hear of it, and after our conversation, I didn't want to give him anything more to worry about.

I needed the bathroom. I rose from my bed, which creaked with each movement. But Nathan didn't wake, and Crystal didn't pop up to say Beltrid's name again. I eased myself out the door and through the back courtyard to find the inn's toilet in a building several yards away.

The place stunk, and luckily the cool night air kept the flies to a minimum. I stayed as long as necessary before working my way back to the room. It must have been in the early hours of the morning. No hint of the sun touched the eastern horizon.

As I approached our door, Cole opened his and saw me. "What are you doing up in the middle of the night?"

I chuckled. "Probably the same thing you are. I had to go."

He shook his head and drew near. "I sensed you were up and couldn't resist taking advantage of the opportunity." He pulled me to him and his lips met mine.

Again, the vision flashed upon my mind of Cole working his way down my neck. Could this be God's way of saying this should happen? It didn't jive with what I'd been taught. Why did the ring show me this?

He parted and stared into my eyes. "Want to come into my room? We can kiss more comfortably in here."

I gazed inside. "All right."

He led me by the hand and shut the door. He reached around me and squeezed tightly on the small of my back. Then his hands slid down onto my rear, and he squeezed again. As before, an energy shot through me, a warm sensation vibrated through my body.

He ran his fingers through my hair. "I don't think we're as likely to be interrupted here. Want to pick up where we left off?"

"I'd like that very much."

He moved his lips toward mine.

"But I'm not ready to unite physically."

He nodded. "I figured as much."

I laid my head on his chest. "It's just, I've experienced too much of God's truth. To dismiss my faith's teachings on morality would deny what I know."

He rubbed my back. "So, you're saying you've heard God himself tell you not to unite with me? Or with anyone?"

"No, not exactly." Actually, the ring's visions could mean it'd be fine with Cole. I didn't know what to think.

He kissed my forehead. "We believe every religion has some things right and some things wrong. None of them could be totally correct on all their teachings. Because you experienced some true and good realities in your religion doesn't mean it isn't wrong in other areas, like physical intimacy."

"But if it's right in important areas, what reason do I have to say it's wrong about that?"

He chuckled. "Your own scriptures give examples of different moralities. Through most of it husbands married multiple wives and in some cases, multiple concubines, purely for the purpose of producing children for the husband."

"But that was a different time."

"Sure, but in your New Testament, the practice still prevailed. They put restrictions on the clergy to not have multiple wives. And the wedding wasn't much more than a big party, which at the end the bride and groom entered a tent and united physically."

I nodded. "Yes, to seal the union. That's what we're taught is its purpose. To join the two into one."

He stared down into my upturned eyes. "I would very much like to be one with you."

I reached up and met his lips. My vision returned, as clear as ever. And on my face, I enjoyed his lips kissing the base of my neck. I studied the scene as I watched him work his way onto the top of my chest. What did this vision mean? The image vanished as his lips parted from mine.

I squeezed him tight. "I would very much like to be one with you as well. But I'm not ready tonight."

He smiled and I thought heaven would burst from him. "We won't go there then. It will be enough for me to hold you and kiss you some more."

It felt great knowing I didn't have to worry about being taken advantage of. I pushed him down onto the bed and fell upon him. His arms enveloped mine and he rolled on top of me. We kissed, and among the vision and the energy coursing through my limbs, my hand found its way onto his rear, and I squeezed.

"I love you," I whispered between kisses.

He answered by kissing my neck and pressing his chest against mine as his hand caressed my body. But he never tried to remove my clothing, or go beyond his loving hugs and kisses.

We enjoyed each other's love until I saw the eastern sky redden through the room's window. I felt a little tired, but energized all at the same time.

I pulled my lips from his. "I'd better get back to my room. I don't want Nathan to worry when he wakes up and finds me missing."

He nodded. "A good idea. I so much enjoyed our time together. Tomorrow night?"

I smiled. "I wouldn't miss it for the world."

We kissed one more time before I slid off his bed, straightened my clothes, and left. I rolled into my bed and it creaked. Nathan groaned and flopped around before resting again. Crystal lay motionless.

My thoughts raced. Cole's arguments rang true, points I couldn't deny. I felt more confused than ever. My vision of him and me continued to invade my memory. And Cole remained true to his word. Several hours of kissing passionately passed, but he refrained from any attempts to get under my clothes. I trusted him. We loved each other so much, surely we could deal with the different religion issue.

I stared at the ceiling and whispered, "God, if this is wrong, you'd better make it clear. I'm not seeing much wrong about it." If only He would state it clearly.

25

Gabrielle opened the tent's flap to let in the morning air. Josh lay curled up on the ground, a dead rabbit laying by his side. He raised his head, and his ears perked up. He leaped to his feet and scooped the rabbit into his mouth. His tail wagged as he stared at her with big, round eyes.

She frowned. She'd better change him back before he chased after something else. "Josh, you're a human."

Light enveloped him and then dimmed. The human Josh sat on the ground, his legs under him, with a rabbit between his teeth. He knocked the rabbit out of his mouth and spit several times upon the ground. "Talk about nasty!"

"Are you ready for some real breakfast?"

He stared up at her. "I've been turned into a big beast, I've even spent a few minutes as a fly one time, but this is the most humiliating animal I've ever been."

She smiled. "We're even then." She reached out a hand and helped him up. She paused and stared into his eyes. "Josh, you just remembered something from your past!"

His eyes widened. "Yes, I did. I remember being a fly. I played the Wheel of Curses at a carnival and ended up trading places with a fly, who wanted to squish me so he could stay a human."

"Can you remember anything else?"

He nodded. "I can remember the spells I used to make the wheel stop where I wanted it to, but someone else prevented it from working as it should. But not much else."

She grunted. "A lot of good that spell will do us." She met his eyes. "Mind telling me why you charged into Silo's wagon as if he were a dragon to slay?"

He rubbed his face. "I thought you were doing...something sexual."

"Sexual? Whatever gave you that idea?"

He rolled his eyes. "When I came up to the wagon, all I heard was, 'Let me get it out. Oh, how big and thick it is! Check this out. Wow, that's long. A whole foot long.' When you started talking about eating it, I couldn't take it anymore. What was I supposed to think?"

She couldn't help but crack a smile. "I see." She pointed a finger at him. "But that still doesn't excuse you. One, you shouldn't charge in to kill someone based purely on assumptions—didn't you see we were looking at a book?"

He shrugged. "I figured the book covered it up."

"Two, even if I were doing what you thought, it's my business. What right did you have to barge in? It's not like you're my husband."

He sniffed. "I feel like I'm your husband."

"It's the link with Sisko causing your feelings. You must control yourself."

He sighed. "I'm trying. Really I am. It's not easy. I'll be glad when I regain my right mind."

Gabrielle breathed deep. "Me too. We'll all be much safer." She met Josh's gaze. "By the way, sorry for turning you into a dog."

He stared at the dead rabbit on the ground. "No harm done in the end. Except I don't think I can ever eat rabbit again."

Gabrielle noticed Silo approaching. Upon seeing Josh, he stopped. "Is it safe to come over?"

She nodded. "He'll behave himself."

He resumed his progress until he stopped by Gabrielle.

Josh smiled. "Sorry about last night." He placed a hand on Silo's shoulder. Silo winced. Josh jerked his hand away. "It was all a misunderstanding. You wouldn't believe what I thought you were doing." He chuckled.

Gabrielle stared at Josh through narrow eyes. "Josh, the whole incident was embarrassing enough. No sense making it more so."

"Of course, you're right." He folded his hands in front of him and focused on Silo. "I'm horribly ashamed about last night. Let me make it up to you with a great breakfast before we get the caravan underway."

They proceeded to enter the tent. Gabrielle doubled over and groaned. Josh put his arm around her shoulders and rubbed her back as she grimaced and gritted her teeth. After a minute, the pains subsided.

She felt her stomach. "I had some pains in the middle of the night too. It's about four or five months along, by standard measurements, in a mere four days."

Josh helped her up. "I'll feel better once we're in Octum. You may need a midwife for this one. A doctor if we can find one."

She nodded. "Let's eat before the food spoils."

They entered the tent.

Josh insisted that Gabrielle ride with Silo. He said that she didn't need jolting around any more than necessary, and the wagon rode smoother. She could tell he did fight his inclination to demand that she ride with him. No doubt Sisko's love influenced his concern for her welfare over whatever jealousy he felt.

She turned to Silo. "How many days till we reach Octum?"

He scanned the horizon as if searching for markers. "I'd say we have at least another couple of days to go." He stared at her protruding stomach. "You gonna make it?"

"I think so, but without much time to spare at the rate I'm progressing." She sighed. "I sure hope I find Kaylee and Nathan there. Not sure if I can continue to chase after them in this condition. But I'll have to if they've moved on."

Silo grunted. "I sure wouldn't if I were you. You have to think about your baby. It's not good having a baby in the wilderness."

She stared at the bulge in her body. "I have a feeling it won't matter much with this baby. This one's destined to come out and be someone special."

"Oh, I nearly forgot!" Silo handed her the reins and dove his upper body into the wagon behind him. He returned holding a book. "While I was cleaning up after your friend's...uh...misunderstanding, I found a book I thought I'd lost. Something I picked up in an obscure town's market. Never seen one like it before or since." He handed her a leather hardback. "Don't think I ever read it. Curiosity purchase mostly."

She studied the cover and read the title: The Secrets of Winged Horses. She jumped from her seat. "Josh! Josh!"

He rode up beside them. "Yes?"

"I have a book about winged horses! We can get it to fly!"

His mouth dropped open. "You do?"

I wrapped an arm around Silo and squeezed. "Thank you so much! This is perfect. We'll be able to get to Octum in much better time this way."

He nodded. "Yes, I suspect you could get there by early tomorrow morning if you didn't stop."

She opened the book and scanned the contents until she found the section titled: How to rise into the air. The command appeared toward the beginning of the section. "Upwards? Is that all we needed to say?"

She scooted to the edge of her seat and called out to Josh. "I discovered the command to cause the horse to fly. You say, 'Upwards.'"

Josh's eyes widened as the horse leaped up and flapped its wings. "Help!" The horse rose into the air and Josh wrapped his arms around the creature's neck.

Gabrielle put her hand over her mouth. "Oh dear." She flipped through the contents and found the section: How To Land. She followed her finger as it wove its way among the words.

Silo stared into the sky, a hand covering his eyes from the sunlight. "He's getting mighty high. Shouldn't you have read how to land it before you launched him into the air?"

She frowned. "I didn't mean to launch him into the air!" She found the command. "Downwards, of course." She cupped her hands around her mouth and hoped Josh or the horse would hear. "Josh, the book says to say, 'Downwards.'"

The horse dove to the ground with Josh clamped to the horses' neck and body. Gabrielle winced when the horse almost hit the ground, but it pulled out at the last minute and braked with its wings until it settled its legs onto the dirt.

Josh rode the horse back to the wagon and pulled alongside. He huffed air in rapid succession. "I didn't ask for a demonstration."

She bit her lip. "Sorry, I wasn't thinking."

He cracked his neck. "At least I'm not the only one who doesn't think all the time."

She turned back to Silo. "Thank you so much. You've been more than generous and helpful. I doubt I could ever repay you."

He shook his head. "It's what I do, Ma'am. You've been a delight..." He glanced at Josh. "If not a somewhat entertaining presence."

She chuckled. "You're worth your weight in gold." She slid off the wagon bench and onto the horse's back and waved.

Silo waved back. "Hope you get a chance to see my snake book again sometime. We barely dug into it last night." He glanced back into his wagon; his eyes widened and he did a double-take. "Where did all this gold come from?"

Gabrielle covered her mouth. "Oh, dear. I really have to watch what I say."

Josh nodded. "He probably deserves it for everything we put him through."

She giggled. "For sure, but if I had worded it differently, I could have turned him into a pile of gold." But she agreed, he deserved it. "Now, let's get this horse airborne."

Josh nudged the beast into a gallop. Gabrielle's muscles tensed as Josh prepared to launch her into the sky with nothing but a few inches of horseback to balance herself on.

"Upwards," Josh's voice rang out.

Gabrielle squeezed him tight and closed her eyes. She screamed as the ground sank away.

"Gabrielle! You're hurting my ears!" Josh cried out. "What's the matter with you?"

She couldn't help but sob if she couldn't scream. "I'm...afraid of heights."

He wheezed. "Great. Do you mind loosening your grip on me? I don't want to fall unconscious up here."

"I'm going to die!" She felt tremors rolling through her body.

Josh sighed. "Maybe we should ride on the ground after all?"

She shook her head. "No, we have to get to Kaylee. Keep flying. I'll manage...somehow."

He grunted. "The question is whether I'll manage or not."

26

"Wake up!"

My dream world faded to reveal Nathan's face. I turned over. "Let me sleep!"

"Kaylee, it's late morning. You're usually up by now."

I rolled over on my back and blinked the sleep from my eyes. "I guess my body needed more sleep than I realized." I let a yawn escape. "Is there any coffee?" If I didn't act guilty, he wouldn't suspect that I'd been up half the night in Cole's arms.

He stepped over to a table. "It's cooled down some." He poured the black liquid into a cup and handed it to me.

I sat up and slurped the lukewarm drink into my mouth. "Um, that's better. Thanks."

He sat at the table. "I have a job."

I raised an eyebrow. "A job?"

He nodded. "Cole said he could only cover a couple nights. We'll need some more money by tomorrow. I found someone who needed a package delivered to Rasor, a small town about ten miles from here. Will take me about a full day of riding to get there and back. I won't return until early tomorrow morning, if I don't stay over too long. But it pays well enough to keep us going."

I rose and sat at the table. "When are you leaving?"

"In about an hour. I'm getting ready to head to the kitchen to eat and stash some extra food for the jaunt." He pointed at Crystal sitting against the wall, staring into space. "Be sure to watch over her. Give her some food and all. She'll pretty much do anything you say, but she needs looking after."

I nodded. "Sure. She's in good hands with me."

He frowned. "You'll have to wake up earlier than noon to take care of her."

"Don't worry, I'll do it." I sipped more coffee.

He wagged a finger at me. "And please, be careful with Cole. Don't take any unnecessary risks."

I smiled, because I knew Cole was safe. "You have nothing to worry about." Time to change the subject. No sense going down that road again. "Too bad the bracelets don't extend ten miles out. You could be there and back in half a day as a winged horse."

He winked. "Yeah, I thought about that. But it would take longer to walk those five miles there and back, assuming I reached the ground before I changed." He rose. "I'd better get moving. I'll see you in the morning."

I jumped to my feet and gave him a tight hug. "Thanks for your help. I'll take good care of Crystal."

He hugged back and smiled. "I know you will." Then he grabbed his pack and left the room.

I sipped the coffee and watched Crystal. I felt sorry for her. I couldn't imagine what she felt, the turmoil she might be going through. I knew the sooner we freed her soul, the better she and we would be.

"You hungry, Crystal?"

"Food."

"Hum, I'll take that as a yes. Stay put, and I'll go grab something from the kitchen."

I spent most of the day taking care of Crystal and chatting with Cole. I didn't have to do much for Crystal—feed her and ensure she didn't wander off. Mostly she sat in the chair, staring into space. A couple hours after lunch, she lay on a bed and fell asleep.

I glanced at Cole. "You know, she'll probably sleep for a while."

He winked. "My thoughts exactly. Let's leave her here and go to my room."

We slipped into the hallway and entered his room. He bolted the door shut. "There, no chance someone will barge in."

He turned and placed a hand behind my back. "I have to ask, have you thought about what I said? Are you all right with more intimacy?"

I stared into his eager eyes. "More intimacy, yes. But to go all the way? I'm still not sure about that."

He nodded. "More intimate it is. Stop me if I go too far, all right?"

I nodded and reached for his lips. Their warmth enveloped me and I shut my eyes. The vision of us together returned, but I flung my eyes wide open. Now the vision showed me lying in the bed next to us, with him atop me! But I kept the kiss intact and closed my eyes again. This must be a sign; it all added up. The ring clearly indicated that I would unite with Cole.

His hand slipped down once again to caress my rear, then it slid up under my blouse and rubbed my bare back. I groaned before I realized it and pulled him tighter to me. With his other hand, he touched my face and let his fingers slide down my neck. His lips followed his fingers, inching down my neck, just as in the vision. Chills raced across my body.

His hand unstrung my outer vest. He started to unbutton my blouse with each swish of his tongue across mine. My pulse increased but found my hand grabbing his, halting his progress. He released my buttons, and ran his hand instead over my shoulders and neck.

I unsnapped his tunic, revealing a muscular chest covered with wisps of hair. His skin smelt of perfumes, and his heart of love. I wrapped him in a hug; a surge of rising energy expanded over my body. I broke our kiss and pulled away.

He raised an eyebrow.

He had to see the desire in my eyes, the flaming fire in my heart. I couldn't deny it any longer. The ring had shown me what should happen. Why should I fight it? What possible harm could arise from melting with him into one? What difference did a church ceremony make anyway? Why put this off any longer?

I eased onto the bed, lay down on my back, and spread my arms wide, dangling off each side. "I'm ready. I'm ready to join to you as one. Now."

He grinned. "Are you sure?"

I breathed deep. "Yes. It is meant to be. I won't stop you this time."

He pulled off his tunic and then climbed onto the bed. He swung his leg over me and straddled my waist. He leaned over, slipped a hand across my back, and kissed my lips. His hand returned to the buttons on my blouse. I closed my eyes as another jolt of energy raced through my body. It exploded between my hips and surged into all my limbs. But then the energy morphed into fingers of revulsion cascading over me in waves ending at my hands.

A thud reached my ears; something hit the floor. I jerked my eyes wide open. A metallic rolling sound echoed through my brain. I jerked my hand up and broke Cole's kiss. A sick feeling grew in my gut as my fingers rose into view.

The ring had fallen off!

This was wrong! So very wrong! How could I have misunderstood? I tried not to overreact. I didn't want Cole to see my fear.

I stared into his eyes. "My ring, it fell off."

He focused on my hand. "I thought you said it doesn't come off?"

I pulled my upper lip between my teeth. "Well, normally it doesn't, but sometimes, it can. I guess the excitement...loosened it a little."

He smiled. "I'll get it." He stretched over the edge and to the floor, and pulled himself back up with the ring between his fingers.

I lifted my hand up. "Thanks."

But he continued to grip it. My heart pumped harder.

He held it up in the afternoon light and turned it over. "A very interesting ring." He stared into my eyes and sighed.

"Cole, please put the ring on my finger. It's important. Please?"

His eyes locked onto mine. Longing desire fought some other demon within them. "I would very much like to continue, because I do love you. But he said the ring would likely fall off at this point." He flipped the ring into the air and it landed in his palm, then he stuffed it into his pants pocket.

"Cole! No, you can't do that. Who's he?"

He frowned and stared at a spot on the wall. "Morgenstern."

"What would he want with the ring? He couldn't use it."

Cole bit his lip. "You know him better as Lucifer, in your religion."

My mouth fell open. No, it couldn't be! "You mean...you worship Satan?"

He nodded.

I stared at him unblinking. This couldn't be happening. My blissful dream veered into a nightmare. I tried kicking at him, but I could barely move my legs. I slammed my fist onto his chest. "Let me up! Give back my ring! Wait until Nathan returns! Wait until Joel hears about this. You'll be sorry!"

His hand landed across my face with a numbing sting. His strong body kept me pinned to the bed. "Get control of yourself. We're taking a trip. Time to deliver the goods."

"I trusted you! I hate you! I hate you!" I flung my arms at his face and connected. He cradled his jaw with one hand, then drove his other onto my head. Darkness swept over me.

27

The walls of Octum proved a welcome relief to Gabrielle. She'd kept her eyes closed through most of the trip, trying to imagine that she rocked back and forth on the swing at her father's house. Memories of the rope hanging from the limb of an old oak tree brought back pleasant childhood dreams: the days before her father and brother became enraged at each other regularly and turned her bright world into a nightmare. A nightmare ended by Sisko.

But she forced herself to keep her eyes open as they approached the city. They had flown all night on the winged horse. It didn't seem to mind. The horse glided most of the way and so didn't expend a lot of energy. But now the stars gave way to the reds and oranges of sunlight creeping over the eastern mountains.

But one lone figure caught her attention. A man on a horse raced toward the gate below them. He left a trail of dust as he sped along, indicating a strong gallop on the otherwise hard soil. He appeared to be a man on a mission, and Gabrielle sensed that his mission might affect hers as well.

She tapped Josh on the shoulder. "Shouldn't we go down now?"

"Uh, what was that command again?"

She whispered it into his ear.

He sat up taller and commanded, "Downward." The horse obeyed and they sank toward the racing man on the ground.

She nudged Josh. "Be careful, it looks as if you're going to land right on the poor guy."

At the last minute, Josh pulled the horse to the left, and they swooshed to the rider's side. The winged horse's hooves connected with the ground. The other rider pulled to a halt as the dust blew past them.

"Mother? What are you doing here?"

The dust cleared and Nathan sat atop the horse. Gabrielle breathed a sigh of relief. "Oh Nathan, I'm so glad I found you. Maybe I'm in time after all."

He wrinkled his brow. "In time for..." He glanced at the city. "Josh, Mother, forget that now. I have to get into town. Something's happened to Kaylee and I don't know what yet."

A knot twisted in her gut. "By all means, let's go."

He snapped the reins and broke the panting horse into a heavy gallop. Josh tried to keep up, but the winged horse, tired from the long trip and carrying two people, simply couldn't maintain the same speed. Still the gate's long, morning shadows stood only two more miles away, and they quickly caught up to Nathan once inside the city's gates. Gabrielle watched Nathan duck into an inn's doorway. A sign hung over the entrance that read, *The Dragon's Inn.*

Josh pulled the horse to a stop in front of the structure. She slid off and sped into the building as fast as her feet would carry her. Fear and hope battled as her anticipation grew. With the help of a couple bystanders, she found Nathan's room. He stood inside it, his head sunk and his shoulders drooped.

On a chair against a wall sat an unfamiliar, black-haired woman. She suspected the lady might be Crystal.

Gabrielle placed her hand on Nathan's back. "Where's Kaylee?"

Nathan shook his head vigorously. "I should have listened to my instinct! I knew Cole was trouble."

She shook him. "Nathan! Where's Kaylee, and who is Cole?"

He covered his face with his hands. "I don't know where Kaylee is. She's gone!"

"How do you know her and this Cole aren't out shopping or visiting with someone?"

"No, Mother. You don't understand." He turned to face her. "Because of the bracelets, I can...Mother!" He pointed at her bulging stomach. "You're...you're..."

"Pregnant. Yes, I know."

"But...how...I mean..." His eyes darted between Gabrielle and Josh.

"You didn't, did you? Are all the women losing their minds?"

Josh threw his hands back. "I had nothing to do with it." He stared at the ceiling. "Well, not directly, anyway, since—"

"Josh! You're not helping." Gabrielle grabbed Nathan by the shoulders and forced him to sit in a chair. "Calm down. This is not Josh's baby. It's your father's child."

He stared at her with wide eyes. His mouth moved as if trying to form words. After several tries, some finally emerged. "I must be having a bad dream, or I'm going insane." He flopped his head onto the table and covered it with his hands. "This can't be happening, it can't."

Gabrielle sighed, then grabbed Nathan's hair with one hand and pulled back. His face emerged from hiding, and she grabbed his cheeks with the other hand and shook him. "Get a grip, son. What's important at this moment is Kaylee. Do you know where she went? How do you know she's left town?"

Nathan blinked his eyes a couple of times and shook his head. "Yes, Kaylee. Like I was saying, the bracelets have connected us mentally. I can sense where she is all the time. The further away she gets, the weaker it becomes, but I could still feel her strongly ten miles away in the city where I delivered a package for some extra money. While there, I felt her emotional state flare into fear and hatred. I could almost hear the words, 'I hate you' flow through my mind. I raced back here as fast as I could. As I approached, I could tell she wasn't here, but I had to see for myself and make sure Crystal was safe."

He met Gabrielle's eyes. "And I can sense she's getting further away every moment. But based on the direction I'm feeling her presence, I know they left down the southwest road. I recall some locals saying it ran to a city called Shore Cliffs about a couple days journey from here."

"Shore Cliffs?" Gabrielle glanced at Josh. "In the vision at the steam house, I flew past a city down the side of a cliff before traveling out to sea and stopping at an island."

Gabrielle blinked back tears that wanted to flood her cheeks. "This Cole, he must be the one in the vision. The one I saw throw Kaylee toward a demon who...who killed her with a sword." She squeezed her eyes shut.

Josh rubbed her back. "God wouldn't have sent you if you couldn't stop it. We still have to try. It's not too late."

Nathan placed a hand over hers and tightened around it. She opened her eyes to see his jaw set and a fire blazing in his eyes. "Mother, he's right. We have to go get her. She saved me once from marrying a demon. Now, I can save her from being sacrificed to one.

"Besides..." He rose from his chair. "Cole doesn't know that we have a real flying horse and a wizard with us, nor does he know that I can sense where Kaylee's at. I think that's one bit of information she never got around to telling him. So once he's out of range from me turning into a winged horse, he'll believe he has all the time he needs."

Josh smiled. "That's the spirit!"

Gabrielle rose from her chair. "Then let's get moving."

Nathan nodded. "Yes, let's do this."

They packed food and supplies. Josh ensured the horse ate and drank plenty of water. Within an hour, the four met in the street.

Gabrielle frowned at getting back on the winged horse again. She met Nathan's eyes. "So, you can't turn into a winged horse yourself right now?"

Nathan ran his fingers through his hair. "No. She's too far away, and judging the time I felt her emotions surge, Cole's had more than a half-day's head start on us. He could be ten or fifteen miles away by now."

Josh patted the winged horse. "Best if you two go on. I'll stay here with Crystal and watch after her for you. That way you can both ride the winged horse and gain on them."

Nathan stared at Josh. "But Mother's in no condition to travel. She looks like she could blow any time now."

Gabrielle grimaced. "Do you have to put it that way?"

Nathan threw up a hand. "Nothing against you, Mother, but Josh's wizardry skills could come in handy once we catch up. Cole apparently knows some magic. Maybe more than he's let on."

Josh peered over the horse's rear. "That's just it, I lost my memory, and my ability to do magic is spotty at best."

Gabrielle laid a hand on Nathan's shoulder. "Besides, I have to go. I don't know how, but I'm to play some part in changing the vision I saw. If I'm not there, Kaylee dies."

"Josh," a voice rang from across the street.

Josh's eyes widened. "That voice, it sounds familiar." He turned to stare at its source. A man approached them, but stopped in the middle of the street. People bustled around him.

Josh narrowed his eyes. "Darek. Your name is Darek. You killed my master, Milnore." Gabrielle watched as Josh's eyes brightened and he straightened his back. A calm replaced the uncertainty that had dogged him since his memory loss. His past must be flooding back in.

Darek grinned. "So nice of you to remember me after all this time." He strolled to the side, keeping his distance. "I've looked forward to this day. Planned for it. To have it so unexpectedly fall into my lap is quite...intoxicating."

Gabrielle watched Josh. Did he remember enough to defend himself?

Darek spat on the ground. "You remember the curse you placed up me?"

Josh nodded. "I get the feeling you didn't learn anything from it."

Darek laughed. "Learn? Why, I've learned many things. Including how to work around your petty little restriction on my magic." He flipped his wand at Josh and a bolt of energy blasted from it. The blast flew around Josh and landed on the raised chest of the wizard. A radiant glow enveloped him.

His lips curled up on the ends. "I simply cast spells on others that I want on myself. I tried to make you invincible to any magic, but now I am!" Darek pulled a sword from his belt. He raised the sword and sped after Josh.

Josh flung his hands out and a force pushed back against Darek's sword, but the energy shattered like glass. The sword smashed through, and fell across Josh's arm. Josh screamed as the sword cut through above his elbow, and blood split upon the severed limb lying in the dirt.

Josh backed up, his stub dripping red, and his face growing paler by the second.

Darek's grin grew bigger and he stepped toward Josh. "I bet your spell will be broken once you're dead." He pulled the sword back.

Gabrielle jumped between the wizard and Josh as she'd done so long ago with her father and brother. She stared him down.

"Mother!" Nathan called out, but her gaze did not flinch.

She placed her hands on her hips. "You will not kill him."

Darek laughed. "And who's going to stop me? You? Stand aside, or I'll run you both through with one blow."

Nathan leaped toward her drawing his sword. He halted when she held out a hand. "Mother?" he whimpered.

She continued to stare Darek down. He shrugged. "Have it your way." He pulled the sword back again.

Gabrielle pointed a finger at him. "You're nothing more than a fly who can't get enough excrement to satisfy the corruption feeding on your soul!"

He laughed. "Such a puny attempt at slander, from a puny woman."

Gabrielle frowned. He didn't immediately change. Could the steam house's power break through his magic? Or would he kill them both before it took effect? If she died here, so would Kaylee on the island.

Nathan dashed forward, his weapon in hand.

Darek thrust his sword at her. She stepped backwards as it sped toward her heart. Another blade broke into her view and smashed with a loud metallic clank against Darek's, knocking it up into the air. Darek's fingers vanished and the sword fell harmlessly onto the ground. Transparent wings sprung from his back, and his eyes bulged out as he shrank toward the ground. A small fly buzzed angrily where Darek had stood.

She whipped around to see Josh lying on the ground in a pool of blood. "Quick, someone get a doctor!" She fell at his side and cradled his head in her arms. "Josh, please hang on!" His dilated pupils stared blankly into the sky.

Nathan dropped beside him with a stick and a strip of cloth he'd ripped from his shirt. He wrapped it around Josh's stump and tied it closed. Then he placed the stick under the cloth and twisted it until the blood stopped flowing. He took another strip of cloth and tied it off. Gabrielle rubbed his shoulders and held him close, hoping her body heat would help him.

Nathan glanced at his mother. "Since when did you get the ability to best a wizard?"

"The steam house."

He nodded and picked up Josh's severed arm. "Better keep this for now. You never know. Help me get him into the bed in our room. Once we get a doctor to see him, we can be on our way."

She nodded.

He gazed into the distance. "Her link grows weak. Soon, I'll not be able to feel her presence."

Gabrielle put her arms under Josh's. "Then let's get moving."

28

I awoke shivering. I lay in a couple inches of snow! I scampered to my feet and soaked in my surroundings. I stood on a ledge high into the mountains. Snow covered everything, and a swirling wind whipped ice crystals against my bare face. It all felt eerily familiar. I was clothed, but my soul, that was a different matter. It lay bare to the freezing cold.

My soul! "This is the ledge in Dad's soul." I spun around and the same cave entrance lay behind me. A little girl emerged from its shadows. I turned back toward the precipice and the vast mountains thrusting their fingers into the sky. I heard Love's feet crunching in the snow as she stepped toward me. Each step echoed, "Guilty." I had failed, and now I would have to face the consequences.

"Kaylee, why do you remain in the cold?"

My teeth chattered, but I didn't care. I deserved this. "This is my soul, isn't it?"

"You're quite perceptive."

I frowned. "Well, go ahead and say it. Tell me how badly I've botched my stewardship of the ring. Tell me how incredible it is that what a demon killing my dad couldn't do, a sweet-talking, good-for-nothing Satan worshiper accomplished with my total compliance."

"Why should I tell you what you already know?"

I fell back into the snow upon my rear and put my head between my knees. "But why wasn't I warned! Why did all the signs point to intimacy with him, including the ring?"

She placed a hand on my shoulder and a pure joy flowed over me. My chattering teeth mellowed, and the snow no longer felt cold. "Kaylee, my dear Kaylee. Why did you assume the ring showed you what should happen? Why didn't you see that it warned you what you could avoid?"

I raised my head and stared over the vast valley hundreds of feet below me. "Warnings? They were warnings?" I closed my eyes and faced the sky. "I don't know. What happened to Dad with Amma caused me to think as I did."

"That was a warning to him as well. The ring didn't force them to get married. They chose to, even as you chose to do what you did. He could have gone on his way and never returned to her."

My eyes watered. "You called me perceptive, but I didn't perceive that the ring warned me. I'm a prideful fool is what I am." I turned to face her. The light, olive-green eyes glistened with tears. She wept for me!

She rubbed my back; tense muscles relaxed as well as the guilt deep inside. "No, you are perceptive. Why do you think you didn't see it?"

I didn't have to think much; I knew. "I wanted to believe the ring pointed me to join with him. I wanted to be freed of the bonds of fear, to experience true love. I focused on what I wanted."

She smiled and I could swear the entire world smiled with her. "You're easier than your father. You practically diagnose yourself."

I sighed and tears formed on the edges of my eyelids. "All the good it did me. I trusted Cole. I allowed myself to be vulnerable, and like those before him, he used me. I don't feel I can ever trust a man again."

Love knelt beside me and stared into my eyes. "No greater love can anyone show, than to lay down their life for another, as our Lord did. Those who believe they control others are the ones to ultimately pity, for they are deluded by Satan."

I nodded. She spoke the truth; it resonated in my heart and soul. Yet... "I've failed. Failed miserably, worse than Dad ever did."

She shook her head. "No, your father did worse. Why do you think he gave you the ring? Because he couldn't handle it anymore. It was pulling him under."

I brushed my hair back behind my shoulders. "He never told me that."

"He never told anyone. But like him, there is still a part for you to play in defeating the enemy."

I raised an eyebrow. "Who? Satan? Me, defeat Satan?"

Love nodded. "You'll know how when the time arrives. But what you need to know right now is don't give up. All is not lost. Keep the faith and let God's wisdom, united to your heart, guide you."

I nodded. My soul already felt better, stronger. "I'll do my best, even though my actions of late haven't been stellar."

She smiled that brilliant smile again. "A little humility introduced into our lives often prepares us to succeed at the more important tasks. You'll do fine."

As if someone flipped a page in a book, the snow disappeared, the sun lit the sky, and Paradise returned to the valley of my soul. But Love vanished, leaving me sitting on the edge of faith, ready to hope once again.

I felt my head bobbing and throbbing against a coil of rope as life returned to my body. Cole sat at the front of the flat-bed wagon, whistling and humming various songs into the bright and chilling air. We headed along a well traveled path; another wagon, headed the opposite direction, pulled away behind us. The land lay flat and mostly barren save for a few scraggly bushes and low trees.

My wrist struggled against cords of rope, and my feet lay helpless in the grip of similar bonds. I examined my fingers and verified that the ring no longer resided in my possession. But I still felt the bracelet rubbing against my breast.

I glanced up at Cole to make sure he still thought I was unconscious, then used my tied hands to pull the necklace from the inside of my tunic. Then I opened the bracelet when the wagon shook to mask the sound of it snapping open.

The hard part proved getting it on my wrist. But I managed to push it against my leg and maneuver my arm into place, and then use my knees to lock it back together.

I hoped it would help Nathan zero in on our location, and when he came close enough, he could turn into his beautiful horse-self and race to my rescue.

I frowned. Nathan had been right about Cole all along. I couldn't believe I, of all people, fell completely and totally into the enemy's trap. But how? I should have felt in my heart the evil from him. I stared at him now and still could not detect evil.

I rolled my eyes. I forgot, I don't have the ring. Of course I wouldn't sense anything.

I thought about rolling off the back of the wagon in hopes he wouldn't notice. Then Nathan would come along to get me. But I knew I couldn't do that. I must get the ring back.

"Cole?"

He swung his head toward me. "I see you've come back to the land of the living. Sorry I had to knock you out, but your hysterics would have attracted unwanted attention and made it harder to slip out of town. I still had to put a spell on you so others wouldn't see I carried an unconscious woman about."

A spell? He knew more than a couple of small tricks. "Cole?"

"Um, what?"

"I didn't mean it when I said I hated you. What you did and said shocked me, but I'm over it now. I do love you." And in truth, I realized I did love him, even if his deception stung. But I hoped it would soften him up.

"Well, um...thanks. But I've not changed my mind. The ring will go to Morgenstern—"

"You mean Satan."

"I prefer my own terms, not your religion's, if you don't mind. But he'll get the ring."

"And what happens to me? Do you get me?"

He turned back to face the oncoming path. "You'll get sacrificed."

I laughed, in the hopes this was a joke. "Sacrificed, right. If you do love me, what's the point of sacrificing me?"

"I told you, the entrance to Hades is the Dying Tree." He turned his head to face me. "It's called the Dying Tree because to open the way to Hades, someone has to die around it."

He was serious! We traveled in silence for a moment. Then I said, "You're really going to have me killed so you can go into Hades and deliver the ring to Satan?"

"That's the plan."

I couldn't accept his words. He wouldn't really have me killed. Would he? "There's one thing I don't understand. How come I can't detect any evil from you?"

He shook his head. "You see, Beltrid played it too obvious. He left himself open to discovery. You could sense something evil in Crystal, and you immediately grew suspicious.

"But Morgenstern is much more subtle than that. You don't feel evil in me, because I do love you. Truth becomes the perfect mask. Morgenstern implanted a command in my mind that would activate when your ring fell off. All I knew up until that point was how much I loved you. So that's all you detected."

Deceived by truth! However, I could use his affection for me. "But if you love me, why would you be so eager to have me killed?"

"It should be obvious. I have a greater love for Morgenstern than I do for you. I'm willing to sacrifice that which I love to proclaim my greater love for Morgenstern."

"Love for him? The one out to destroy your soul? To pull it into Hell itself?"

He glanced back at me. "Hades."

"No, I'm talking about Hell. The fiery presence of God. That's what you're afraid of. Doesn't that speak volumes about who is really God?"

"Why do you think we want the ring? It's to hide His presence, bury His presence, destroy His presence so that Hell itself dwindles into a mere vapor of steam."

"You fear God, then." I watched his head bob with the road's bumps.

"If you don't, you're stupid. I want to live out from under His fear. That's what all who follow Morgenstern want. And with this captured ring, we will finally have that freedom."

I shook my head. "Sometimes freedom means embracing those restrictions as guides to a fuller life. Getting out from under them only results in the ship sinking upon a rocky shore."

He sighed. "You don't understand."

I smiled. That tended to be the response when someone couldn't come up with a good answer. "No, I guess I don't understand your point of view, Cole. And though I love you, I don't want to understand anymore. Because I too have one I love. One who I'm willing to sacrifice everything for, including you."

He gave no answer but silence. I lay back without further conversation as well. The wagon wheels creaked along while birds sang various songs. For the first time, I realized that those visions, or warnings, as they were, would likely never come true. The gulf between our two religions widened considerably at several key points, the most critical of them about who

God was.

I stretched as best I could. "I don't suppose you plan on feeding me anytime soon? I'm hungry."

29

Gabrielle felt bad about leaving Josh in his condition. The doctor bandaged him up, but said it would take some time for his blood supply to build back to normal. Josh regained consciousness quick enough and told them that he wanted his severed arm to remain with him. A strange request, but he insisted and so they did.

The innkeeper promised to watch after him and Crystal. Nathan could no longer sense Kaylee's presence, heightening the desire to get underway. He hoped to pick it up again, so once Gabrielle felt Josh would survive and be cared for, Nathan helped her onto the winged horse, then slid on himself and took the reins. They lifted into the sky to chase after Cole and Kaylee.

Gabrielle tightly wrapped her arms around Nathan's chest and kept her eyes shut as they glided through the air. She decided to extract some information from Nathan. She wanted to find out about Cole, and it would keep her mind off the reality of being hundreds of feet in the air. Apparently Nathan entertained questions as well.

"Mother, is the baby really Father's?"

"Yes, though I know it's hard to believe."

He laughed. "After all the events I've witnessed the last few months, I doubt anything could surprise me. But I have to ask: how could it be when Father has been dead more than two months?"

She cleared her throat. "Josh lost his memory. Without it, he couldn't control the magic within himself. His link with Sisko caused him to have Sisko's feelings for me. When I realized the truth, I spoke it, and Josh turned into Sisko. Their souls exchanged places. I spent a day and night with him. One thing led to another, and now I'm pregnant."

He turned his head around and caught a glimpse of her. "You spoke it and it happened? Just like that?"

She smiled. "While in the steam house, I gained the steam house's ability. A messenger named Joel told me if I spoke the truth, it would be revealed. If what I speak isn't true, then nothing happens."

"Joel? Wow. He really gets around."

She chuckled. "So it seems."

Nathan remained silent for a few seconds. "How long ago did Father appear?"

"About six days."

"Six days! It looks like you're seven or eight months along!"

Leaning over her stomach, she rested her head on his back. "I know. The baby has an accelerated growth rate, about a little over one month for every day. When it has growth spurts, it's painful."

The wind churned around them in sudden gusts, whipping her hair back and forth.

"Mother, hold on!"

She involuntarily flung her eyes open and regretted it. A black mass, much like the one in her vision, raced up behind them. She clamped her legs around the horse as tight as she could and held onto Nathan.

The wind slammed into them. It shoved her sideways, and she felt the horse's back sliding under her. "Nathan!"

He reached back and pulled her up with one hand. With the other he held onto the reins. Meanwhile, the horse lost its balance and careened downward in a spiral. It frantically tried to regain its lift. Gabrielle held on as tightly as she could as each blast of wind pushed her one way, and then the other. The world spun around her.

The blackness passed and the winds died. The horse caught the air and pulled out of the dive.

"Mother, we're all right! You can stop screaming in my ear!"

Screaming? Yes, she had been. "Sorry." She swallowed to wet her raw throat, glanced about, and relaxed. After hanging on through the gale, she didn't feel as likely to slide off. Still, she avoided glancing down.

She pointed at the darkness receding ahead of them. "That's the darkness I saw in my steam house vision. It knocked Kaylee off your back."

"That did happen. And Kaylee said she saw your hand and face reaching out from the sky to grab her."

Gabrielle shuttered. "How strange, because that's what I tried to do in my vision. To think she actually saw me. Any idea what the blackness was?"

Nathan breathed hard. "Not the slightest. But after that, our horse will need a rest. Besides, we've been flying for hours and it's getting dark."

He angled downwards and landed in a clearing a few yards from the road. They set up camp and prepared a simple meal of broth, cheese, and flat bread.

Gabrielle stared at the dancing flames of the campfire. "So tell me about Cole."

"He's a priest from Morgoth, whose god is called Morgenstern, and Kaylee has fallen madly in love with him. Or, at least she did. I'm not sure how she feels about him now."

"Can you still sense her?"

He nodded. "Yes, and it's stronger now. We've made progress."

"How is she feeling right now?" Gabrielle bit and chewed some bread while Nathan thought about it.

"I can only sense her stronger emotions, but if I were to put a label on what I'm picking up from her, I'd say hopeful."

"Hopeful? Do you think she went with him willingly?"

He shrugged. "He had captivated her love, he could have convinced her to run away with him." He paused as he thought. "But that's not the emotion I felt from her when they left. I don't think she willingly followed him, and I know she wouldn't have willingly left Crystal to fend for herself."

Gabrielle smile. "I hope I instilled in her more responsibility than that." She frowned. "But Kaylee in love? With a priest from another religion? That doesn't sound like her at all."

"And Mother, they kissed a lot. One time I woke up and noticed them together on the other side of the campfire. She let him squeeze her rear! Kaylee! Can you imagine?"

Gabrielle shook her head. "My little girl destined to be a nun and didn't want to have anything to do with men, in love with one? Despite all I've experienced these past few days, that is the hardest to believe."

He laughed. "Who knows how far they would have gone. But Crystal popped up from her sleep and said, 'Beltrid.' You should have seen

Kaylee fly out of her bed. I barely controlled my giggles, but I did and I don't think she ever knew that I saw the whole scene. I didn't want to embarrass her."

Gabrielle chuckled with him. "You're a good brother, Nathan. And you'll make Crystal a good husband someday, provided you're able to get her soul back. I'm proud of you."

His face reddened. "There was a time I wondered if I'd ever make it. Then Kaylee pulled me through. I hope I can do the same for her now that the situations are reversed."

Gabrielle thanked God for Nathan's character. Pride welled up for him. "I'm sure you will."

My body complained with each bump and jolt of the wagon on the dry road. Occasionally people would pass by going the other way, but they never noticed me. Most likely due to Cole's spell. Nor did I feel right getting a stranger involved anyway. Cole had hidden much from me. I didn't know the full extent of his power.

The trees thickened, and a bridge appeared on the road ahead of us. It stretched for several yards before bending around a set of trees in what appeared to be a small swamp. The horses' hooves clopped loudly as they stepped upon the wooden bridge. It took several minutes to cross the boggy waters of the delta flowing toward the sea. The smell of musty water attacked my nose; the metal of the wheels echoed against the wooden bridge into the stale air as we traversed the distance.

About a mile past the bridge, Cole pulled the wagon to a halt and slid out. "This is a good place for a rest. It'll get dark soon, and we're in no hurry. We'll set up camp here."

I didn't respond. Our last conversation had proved fruitless. Maybe if I tried a different tack? Theological arguments rarely win a person over.

He leaned against the side of the wagon and stared at me. "Um, um! Seeing you lie there causes me to regret we couldn't have continued."

I decided to play on his feelings. "Satan must have offered you some deal to be willing to give me up. How much am I worth to you? What did he offer?"

He smiled his disarming smile. "The usual. Rule over a kingdom, important place in his dominion once established. All the women I could want."

"I'll bet there'll be none like me."

His smile faded and his gaze focused beyond me. "I suppose not."

"You know what I want?"

"What?"

"I really wanted you back in Octum, in the inn. And I still do, but done the right way. Why would you want the pressures and headaches of running a kingdom and answering to someone like Satan? Instead, you could have a wonderful life, married to me. We could live our lives together, enjoying each other's company and love. Raise a family and treasure each moment. Do you value Satan's promises over me?"

He stared at me. Several seconds passed, and I wondered if he would say anything.

But his eyes blinked and he sighed. "I long for such a life. But I've sworn commitments to Morgenstern. I can't break those."

I frowned. "Why not?"

"Because if I did, I wouldn't be alive to enjoy such a life and marriage as you propose." He pulled away, moved to the back of the wagon, and pulled out the bedrolls. "So, whether I like it or not, you're his sacrifice, and I can't have you."

Cole froze as if listening intently; he spun around and gazed into the sky. Upon the evening dusk, a darkness much like the one Nathan and I had encountered a few days ago sped toward us. Cole stood in the middle of the road as the blackness changed direction and swirled over his head. Then like water flowing through a hole, the darkness formed a funnel and spouted down like a tornado.

Cole stretched out his right palm and held it up toward the sky. The winds whipped my hair around as the funnel narrowed until it rested in Cole's palm. Then the whole darkness drained itself onto his outstretched hand. The last of the swirling black sank between his fingers, leaving a translucent, black ball resting in his palm.

Cole peered into it. A flash of energy bolted from its blackness and landed on his forehead. His body lit up as the energy flowed though him and back to the ball over and over again. But within seconds the lightning stopped, and Cole's appearance returned to normal. Except now he didn't smile. Instead, a frown, mingled with clenched teeth, stared back at me.

He pointed back the way we'd come. "It's not my fault what happens to them, you understand. I'd hoped we'd be able to leave and they wouldn't know what route we left by. I don't know how, but your brother is following us."

I raised an eyebrow. "How do you know that?"

He held the small ball up. "This is a messenger of Morgenstern."

"The blackness?" I shuddered. The darkness that knocked me off Nathan several days ago must have been a message warning Cole about my arrival in his city, with instructions to trap me. Except Satan didn't count on the effect of Cole falling in love.

"Yes. Apparently he and a woman are riding on a winged horse."

Nathan riding on a winged horse? That didn't make sense. Where would he get a winged horse? And why would he decide to carry Crystal with him? Maybe afraid to leave her by herself or in another's care?

Cole reached into the wagon and grasped my arm.

"Ouch, careful!"

He jerked my hand up and pulled down my sleeve. The bracelet glowed a deep red, reflecting the sunset. "I don't suppose you've told me everything about this bracelet, have you?"

I stared into his eyes but said nothing.

He grabbed the bracelet.

"Cole, don't! You don't know what you're about to do."

"You wore this on a necklace when I knocked you out. Couldn't miss it lying across your chest." He stared into my eyes. "You put this on for a reason. Tell me why."

I couldn't risk telling him anything that he didn't already know. If he knew Nathan could find me because of the bracelet, he'd take it off anyway.

"Please, Cole. Trust me. It could cause his death."

He frowned. "I figured it was magical." He pulled back and yanked it off. The clasp bent out of place as it broke apart.

I jerked by head away from him and whispered a prayer. I hoped Nathan flew on a winged horse instead of being one. Otherwise, he could be falling to his death at this very moment, and there would be nothing I could do to save him. But if I could get the ring back, race to find him, maybe I could.

Cole stood, my arm in his hand, and checked out the bracelet. If Nathan and Crystal were falling to their deaths, I had seconds to act.

Using his grasp as leverage, I pulled myself up toward him and swung my heels up against his head. He staggered back. My feet dropped to the ground and I slid off the wagon.

Cole wiped blood from the side of his mouth. "You don't want to do this. I don't want to hurt you."

"Hurt me? You plan on sacrificing me."

"But it doesn't have to be painful. This will only cause you pain and suffering." He stepped closer.

I swung my tied hands upward and connected with his jaw. He fell against the wagon. He rubbed his chin and smiled. "You're feisty too."

"I excelled in feistiness growing up."

He drew a sword. "I can't kill you, but I can give you pain if that is what you want."

I stared deep into his eyes. "What I want is you."

He swung his sword up behind his back before bringing it down in front of him. I slid to the side and the blade whooshed past me. I grabbed the side of the wagon, launched my feet into the air, then pushed out toward his head as hard as I could.

My feet connected. He placed his free hand on the side of his head and tried to shake off the confusion. Upon landing on my feet, I swung out and hit him in the stomach.

He bent over and gasped. But before I could do anything else, he pulled a wand from under his coat and a bolt of lightning shot out. The force smashed me off my feet and sent me flying through the air. I crashed on the ground and rolled to a stop, arching my back from the ripped skin throbbing with pain.

He stood over me and watched as I struggled to sit up.

I fixed my eyes on him, then stared at the wand in his hand. "I should have known you knew a lot more magic than you let on."

He rubbed his jaw. "I told you I didn't want to hurt you. Give up?"

I squeezed my eyes shut and a tear etched its way across my cheek. If Nathan and Crystal did fall, they would have hit the ground by now. *Lord, keep them safe.* "I give. But I had to try. The consequences of following through on your promises are staggering, not only for us, but for all who live in this world."

"And the consequences of me not keeping my promise are also staggering, at least to me." He scanned the sky. "We no longer have the luxury of traveling at a leisurely pace. We'll ditch the wagon and both ride the horse all night. That should keep us ahead of them."

He pointed his wand to the sky. "But to make sure..." He recited some words I couldn't make out. A black wall materialized from the swamp behind us and rose toward the sky like vast columns of smoke. It reached over the clouds and each end disappeared over the horizon. The mass of black fog flashed with light and then it disappeared, leaving no evidence of its existence.

"What is that?" I asked, hoping for reassurance.

He proceeded to take the horses off the wagon. "The Wall of Confusion. When your brother and his friend fly into it, they won't know up from down."

"You're not going to kill them, are you?"

He shrugged. "I don't want to, but I have to defend—"

"What you've stolen from me?"

"What will gain my freedom." He huffed.

I frowned and shook my head. "You will not gain freedom with Satan, only further bondage."

He grabbed a chunk of cheese and crammed it into my mouth until it could hold no more. "There, suck on that for a while and stop talking."

He threw me over his shoulders and shoved me onto the horse's back. He settled in behind me and took the reins, his arms around me. The warmth of his body on my back helped remove the cold edge of the night air. Then we galloped down the road, the moonlight to guide us.

31

Nathan chewed on a piece of dried meat as the fire crackled in the light of the waning sun. Gabrielle watched him with interest. She couldn't get over how much he'd changed. Before her imprisonment in the crystal, he acted touchy and closed off from everyone. This trip provided the first chance to spend significant time with him since then. Now his attitude and actions bore the mark of maturity and steadfastness.

She swallowed a bite of meat. "How have you and Kaylee been getting along since leaving Reol?"

"Pretty good. Except lately she's been distracted by Cole. I've tried to talk sense into her, but apparently it didn't work."

"How did she take it?"

He stared at the red lining on the clouds, watching the sun sink away. "A lot better than I did when she tried to tell me about Crystal a few months ago. But she ended up agreeing with me because she didn't want to talk about it. She keeps forgetting that I can feel what's going on inside her."

Gabrielle smiled. "What's new? We do that with God all the time." She winked.

He chuckled. "I guess so." He downed a gulp from his cup and then paused as if listening. His eyes met hers. "Kaylee's getting further away. And I'm sensing that she's...worried."

"Worried? Worried about what?"

He shrugged. "I don't know. But if we want to keep up with them, we'd better go. The night is dark. Safer not to fly, but we can stay on the ground."

Gabrielle sighed. "I'm thinking he might be onto us following him if he's willing to travel through the night."

Nathan frowned. "You're probably right."

They folded up their bedrolls and prepared to continue the journey. Soon, the horse trotted along the barely visible path as clouds moved over to cover the moonlight. Minutes flowed into hours as darkness gave little hint of progress.

Gabrielle's eyes drifted shut, only to jerk open when she felt herself about to fall off the horse. It felt the night would never end. But eventually the sun rose over the eastern horizon, landing on Gabrielle's half-closed eyes. The trotting of the horse against the ground had lulled her to a near sleep.

Nathan jabbed her in the side with his elbow. "Stay awake. I think it's light enough I can fly now." He pulled up on the reins. "Upwards!"

Gabrielle's eyes jerked open as the horse leaped into the air and its wings flared out. She squeezed Nathan's waist tighter. "Don't let me fall asleep up here. I'd hate to fall to my death."

"You worry too much. You've been flying around on a magic carpet and on this winged horse, and not once have you fallen off."

"I can't help it." She closed her eyes. "Though I'm getting better."

Nathan pointed ahead. "Looks like there's a marshy area ahead, a river branching out as it reaches the sea. It probably slowed Cole down, but we'll fly right over it without a problem."

"Good, cause I don't need any more problems." Gabrielle cracked her eyes open. She discovered the interesting landscape below them took her mind off the fact she might fall off the horse. The marshes held a special beauty from this high up.

The trees and slow moving waters crept under them as the horse beat its wings every few seconds and glided on wind currents in between.

Gabrielle froze. "Nathan, something's not right."

"What do you mean?"

"There's a danger here. I can feel it. Turn around!"

The horse neighed and flapped its wings erratically. Nathan started to slide off the horse as his hands grabbed at air. "What's happening, everything is spinning!"

Gabrielle tried to hold Nathan in place, but the horse dropped several feet in one second, then banked wildly and shot upwards as if from a slingshot. Nathan's weight pushed against her and she started to slide to the rear of the horse.

"Nathan!" He and the horse both acted dizzy, but why didn't it affect her? The steam house maybe? But at this rate, it wouldn't matter.

The horse reached a peak and then dropped into a dive. Gabrielle's legs couldn't keep a grip on the horse's body as it plunged downward. She flew off, holding Nathan in her arms.

"Mother!" Nathan called out as the air rushed past them. "Push me away. If Kaylee has her bracelet on, I can turn into a winged horse and save us."

She nodded and shoved him. His body spun as he fell away from her. The wind flapped her dress in rapid beats and pulled back her cheeks as the ground drew ever closer.

She waited for a few seconds but Nathan didn't change. Kaylee probably didn't have her bracelet on. Strange. Now that she plunged toward the trees below, a calm settled over her. At least death wouldn't be painful and slow. If God wanted to save them, He would. If only she could change Nathan into a winged horse.

Her eyes widened—Yes! She cried out though no one but God could hear her, "Nathan is a winged horse!"

Light flooded Gabrielle's eyes. She shielded them, and when she peeked between her fingers, the most beautiful white horse caught the air and dived toward her. She glanced down; the trees of the marsh raced up to meet her. Nathan flew under her and she landed on his back, knocking the air out of her chest. Her fingers clawed at his soft hair as she slid to the side.

Nathan banked under her and popped her into the air, she collapsed onto his back and wrapped her arms around his neck as they swooshed over the tops of the trees.

You all right?

She heard him in her head! "Not all right, but I'm alive though my nerves are in shambles." She struggled to get her body to calm down and her breathing to slow.

How did I turn into a winged horse? I said "upwards" several times, but nothing happened.

She smiled. "I changed you."

You? Amazing! I'm impressed.

"Don't be. I didn't earn the gift, or want it. But I got it." She relaxed and felt better already. She lifted an eyebrow. Relaxed? On a flying horse way up in the air? She watched the ground sailing beneath them and it no longer frightened her.

Don't fall asleep up there.

"I'm not. My near death drove all sleepiness from me."

He turned his head back so that one eye watched her. *But you're not tense.*

She patted his neck. "No, I'm not."

Kaylee could usually hear me in her head. Maybe she's hearing my thoughts. If so, Kaylee, we're coming. Hold on!

Gabrielle hoped she could hear. Her stomach growled and her body, while temporarily pumped from the excitement, felt weak. At some point they would have to stop to eat, and sleep would overtake them. But she didn't want to now. Not if Cole wouldn't stop.

Nathan bobbed his head. *Do you need to stop?*

She leaned to his ear. "I only have one word to say to that." She thought she would never hear herself say this. "Upwards."

He neighed. *Upwards and onwards it is!*

My eyes cracked open as Cole's horse slowed to a stop. I must have fallen asleep, but why hadn't Cole's eyes grown heavy? He must have used magic to keep himself and the horse going. Nathan wouldn't be able to duplicate that.

Hold it! There it was again. I thought I had been dreaming, but now fully awake, I heard Nathan talking to someone. But how could I hear him? He couldn't be...hold on, he just said he was a winged horse! He'd turned into a winged horse? But how? Who?

And who did he carry on a conversation with? What other women could be with him besides Crystal? She was in no shape to chat with last I knew. And how would Crystal have obtained the ability to change Nathan into a winged horse? A relief flooded over me knowing he still lived, even as questions and confusion attacked me.

Yet, I could hear Nathan's thoughts in my head, like listening to one side of a conversation. I smiled. Nathan spoke to me, hoping I could hear him. My knight in shining white "armor" rides to the rescue. "I'm holding on," I whispered.

"What's that?" Cole hopped to the ground.

I swallowed. "Said I'm holding on, I won't fall off the horse."

He shook his head and then gazed at the trail branching away from the main road. He pulled out the black ball and held it to his head. As before, a thread of energy crackled in the air and poured into his skull. He closed his eyes for the few seconds it vibrated. Then it stopped and he opened his eyes again.

Cole stuffed the ball back into his pocket. "Damn it all!"

I smiled. Nathan and his friend, whoever she was, still followed us.

He stepped to the horse and stared into my eyes. "Who is this woman with Nathan?"

I shrugged. "You know as much as I do. My best guess is Crystal, though I don't know how. Her soul is still in Hades. Right?"

He stomped his feet. "Whoever she is, she's making this more difficult than it should be."

"You still have time to give up and be my husband before my brother catches up to you."

Cole laughed. "Your brother? Do you really think he would stand a chance against me? You've handled my sword and killed him with it, not knowing what you're doing."

My head sank. Against Cole's magic, Nathan didn't stand a chance. For his sake, she hoped Cole could lose him, because she knew Nathan would try despite the odds if he caught up to them.

He gazed down the side road. "If knocking them out of the sky won't work, maybe deception will."

He jumped back on the horse. "No time to waste, let's go!" He flipped the reins and the horse broke into a strong trot. He guided it onto the road branching toward the east.

We traveled almost two hours when Cole pulled the horse to a stop. He scanned the area. "Perfect."

He dismounted and stepped a few feet away, then grabbed his wand and cast it into the air as he muttered a spell. He swept the area with it; the air shimmered with energy and then died off.

"And one last touch." He said another spell under his breath and pointed his wand at the horse's hooves. Radiance beamed around them. Cole swooshed his wand over the horizon, and I saw hoof-prints appear in the dirt as if an invisible horse galloped off into the distance.

I re-checked the horse's hooves and notice they now floated over the ground. This didn't look good.

"What are you doing"?

"Trying to keep your brother and his friend from getting killed." He pulled himself onto the horse's back and whispered in my ear. "See, I'm not bad."

I huffed. "Am I your first sacrificial virgin, or have you had many?"

He ignored the comment and spurred the horse into a gallop. We shot across the open plains where no road existed, leaving no tracks in our wake.

"I'm hungry."

"Of course you are." Cole laughed.

I didn't see it as anything to laugh about. "Seriously, I need something to eat. Perhaps you can go days without sleep, food, or water, but I can't."

He pulled the horse to a stop by a rock and dismounted. "The last diversion should work. We don't have to move as fast, so why not eat?"

He helped me off the horse and untied my hands.

I rubbed my wrists. "Thank you."

"You need your hands to eat, and there's nowhere out here to hide." He wagged a finger at me. "Remember, I would have no trouble tracking you down."

I nodded. Internally I thanked him for reminding me.

I set up a fire, while he used his magic to catch a rabbit, luring the creature into his arms before breaking its neck. I skinned it and roasted it. Succulent flavors drenched my mouth when I bit into it, and my hunger took over. The meat disappeared before I knew it, and Cole ate a fair portion himself.

I tossed a bone into the fire. "Very good!"

He nodded and patted his belly. "I have to admit, that tasted good." He stretched and yawned.

Sleepiness crept upon him. With a full belly, it might not take much more to send him into dreamland. I thought for a second and decided a good lullaby would be in order. I sang in a soft, sweet voice as if to a baby.

The sun is falling,
The sun is dimming,
The sun is closing its eyes.

The dog is rolling,
The dog is yawning,

The dog is closing its eyes.

The cloud is weeping,
The cloud is drifting,
The cloud is closing its eyes.

The clock is ticking,
The clock is whirling,
The clock is closing its eyes.

The babe is nodding,
The babe is jerking,
The babe is closing its eyes.

Hearken to the eyes of life.
Hearken to the eyes of beasts.
Hearken to the eyes of things.
Hearken to the eyes of babes.
Close your eyes and sleep.

As I sang, he nodded off and snored. I stared at him. Why did it have to end this way? Why did the man I fell in love with worship Satan?

I glanced at Cole's horse munching quietly on a clump of grass. I could hop on the horse and ride back the way we'd come, find Nathan, and we could return to save the ring from being given to Satan. He'd have to spend time finding another sacrificial victim to open the way into Hades.

I bit my lip. If I could get it now, the problem would be solved. He couldn't kill me, Satan wouldn't get the ring, and I could continue with the ministry of the ring. But how to get it out of his pocket without waking him?

My eyes jumped from spot to spot around me, seeking anything I could use. Then my eyes landed on a stick with a small spout branching off of it, perfect to use as a fishing tool.

I retrieved the stick and broke off the parts I didn't need, but left a stub of a branch to create the hook. I slid the hook toward his pocket. I pushed it in carefully, doing my best not to jab him awake.

I did this for a few minutes. At one point, he groaned. I froze, hoping he didn't wake up. But he rolled over and continued snoring. I continued fishing until finally, I saw what I longed for dangling from the end of my makeshift fishing pole.

I pulled the ring from the stick and held it between my fingers. I smiled. At last! I pulled the ring to my left hand. Before it could reach my ring finger, a force blocked it. I pushed harder and still I could not break the force to slide the ring on.

"You must not have thought too much of me if you believed I wouldn't have protected the ring." Cole sat up and stared at me. He held his hand out. "Give me the ring."

I clenched my fist tight. "I don't think so. This belongs to me, to God. Not you or Satan."

He shook his head and closed his palm. I felt the ring vanish from my hand. He opened his fingers; the ring rested on his palm.

I stomped the ground and gritted my teeth. So close!

He rose to his feet. "You could have killed me or taken the horse. Why didn't you?"

I met his eyes and drew near to him. My arms slipped around his neck, and I held my lips from his with barely a paper's thickness between us. "I didn't kill you because I could never do that. Not on purpose. I love you, even now, and unlike some people I know, wouldn't dare allow you to be killed."

He blinked.

"I need the ring back. Please? I'll do anything you want. I'll serve you for the rest of my days. But please restore the ring to my finger, where it should be."

He held it up and shook his head. "I think by order of the ring itself, you lost that right when you sinned."

"Sinned? That's not what you called it at the time."

He smiled. "It's not in my religion, but it is in yours, and the ring comes from yours." He stuffed it back in his pocket. "No, I have a duty to perform. Once I'm finished, I'll be set for life."

My heart grew heavy. "No, you'll not be set for life, but for death. I'd hoped we could spend eternity together, but maybe it's not meant to be."

He loaded the pack. "Maybe not."

Soon we remounted the horse and trotted once again across the barren coastal plains.

Nathan circled above a fork in the road before landing.

"I feel like we should continue straight." Gabrielle slid off his back to walk her soreness off.

But I can feel where Kaylee is, and she's down this road to the east. Are you feeling anything different?

Gabrielle sighed and shook her head. "Pure intuition. Maybe a steam house intuition, but nothing solid I can point to."

Nathan stared down the road branching from the main one. *I don't think I can go second-guessing what I feel without good reason. I say we follow this road branching to the east.*

She stretched. "I suppose you're right. I doubt he could easily deceive your link with Kaylee. After all, he's not a wizard or anything."

Nathan stared into the distance and didn't respond.

"Nathan, he isn't, is he?"

Nathan's head drooped. *He said he knows a little magic. He did some small things, cut some ropes and created light in the caves, but I did wonder if he told us everything. It's possible he's a full-fledged wizard.*

She bit her lip. "A possibility isn't enough reason to ignore your link with Kaylee. Though my intuition says to go straight on the main road, we'll follow yours. I hope you're right."

Me too.

Gabrielle climbed onto Nathan's back. He galloped for five steps before leaping into the air and catching the wind in his wing.

Forty-five minutes oozed by as they followed the trail. Though

Gabrielle couldn't put a finger on it, everything in her told her to head to Shore Cliffs. Something felt wrong about following this route. If only she could point to something solid.

Look down there. I'm sensing they entered the cave up ahead.

She studied the direction his head indicated. She could see evidence of tracks leading to its entrance. "Are you sure? This doesn't feel right to me."

Positive.

Nathan glided downward until his hooves landed on the ground at the cave. Gabrielle jumped off his back and studied the area. "Why would they go into a cave?"

He neighed. *Maybe it's the way to Hades.*

Gabrielle pushed a stray hair back. "I don't think so. You said he called it the Dying Tree."

Yes, but it could be a metaphor. It might not be a real tree.

She shook her head. "In my vision, I did see a real tree on an island. I don't know if it's the way into Hades, but it looked the part and a demon stood guard before it. I don't think this is it."

Then how can we know? My sense tells me she's under the ground.

Gabrielle thought for a moment. If this were a deception, he would be able to fool Nathan but not her. He doesn't know about the steam house's gift to her and wouldn't have known to block it. Just as the confusion over the marsh didn't confuse her, only Nathan and the horse. She opened her eyes wider. "The confusion over the marsh you experienced, that must have been Cole's doing. He is a wizard."

Gabrielle stood taller. "This is not Kaylee's path." A wind swooshed by. The horse prints in the dirt vanished. Gabrielle met Nathan's eyes. "Now where do you sense Kaylee?"

His head bobbed up and his eyes grew wide. *That she's not under this ground, but off to our south.* He stomped his hooves onto the ground. *They're headed to Shore Cliffs. You were right!*

Gabrielle jumped onto his back. "Luckily, he doesn't know of me and my ability. No time for fretting over it. Let's go get them."

Nathan launched into the air once again.

196

Much to her surprise, Gabrielle realized she had been sleeping on Nathan's back, way up in the air! Nathan's wings beat every few seconds. Sometimes there would be long pauses as he glided on the winds.

An updraft bathed Gabrielle in warm, dry air. Nathan rode it for a couple of minutes. Then they dropped a few feet, then a few more feet. Nathan's wings fell limp.

"Nathan!"

They plummeted toward the earth; Gabrielle's stomach lurched. She slapped Nathan's neck with her palm. Nothing happened. She reared back and slammed her hand behind his ear.

His eyes cracked open, then flung wide open. *Oh no! I'm so sorry.* He spread his wings and pulled out of the dive. *I must have fallen asleep.*

Gabrielle panted. "I'm glad you simply fell asleep instead of dying. Why don't we set down?"

But Kaylee!

"We won't do Kaylee any good if we're puddles of flesh, bones, and blood on the ground. Apparently Cole's using magic to keep him and his horse awake and running. We don't have that luxury."

But what if we're late? What if Kaylee dies because we rested?

Gabrielle thought for a moment. "There's one thing I've learned in my life. If God wants us to get there, He'll make the way." She pointed to a stream flowing below. "Let's land there. I've had some sleep, and I'll let you take a quick nap and wake you in thirty minutes. With a little water, food, and rest, you'll feel better."

He nodded and banked for the stream. *At least from what I can tell, Cole and Kaylee aren't on the main road either, so he must have detoured onto this side road for a ways before diverting back toward Shore Cliffs. And they feel much closer now. I think we can gain on them before they reach the city.*

Gabrielle smiled. It appeared they would reach Kaylee before the island. She might yet change the steam house's vision. Then she wondered what she could do when they reached them. If Cole could use magic, what chance did they have to defeat him? She'd have to trust God to direct her when the time came.

I could hear Nathan's thoughts. He and his friend had figured out Cole's deception and would catch up to us before we reached the city. The thought gave me hope, but also fear. Cole's magic could destroy both of them easily. How could I help? Maybe keep him distracted so he wouldn't check his ball and discover that his deception had failed? The more of a surprise, the better.

Cole didn't hurry now. The horse trotted along at a brisk pace, but Cole didn't force the horse to sustain a gallop with magic as before. He must have thought his trap would send Nathan several hours off our trail. An idea of how to keep him occupied popped into my mind.

I huffed and ended with a grunt. "This is so unfair." He didn't respond. "I find the one man who I felt totally safe with, am willing to spend the rest of my life with, and his only desire is to sacrifice me to Satan."

"That's not my only desire. I do love you." He shifted his weight.

"Your actions say different."

He sighed. "You believed I loved you before losing the ring."

I half believed he did love me still. I frowned. "You pretended to love me for the ring. You didn't mean any of it."

He remained silent for a moment. "Like I said before, the deception worked because it was all true. I do love you, and I would never have forced myself on you. Even if the ring hadn't fallen off and you changed your mind, I would have gladly waited until another day to unite with you. But the ring did fall off, and a promise to Morgenstern is one that cannot be broken without resulting in death."

I leaned back into his chest. "You're right. Satan has no grace for broken promises and failings. At least God forgives and brings life."

He didn't respond. It nurtured a hope in me that I could break through to him. "To know how deeply you feel for me, what we could have had together, and you're willing to throw it away—the pain is numbing. All because Satan, who can't stand God's presence or live in it, has deceived you into thinking he can win against God. He's painted a false picture of who God is."

"No, you're the ones who are deceived."

I shook my head. "Look into your soul, Cole. If you're honest, you know the reality I speak of resonates from there."

"We can't live in the fire of His presence."

I smiled. "My dad's time with the ring and my own say we can. I've experienced His fire, and it is joy unending, peace beyond measure, freedom to dance in the fire. The way to no longer fear the fire is to join with Him and live in it instead of die from it."

The clop of the horse's hooves on the soil echoed in the slight breeze for several minutes. Cole pulled the horse to a stop and climbed off. He helped me down, then stared into the distance, his back to me.

I waited, and then decided to find out what thoughts ran through his brain. I slipped around to face him; his eyes blinked back tears. I wrapped my arms around him and waited for him to speak.

He wiped his eyes with his left sleeve. "I so much want to believe what you've said."

"It's reality. All you have to do is believe in reality."

He thrust his arms into the air and stared into the sky as if talking to God directly. "How! How do I know it's reality?"

I felt my eyes watering as I watched him struggle. "Did Satan create this reality?"

He shook his head.

"Then how could he define what reality is? If he could, he'd be god."

His wet eyes gazed into mine. His mouth sank into defeat. "I can't change my course now. Not after all I've invested with Morgenstern. But I'll promise you this. Once I've handed the ring over, I'll seriously consider changing, if for no other reason, in memory of you and your affect upon my life."

He grabbed my shoulders and held me before him. "Because, if what you say is true, I'd rather spend eternity with you in His fire than with Morgenstern."

I smiled weakly, but inside I realized I would not deter him from his current mission. "At least that's something, and the most important part too."

He drew me to him and his warm lips locked onto mine. A vision of a tree, and a demon with a sword blossomed into view, and Cole pushing me forward. I jerked back as the demon drew his sword and prepared to kill me. I didn't want to see what happened. I had to hope this warning could be changed. Love said it could.

He stared into my eyes. "What's the matter?"

I held his gaze for a moment. "That's the saddest kiss I've ever felt."

"It's my pledge to you of my promise. And as you know, I don't break my promises."

I buried my head in his chest and prayed that somehow God could change the vision I'd seen. We stood there, holding each other as the breeze caressed my wet cheeks. And I knew he thought the same thing I did. We both wished this could turn out differently.

A swooshing noise sounded in the distance. At first I didn't think much about it. But the beat of wings reminded me of...Nathan! Cole appeared to notice it about the same time, and we spun around to see a shining white, winged horse landing as a woman sat atop him.

My mouth dropped open. "Amma! The other woman is my mother!"

Cole glanced down at me and back at her. "She's your mother?"

I nodded.

He groaned. "This complicates things."

I widened my eyes; I couldn't believe it. Amma was pregnant! And from the size of her stomach, not too many days from delivering. But how? She didn't show a few weeks ago when we left Reol. But more importantly, who? "This complicates things a lot."

Amma dropped from Nathan's back. "Nathan is a human."

A light enveloped the horse and Nathan's human form appeared as the light dimmed.

I leaned upon Cole and stared at Amma. How did she change him by merely speaking it? Had reality taken a left turn into crazy?

Nathan drew his sword. "Unhand my sister, you two-timing fake!"

Cole drew his from its sheath. "You don't need to do this."

I thrust my hand out. "Nathan, stop! Remember what happened last time with his sword? I can't heal you now. Cole has the ring!"

He glanced at me and rolled his eyes toward the sky. He mumbled something as he focused on Cole. "I have to do this. It's all I have to offer."

I groaned. Men! I didn't want either of them hurt or dead. But I knew Nathan didn't have a chance with Cole. "Please! Back off for my sake!"

Cole nodded his head. "I'd listen to her if I were you."

Nathan gritted his teeth. "No one abducts my sister for some virgin sacrifice ritual while I live and breathe."

Cole's left eyebrow raised. "So you know about that, do you?"

Nathan growled and thrust his blade toward Cole. He parried it without any difficulty and slid his blade across Nathan's chest, nicking a rip in his tunic.

My shoulder muscles tensed. Cole's playing with him! But for how long?

Amma finally spoke up, "Cole, I cannot allow you to kill my daughter."

He answered her while keeping his eyes trained on Nathan, "I understand your sentiment, but neither can I allow you to prevent me from fulfilling my mission."

Nathan thrust another stab at Cole. He stepped to the side and slapped Nathan on his rear with the flat of his blade. Nathan gritted his teeth as he gained his feet and skidded to a stop.

Amma's eyes narrowed. "Cole, you love Kaylee no more than a dog its food!"

Nathan held back as if waiting for something to happen.

Amma's face fell. "You didn't change—you do love her!"

"With all my heart."

"Then why sacrifice her?"

Cole sighed. "I sincerely wish I didn't have to, but I've no choice in the matter."

She frowned. "There's always a choice."

"No good choices."

Nathan stomped a foot. "I have a choice!" He swung his sword from the side, but at the last minute he angled up toward Cole's heart.

Cole jumped back as the tip ripped through his clothes and left a slash of blood rising to the surface. He clutched his chest and gritted his teeth. He drew out his wand.

"No, Cole! Don't!" I yelled.

He mumbled a spell and whipped his wand into a circle. Amma and Nathan froze and then dissolved into nothingness.

I jumped to him and pounded on his chest. "What did you do to them! You didn't kill them did you?"

He pulled me into his chest. "No. I sent them away where they can't possibly interfere." He met my eyes. "It would take a miracle for them to reach the island in time."

A miracle would do. I'd seen enough of them to know they could happen. But would it? Am I to be a martyr who changes Cole for the better so he can spend the rest of his days in the service of God? Whatever God's purpose—I would finish it. I owed Him that much.

35

Gabrielle stared at Cole as he waved his wand toward her and Nathan. She couldn't move. Then a flash of light blasted across her eyes and as it died out, a busy street emerged into view.

"Look out, Lady!"

She spun around to see a horse drawn wagon barreling down on her. The man pulled back on the reins and yelled out, "Whoa!"

Gabrielle jumped to the side in time to let the horses, skidding to a stop, slide by her. She stepped to the side of the wagon.

The man pointed at her. "Lady, you can't be jumping in front of horses on a busy street! You nearly caused my heart to stop beating."

She doubted he would believe her if she told him the truth. "Sorry, Sir, But can you tell me what city this is?"

He wrinkled his nose. "You're here and you don't know where here is?"

She rolled her eyes. "Would I have asked if I knew? Can you please tell me?"

He flung his hand into the air. "Why, Octum, of course."

She glanced down the street and saw the sign for *Dragon's Inn* not far away. She slammed her hands onto her thighs. "All the way back to Octum!"

The man in the wagon raised an eyebrow and shrugged. He shook the reins, and the horses continued down the street.

Gabrielle heard a series of screams from a building close by. She whipped around in time to see Nathan exiting a doorway. A couple of scantily clad women held onto his waist and neck. A few others peeked out the door holding towels around their bodies.

One of the women danced in front of him, stopping his progress. "Oh, please. We're sorry we screamed. Won't you please come back inside?"

Nathan peeled their hands off of him. "Sorry, I'm not interested." He slipped around her as she stomped her foot on the ground and frowned.

His eyes caught Gabrielle's. "Oh, Mother." His face turned red. "One minute I'm facing Cole, next I'm surrounded by a bunch of naked women in a bath house. Where are we?"

"In Octum."

He stomped his feet. "Octum! Now Kaylee's doomed."

She sighed. "It's looking more that way all the time. But she's still alive right now. We have to do something, find some way to get back there before he kills her." She headed toward the inn. "Good thing Cole doesn't know about Josh. Let's see what his condition is. Maybe he can help."

They entered the inn and worked their way through the crowded tavern and back to the rooms. She knocked upon the door.

"Come in."

She pushed the door open.

Josh sat at the table with Crystal, eating roasted beef and enjoying a mug of ale. His eyes lit up on seeing Gabrielle. "Great! You're back so quickly. Where's Kaylee?"

Gabrielle shook her head.

Josh's grin fell. "Is she...dead?"

Gabrielle dropped into a chair while Nathan pulled another one up beside Crystal, then sat beside her and held her in his arms.

Gabrielle grabbed an empty mug and poured some ale into it. "No, not yet. But unless she can change his mind, she's as good as dead." Gabrielle froze. "Josh, your arm? It's not severed."

He held it up. "Yes, I recalled the spells to heal and restore limbs. Ever since my encounter with Darek, I've remembered more and more about Milnore, my master, and what he'd taught me. Much of my memory has returned. So I reattached my arm and it's as good as new." He wiggled his fingers to prove his point.

"What about your flying carpet?"

He frowned. "No, I can't recall that spell yet. It wasn't a common one."

She twisted her mouth. "What about transport spells? It turns out Cole is a wizard. He used a transport spell to send us back here. Can you reverse it?"

He nodded. "I recall the spell, it's a basic one a wizard learns. But I need a clear picture in my mind of where to transport—"

"Oh yes, I recall you saying that when we left Reol." Gabrielle leaned back in her chair. "Guess there's nothing we can do. Even if I turn Nathan into a flying horse and we fly hard and fast the whole way, it would take us at least a day to get there. By then, Kaylee will be dead."

Nathan waved his hand to get their attention. "But I have a clear picture in my mind of our last location. You do too."

Josh sat up straight. "He's right. I can pull the memory from your head and use it to transport you back." He snapped his fingers. "Excellent idea, Nathan."

Nathan smiled. "And you can come with us. We'll need a wizard to fight a wizard."

Josh winced. "Problem is, I'm not very strong yet. And while I'm recalling more and more spells, I might need one I can't recall. With reduced strength and not totally together mentally, I probably wouldn't stand a chance against an experienced wizard."

Gabrielle leaned over the table. "But Josh, you're the only chance we have. Couldn't you at least try?"

He shook his head. "You don't understand. It will take nearly all the strength I have to transport you two. I doubt I could send us all three back until my strength returned."

"But the Harrower? Remember, you said you were the most powerful wizard in the world?"

He shrugged. "Yes, I am, but if my body is weak, it can't handle the power. If I transport all three of us, I'll likely die in the attempt. Then you'd still be short one wizard. It's too dangerous to risk it."

Nathan bit his lip and stared at the ceiling. "I can't believe I'm saying this, but maybe it would be better if Josh went and I stayed. I felt pretty useless against Cole. Josh would at least have a chance to do something."

Josh shook his head. "That won't work either. Once there, Gabrielle will need your ability to fly to the island in quick time. And if transporting all three of us would kill me, it would certainly kill me to transport two of us and a winged horse."

Gabrielle pointed at Josh's cloak. "But you can expand one of your balls into a winged horse when we get there."

His left eyebrow raised up. "Yes, I suppose I could." He stared out the window a few seconds. "All right, I'll do it. But keep in mind, I'm not in good shape and I can promise nothing in defeating this Cole fellow. I might end up dead getting two of us there. Nathan would have more stamina for the trip and I can continue to recuperate here. But I'll go if you both want me to."

Nathan's head sunk. "Aside from my ability to fly, I didn't make much difference. Cole literally played with me as I tried to kill him with my sword." Nathan met Gabrielle's eyes. "He could have easily killed me, but he didn't."

She stared back. "I think it's because he does love Kaylee and didn't want to kill her brother or mother." She smiled. "Too bad he's on the wrong path. He'd fit right into this family."

Josh rose from the table, hobbled to a bed, and grabbed a cane from beside it. "If we're going to do this, the sooner the better."

Gabrielle stood up. "What do I do?"

"Make sure you have anything you want to take with you. The rest I'll do." He stared at her stomach. "How's our baby...I mean, your baby doing?"

Gabrielle glanced at Nathan and bit her lip. "It's his link with Sisko coming through." Nathan stared back at her without saying a word. She met Josh's eyes. "The baby is doing fine. I think its growth rate has slowed. I've not had any pains for a while. But I feel as if it could come at any time."

He nodded. "It looks that way too."

Nathan wrapped his arms around her shoulders and squeezed. "I fear I'll never see you again."

She pulled his head onto her shoulder and rubbed his back. "Even if I die in this attempt, that will not be true. Stay true to God and I'll see you in Paradise at least."

"But if you do die, I'll miss you all the same."

She smiled. "You'd better, or I'll have a thing or two to say when you get to Paradise."

Nathan pulled back and a slight smile crept across his face, but his eyes watered. He grabbed Josh's arm and hand. "Take good care of them, and may God be with you."

"And may God be with you as well. I'll do my best." Josh turned to Gabrielle. "Ready?"

She gathered some supplies into a pack and slung it over her shoulder. "Ready."

Josh placed a hand on her head and closed his eyes. He recited a spell. She could barely hear the words but felt an icy finger probing her mind. She shivered as Josh explored, seeking for the memory she held.

His probing paused. "Is this the one?"

An image flashed before Gabrielle's mind of Nathan with a sword in hand, attempting to kill Cole, and her and Kaylee standing to the side. "Yes, that's the one."

Josh wrapped her in his arms and mumbled another spell above her ears. The room faded from her eyes.

A vast plain dotted with low lying trees, shrubs, and cactus materialized before her. She felt Josh slouch in her arms. She shook him. "Josh, Josh, are you all right?"

His eyes flickered open. "If you call feeling like warmed over eggs all right, then I guess I am."

She prayed a quick prayer for him. "Can you fly on a horse?"

"I can't even stand up. Maybe I should eat something first."

She lay him on the ground. "You were eating roasted beef when we found you."

He nodded. "But I need more. I told you I would be near death by the transport. I can't promise I'll be able to do anything to Cole. At least the balls contain their own magic and will require nothing from me."

His shaking arm reached inside his cloak and pulled one out. He handed it to Gabrielle. "Can you throw this for me?"

She took it and gave it a toss.

"Expand to a tent." Josh said as it flew from her hand.

She watched as his tent blossomed upon the ground where the ball fell. "When can we go?"

He nodded. "At least an hour, maybe more."

Gabrielle frowned. "We may not have even an hour to spare."

"And if I don't gain my strength back, getting to her won't do us any good. Now, can you carry me into the tent and fix some food? I can cast some spells over it that will speed up the process once I gain some strength back."

"Carry you? In my condition? You can't be serious."

He studied her. "I suppose getting past your stomach would be a challenge."

She chuckled. "My stomach? The steam house didn't increase my strength, you know."

He smiled. "No, I guess not. Drag me then."

She shrugged and grabbed his outstretched hands. As she pulled him toward the tent, she worried whether he could do much of anything. He'd better gain some strength back fast. Kaylee's life certainly hung by a slim thread now. Very slim.

The crash of waves greeted my ears as we approached Shore Cliffs. I expected to find a large city. Instead, the coastal road passed through a town of five buildings facing the cliff where it intersected with the road from Octum from across the plains.

As we drew near, I noticed a strange contraption. A platform about the size of four buildings hung over the cliff and appeared to be supported by a series of ropes threaded through a network of poles fastened to the ground. On each corner of the platform, hollow tubes rested around wooden beams receding down the cliff face.

I pointed at it. "What's that?"

Cole followed my finger. "A vertical transport. It moves people and goods up and down the cliff, to the city below."

I raised an eyebrow. "The city below?"

He chuckled. "You'll see."

We joined the coastal road and he nudged the horse closer to the edge of the cliff. Its face dropped at least a hundred feet before meeting the waters of the bay. I dropped my mouth open, for sitting over the surging waves, built upon an intricate system of piers and walkways, lay a massive city. Houses, stores, banks, government buildings, everything resided on piers tied off to the face of the cliff.

On one side of the vast city, the piers provided docking areas for ships, and many worked hard to load and unload the cargo from them. The citizens themselves resembled a hive of bees all buzzing from place to place.

"Quite impressive, isn't it?" Cole rested his chin on my shoulder.

"Yes, I've never seen anything quite like it. But what happens when there's a storm?"

"The people go up. Aside from the vertical transport, there is a narrow set of stairs cut into the cliff face as well. The people pitch tents up on top and let the storm pass. Then they return to fix whatever damage they find."

We pulled up to one of the buildings. A man appeared at an open half-door. "What can we help you with today? Have any cargo needing shipped?"

Cole shook his head. "Two passengers to the island of Pluto."

I winked at the man. "It's our honeymoon!"

Cole jabbed me.

The man's eyes widened, and he leaned over his counter. "Do ya know what's there? If'n I were you, I'd not set foot on that godforsaken bit of land pokin' from the sea."

Cole frowned. "It's godforsaken for a reason. Now are you going to sell me tickets to it or not?"

He shook his head. "Sure, I'll be right happy to send you down the river, or sea is it may be. But you'll get no refund from me!"

He stamped a couple of tickets and held them out.

Cole stared at them. "Only one needs to be a round trip ticket. The second will be one way, please."

The man narrowed his eyes. "Heading to the Island of Pluto with a woman, and you need only one round-trip ticket? Sounds mighty suspicious to me. Such a request may compel me to notify the proper authorities."

I stared at Cole. He could do any number of things to the man. Cole gritted his teeth and then relaxed. "Two round trip tickets will be fine." Cole forked over the cash. Then pulled out a couple more bills. "And if you can take care of my horse while I'm gone, I'd appreciate it."

A grin spread across the man's face. "Sure, I'll take care of her for ya. And I might even feed her if you's can throw in a little more." He smiled. "For expenses, ya know."

Cole shook his head and shelled out another bill. The man handed Cole the tickets and commanded someone from the back room to take the horse to the stables.

Cole led me to the platform and I stepped onto it. Several groups and couples filled the area, gazing around in awe. Others rested on benches as if they'd done this many times.

The platform rocked slightly in the wind, and occasionally a gust racing up the cliff would push the floor upward enough to create an unsettled feeling.

I peered over the side to the city far below. "I feel more secure riding on a winged horse."

A bell rang through the air, and a man closed the gate leading onto the platform. The poles creaked, and then the whole floor sank. I gasped for a moment before adjusting to the drop. I wondered what would happen if any of the ropes broke.

The trip down took several minutes. The sound of the sea lapping against the cliffs calmed me, but as we drew near the piers, the noise of the crowd grew until it provided an off-beat backup to the waves' music.

The platform settled upon the city's walkways, and the gate opened. The crowd flooded out while others waited in line to enter.

Cole held my hand as we strolled down a busy "street" of the city. The sound of boots and sandals clomping on the wooden piers mixed with the chatter of the crowd and the crash of waves. The smell of salty air hung heavy around us while sea gulls squawked over the city, searching for food left by the crowds.

Cole turned to me. "I suppose you deserve a last meal. We have a while before the ship leaves, and I know the perfect place." A smile spread across his lips.

"Great, I am hungry."

We dodged in and out of bodies and around a couple of corners. Cole had obviously been here before. He led me to a storefront. Nailed over the doorway, a sign read, *Soulful Seafood*. We entered in. A woman wearing a long, tight dress led us to a table. The room light flickered dimly about us.

Once seated, she asked, "Do you know what you want, or do you need a list?"

Cole leaned back. "I would like the salmon-for-two special, please." He glanced at me. "Is that fine with you?"

I nodded. "Sounds delicious."

"It is." He focused on the lady again. "And bring us some clams and a bottle of your best wine." He pulled out a couple of bills and pushed them into her hands.

She smiled. "I'll get right on it. Thank you, sir." She scurried off.

A candle flame from the table cast fleeting shadows over Cole's face. "I don't get it."

"Get what?"

He cast a hand my direction. "You're about to die in a few hours, and yet you don't act like you fear it. You're even cutting jokes like you did at the top of the cliff."

"I get it from my dad." I shrugged. "It's simple, really. If this is my time, then I'll die as a martyr, showing the joy of God in my soul." I locked onto his eyes. "I'm willing to die for you, Cole. Though I would very much love to stay here and make a life and children with you, I have much to look forward to in the next life."

He frowned and stared at the table. He couldn't say the same words! He planned to kill me to avoid Satan killing him.

He rubbed his forehead. "That's just it. I fear the next life, what it might bring. To not fear would be total freedom."

I nodded. "Exactly. If I'm to die, then it is my time to die. If not, then God will rescue me."

"How can you be so confident that you'll like what you find on the other side of death?" His eyes peered into mine, searching for an answer.

"Because I've experienced it." I gazed into the distance. "I'll never forget what happened in the steam house with my dad. One taste of Paradise, and you'll never doubt again."

He reached his hands across the table and enveloped mine. He caressed my fingers in his grip. "I know it may not seem like it, but I do love you. You're an amazing woman. I know I'm the biggest fool for giving you over to Morgenstern. But I can't avoid it. I don't break promises." A smile grew across his face. "But I can say, I've experienced a taste of Paradise after all—in you."

I felt heat rising in my cheeks. "I hope you make it to Paradise. But for now, I'm enjoying our time together."

His lips turned up, but I could see the doubt in his eyes. He nodded. "Yes, I suppose we should enjoy our remaining time together. It may be all we have left."

I stared into his eyes and sensed regret in them. I felt more sadness for him than I did for myself. He was trapped, unable to fulfill his own will, and based on what I knew of Satan, would never fulfill his master's either.

Fear of God had trapped him into fear itself. And it had ruled his life.

The food arrived. We talked and ate, but mostly we stared into each others eyes and held hands. We couldn't discuss a future together, not even in Paradise. Even though I had successfully caused doubt to rise in his mind and stoked his desire for me, it didn't matter. He would fulfill his promise. His own comfort and desire wouldn't deter him from it. I found it to be an attractive quality about him.

I placed my hand on his and squeezed. "Cole, I think you're an amazing man." I smiled and he returned the affection. But I could see guilt clouding his eyes. I did get to him, and maybe once I died, it would be enough to send him down the right path. I squeezed his fingers as I prayed for his soul.

Our meal together ended way too soon, as I knew it would. Cole and I worked our way through the crowds until we arrived at the ship headed to Pluto. I'd never been on a sailing vessel before. The back and forth motion on the ship rocked my stomach, stirring a queasiness up my throat. But it passed before we left the bay. Then the higher waves of the sea ignited the nausea all over again.

I stood at the railing of the ship, watching the water swirl and slash against the hull. Cole stood by my side. I wondered if he feared I would jump to attempt an escape, but we both knew he could easily fish me out if I tried. No, my destiny lay at the Dying Tree. It would be up to God to save me from being killed, if that was His plan. Otherwise, I'd see Dad much sooner than I had originally planned.

Dad's descriptions of Paradise, inadequate as he said they were, filled my mind. I knew another exciting life awaited me on the other side of death. One I would enjoy much more than this life. Desire to be there bubbled up, and the pending death didn't hold the fear it should have. If God needed me to die to fulfill his plan, I was ready and willing.

Cole placed his arm around my shoulders. "Hypnotic, isn't it?"

I smiled. "Yes. I keep imagining that under the waves there is a vast civilization watching us float by. A world we're totally oblivious to. I wonder what their lives would be like, how they breathe, what kinds of games their kids play."

Cole chuckled. "You have a very active imagination."

"And you don't?" I feigned surprise.

He smiled and stared at the approaching island. We'd been at sea for nearly four hours while the dot on the horizon grew into a full-sized land mass, small though it was.

Tree trunks stretched upwards for several feet before disappearing into a dense foliage. Dark tan sands lined the beach while a group of clouds hovered over the land as if created specifically for this spot.

The ship cast anchor and they lowered a boat to the water. The captain called to us. "We're ready to take ya to shore."

Cole's eyes grew cold, and his jaw set. He refused to meet my gaze. His black hair waved in the breeze. He grabbed my arm and pulled me along. "Come, let's get this over with."

The boat carried us to shore, the only passengers disembarking at this location. I didn't blame them. The island engendered feelings of doom.

We left the shore and foraged through the underbrush along a rarely traveled path, which grew hard to discern in places. After an hour, the branches and leaves parted to reveal an open area around the center of the island. In the middle of the clearing stood an old tree. I'd never seen a tree like this one. A blackened tree trunk as big as an elephant rose from the ground. Its branches twisted in all directions. No leaves dangled from them. It appeared a fire had burned it, and this skeleton of a tree stood alone and dark.

That alone soaked my bones in dread, but the horror wielding a sword in front of the massive tree stole my breath. A demon! A thin but solid frame wore a dark breastplate. Deep red eyes burned from under a heavy and wrinkled brow. Its thin mouth curled up as we approached.

Memories of Beltrid, and his attempt to trap me in my mind, forced their way to the surface. Despite my brave words to Cole, I couldn't help but shake in the face of death.

The demon's face flared with heat and he raised his sword in anticipation. Yet he didn't move forward, as if he waited for one of us to cross an imaginary line in the dirt before he would be allowed to strike.

Cole wrapped me in his arms. "Please forgive me for what I'm about to do."

I felt a calm rush over me. "Of course I forgive you. I'm ready."

His eyes watered and he bit his lip. Then he breathed deep, and flung me toward the demon.

I stumbled and crashed upon the ground at the demon's feet.

The creature lifted his sword and brought it down upon me. I rolled to the side instinctively, and the sword stabbed dirt. I leaped to my feet and scurried out of the demon's circle. Cole's jaw set and his eyes narrowed.

I dusted myself off. "Sorry. But if I'm going to die, at least let me die willingly rather than being tossed into it like food to a dog."

He bowed his head. "I'm sorry. You're right."

I pulled my shoulders back and took a step toward the demon. I glanced back. "I'm doing this for you, Cole. And for God." I refocused on the demon licking his lips. My legs quivered and I closed my eyes. *God, please use my death for your purpose. And please save Cole.* I felt my legs strengthen. I opened my eyes and stepped forward.

A whooshing noise broke the quietness of the island. I spun around to see a brown flying horse drop to a landing. Amma slipped to the dirt along with her hard-to-miss stomach. Josh also slid off! Excitement raced over me. If anyone could deal with Cole, it was Josh.

Amma held up a hand. "Kaylee, don't move!"

Josh approached Cole. "I understand you intend to harm my friend's daughter?"

Cole gritted his teeth. "I don't know how you arrived back here so soon, but another trip you cannot make in a few seconds!" He slipped his wand out and recited a spell as he drew circles around the two of them.

Josh threw his hands up and sparks showered around him and Amma as if Cole's energy hit an invisible shield. But Josh's legs shook from the effort.

Cole frowned. "So that's how you've returned so quickly. You have a wizard with you." He thrust his wand toward Josh and a ball of energy raced from it.

Josh shot his own fiery blast. The energies collided and a light flashed from it causing me to shield my eyes. Josh flung his hands at Cole. An invisible force knocked Cole off his feet, and he crashed to the dirt.

Then Josh stepped back. His legs shook and his arms quivered. He groaned and his eyes glazed over as if seeing into another world.

Cole rose to his feet, his eyes focused and his jaw set. He thrust his wand at Josh, and a surge of energy blasted from it. Josh watched it speeding toward him. My mouth fell open; Josh could barely stand!

The blast plowed into Josh, and flung him several feet back before he smashed into a tree and collapsed upon the ground. He groaned and rolled around as if to get up. But his arms gave way.

Amma cried out, "Josh!" She rushed to kneel beside him. Her eyes watered.

I wanted to grab the ring from Cole and heal Josh. I wanted to do something, but what? I felt helpless.

Amma helped Josh sit up against a tree. Then she stood and stepped toward Cole.

Cole pulled his wand up again.

She held up a hand. "Cole, please wait. You win. I only ask for one last moment with my daughter. You wouldn't deny me that, would you?"

He held the wand in place for a moment before his cold eyes warmed. He lowered the wand. "You may say goodbye to her."

She rushed to me and wrapped me in her arms. Her bulging stomach pushed at my own. Tears watered her eyes but a soft smile caressed her lips. "I'm so glad I arrived in time."

A knot caught in my throat. I would miss her. "Me too. But I wish Nathan had come along. Please tell him I'm sorry I didn't listen to him. If I had, I wouldn't be here now."

She lifted my head from her chest. "You'll understand when I say I long to see you in Paradise one day."

I smiled. "Yes, definitely."

She breathed deeply. "Sorry for leaving you so soon."

"What? You don't mean—"

She shoved me back and my feet stumbled. I fell onto my rear with a thud. Though pain shot through me, it felt like a distant throb. For I watched helplessly as she fled toward the demon. The creature plunged his sword through her chest and it protruded out her back, stained with her blood.

"No! Amma!" I scrambled to my feet and raced to her.

The demon started to pull the sword out of her, but his dark blade glowed, then a burning white light shot up the blade and enveloped the demon. It screeched but didn't let go, perhaps couldn't. The white light worked its way through the beast like cracks appearing over its skin. The light burst through the openings and grew until the demon radiated brighter than the sun.

Cole dropped to the ground and covered his head. I stared into the light without pain. I recognized it. It was the light of Paradise. It resided in Amma! The light dimmed, leaving a pile of charred remains where the demon stood, and Amma collapsed beside it with the sword still in her chest.

I knelt beside her, and laid my head on her stomach to cry. The baby? What would happen to it?

Before I could think about it, Cole's hand grabbed my arm and pulled me up. "We're all going in." He grabbed Josh's arm as well and lifted him up.

The tree groaned and shook. A crack appeared at its base and rose upwards in erratic zigzag patterns. As it did, it opened wider and whiffs of smoke puffed from it. A rotting smell filled the air. When it stopped, a small doorway beckoned us to enter.

I jerked against Cole's pull. "My mother! Cole, please give me the ring, I need to heal her!"

He didn't answer, instead he pulled Josh and me into the tree.

"Cole! Please don't do this!" I kicked and hit him, but he stoically received the blows. His grip didn't relax nor did he acknowledge my protest. Rough-hewn steps descended inside. The darkness swallowed us whole.

38

A light flickered on. Cole moved ahead of us as a flame floated in the air before him. I let Josh lean on me. He smiled weakly as we stumbled behind Cole. Shadows of tunnels and rock formations of various sizes flashed around us. For an hour or two we dropped into the bowels of Hades.

I didn't say anything and neither did Cole. His eyes displayed a steely, cold gaze. He didn't acknowledge me; the only words he said to me: "Move faster."

I wanted to cry. I wanted to run back to Amma, and see if I could save the baby at least. But I knew if I tried, Cole would easily pull me back. So I didn't do any of those things. I focused on the task at hand, whatever that might be. Maybe now, I could free Crystal's soul for Nathan—if I could figure out how.

The passageway widened as the bottom of the descent approached, and then broke into a large cavern. An eerie, reddish glow emanated from a large hole in the center of the cave. A noise of millions screaming from far away echoed from its depths.

I broke the silence. "Cole, what are those voices?"

He stepped to the edge of the precipice and stared down. "Souls trapped in the vortex of Hades. Come and see."

I crept toward it, glancing at Cole as I did, but keeping my eyes trained on the giant hole. As its depths shifted into view, I saw a swirling mass of ghostly faces and bodies, stretched and distorted. The vortex sank into the depths of the earth, Hades, wherever it led.

I gasped and pointed. "I see Crystal in there." Then my eyes widened. "And Amma with her!" I swung my eyes up to meet Cole's.

He nodded. "Everyone passes through here. Not all escape. Guilt over some sin, some wrong, causes them to give up."

"But Amma? She wouldn't give up."

Cole cocked his head to one side. "Maybe not. She might eventually escape. Those closest to your God have the easiest time of it. Like you, they aren't afraid of His presence and go to meet it with joy. We always called them fools for meeting Hell head on."

The swirling millions below saddened me. "You speak as if that's the past. Do you think differently now? Have you become a fool too?"

He sighed. "When sickness becomes the normal reality, health can appear its perversion. Those who are healed, escape."

I stared at him. "Healed?"

"Yes. That's what you call it, isn't it, when a person who can't see God's reality finally sees it? Everyone who remains in this vortex stays because Satan has convinced them that what you call a sickness of the soul is the only reality."

I stared intently at his eyes. "And you? Do you see His reality now?"

He stared into the vortex, but remained silent.

I glanced back to see Josh sitting against the wall. He still didn't appear very strong from his battle. I would probably get little help from him in here.

A voice echoed from across the cave. "I see you have returned. Do you have it?"

I jerked my head toward the voice. A shining white creature approached. A dazzling light gleamed from him, causing pain to stare directly at him. I'd felt this light before. Paradise. Not the real one, but the city. Outwardly, it appeared to be the same light. Inwardly, it was ever so slightly off.

I pointed at him. "Cole, is that—"

"Yes, it is who you call Satan."

The being glided around the hole to where we stood. A serene smile beamed at me. "So, we finally meet face to face. The one who has finally given us the ring."

A surge of guilt careened through me, recalling my rationalizations, my justifications, and my willing act to violate what I knew to be right. By my sin, I had handed the ring over to the enemy. A heat burned around me as if I could feel its fingers reaching for me.

No! Paradise resided in my soul after the sin. God had forgiven me, how could Satan change that? "Yes, I did sin, resulting in Cole obtaining the ring. But you fool yourself if you think you can hide God's presence with it."

He laughed. Not a particularly evil laugh, more like one that feels pity for those in ignorance. "And who are you to speak with me so? Do you not know what I can do?"

I stared at him squarely in the eyes. "It's doesn't matter who I am because I'm not the one who will defeat you."

He faced Cole. "She has some spunk. But we have a more important transaction to make, you and I."

I scooted into his line of sight. "Excuse me? I have a friend in your vortex there. Please release her back to her body, which isn't dead."

He raised what would be his eyebrow, but he didn't have any. "Not dead? Now that's odd." He snapped his fingers. "You speak of Beltrid's plaything. Foolish demon. I tried to train him in subtle ways, but he wouldn't listen. You can see the results. He failed, and I have succeeded."

I frowned at his arrogance, but I guess they didn't call him Satan for nothing. "Yes, Crystal. She shouldn't be in there. Beltrid never released her before he...went—"

"Yes, yes. To the abyss. Serves him right for failing." He glanced at the swirling cyclone of souls. "We'll discuss it after I have what I want." He turned back to Cole. "Do you have it?"

Cole nodded. "Yes. It is not here, but I can get it easily enough."

A flash of rage fled across Satan's face. "Not here! Do you dare to bargain with me?"

"You promised me a kingdom, wealth, and glory if I brought this ring to you."

"And those you shall have. Now provide the ring."

"I would like to have a deposit before I release it."

Satan's body warped as if heat wrapped around him. Red waves rolled down his arms and enveloped Cole.

Cole collapsed onto the floor in pain, holding his head in his hands as he cried out through gritted teeth. My legs grew weak watching him suffer. But what could I do against such raw power without the ring?

Satan smiled. "You'll have your deposit! A corner of Hades to rule, and all the gold you could ever want sitting useless in your little kingdom."

Cole held a hand up. "Please, stop! I'll give you the ring. I'll give it to you!"

Satan's pure whiteness returned and Cole sank in relief, breathing heavily.

He struggled to his feet and put a hand in his pocket. "I've got it with me, right here."

Satan held out his palm and Cole pulled his fist from the pocket. His hand trembled, but he paused.

"Give it to me!"

Satan couldn't take it; the ring had to be handed over willingly. Like I had done with Cole, like Beltrid attempted to get me to do. Satan operated under restrictions too!

Cole opened his fingers; the ring glowed red upon his hand. Satan reached his palm out for Cole to drop it in. Cole's palm turned slightly, but then he paused. His jaw set. "You broke your promised payment. I am no longer required to keep my end of the deal." He closed his fist and waved his left hand over it. His fingers spread—the ring no longer lay on his palm!

The ring materialized before me, floating in the air, the red glow of the cyclone reflecting from its surface. I reached out and grabbed the ring.

Cole yelled to me, "Kaylee, put it on, quickly! At least you'll be protected!"

I grasped the ring between my fingers and slid it over the tip of my finger, but my heart said no. The ring hovered over my fingernail. No? Once on my finger, all would be back the way it should. Then I'd have a chance to defeat Satan, heal Amma, Josh, and free Crystal. Merely push it down, and the nightmare would end. But a voice yelled "no" from deep within. It made no sense.

Dad's words echoed from my memories when he gave me the ring: "Never, ever use it on your own volition. Always wait for God's direction, and always, always ask Him." God said no. I would obey.

A laugh echoed against the distant screams of souls. I jerked my head up to see Satan's eyes trained on me.

A blissful smile broke forth upon his face. "You can't do it, can you?"

Did Satan cause the voice to say no? Did he trick me?

"Kaylee, please, hurry!" Cole's eyes reflected the fire in his soul. "Save yourself!"

Satan held out his hand, and Cole gasped as if he could no longer breathe. Satan smiled as he watched Cole suffer. "This is what happens to traitors!"

Cole crumbled to his knees, then fell over on his side, his hands wrapped around his neck.

"Stop it!" I cried. I moved the ring down my finger, but halted again when the voice cried out to stop.

A grin spread across his face. "Then give me the ring, and I'll spare him."

Once again, the decision to give up the ring in exchange for those I loved stared me in the face. Tears welled up within me. What could I do? I couldn't give it to him, but I couldn't let him kill Cole, and then Josh. Yet something prevented me from putting the ring on to heal them.

Satan thrust his hand outward; Cole's body stopped moving and fell limp.

"Cole!" An overwhelming urge filled me to jam the ring onto my finger, and race over to heal Cole. I couldn't let him die!

Anger poured over me and then despair. The voice said no. It had never been wrong before. The reality sank in. Satan would never allow me to leave with the ring. If I put it on, I would be trapped here forever. I pulled it off my finger and clinched it in my palm.

Satan stretched out his palm before me. "Give me the ring."

"Why don't you just kill me and take it, like Cole?"

He raised a hairless eyebrow. "I don't own you like I did Cole. For a moment, I thought I would. But if you want to leave here, you have no choice. Make this easy on yourself, and hand it over."

Defeat rolled over me. Tears mixed with sweat and despair. No other option lay before me but to release it. I prayed that God would forgive me, but I saw no way out if I couldn't put the ring on myself.

I nodded and slipped the ring between my index finger and thumb. I stared at his waiting hand, his fingers wiggling in anticipation.

Joel's words rushed back to me. I would pass the ring on, and I would know when and who. My breath froze as the reality cascaded over me. My heart confirmed it. The ring's final destination stood before me!

I gazed into Satan's fiery eyes and smiled. Peace settled over me as I stared death in the face. "You want the ring, you can have it."

I jammed it onto Satan's finger. It slid on and locked into place. The ring had found its final home!

I fell backwards as Satan's light grew to a deep brilliance before it imploded back into him, somewhere deep within the fallen angel. He writhed upon his feet as he jerked around. He grabbed the ring and worked to pull it off, but it would not budge. He now wore the ring and the ring would not let him go.

I watched the fullness of the ring's curse become a reality. His screams broke dust from the upper cave wall and fragments of rocks fell around me. Cracks appeared over Satan's body, and a red-blue heat enveloped him until he burst into a flaming inferno. Yet the fire did not consume him, but burned continually. He cried out for mercy from the presence of God. The One Satan wanted to bury deep into Hades, had instead buried Satan deep into His fiery love.

I rose to my feet and dashed toward Josh. The whole cavern would collapse about us if we didn't leave. But before I could reach him, the ground jerked from under my feet; I collapsed onto the cavern floor. A crack widened between Josh and I, bursting forth flames.

Another violent earthquake shook the vast expanse, causing rocks to pour down around me. I knew this would be the end. We'd be buried alive in the depths of Hades.

I struggled to my feet once the rumbling subsided. Josh rose upon shaking feet. "Hold on. I'll try and transport us out of here!"

I searched for Cole's body, but the rubble already obscured it. My heart broke. Maybe I would see him in the next life, if his last act of love had earned him a martyr's crown.

The rocks continued pouring down. I struggled to stay on my feet and dodge the falling debris. A pillar of light burst forth from above. My eyes shot up to see a brilliance pour into the dim confines of Hades. It blasted through the darkness and down into the cyclone of souls swirling in its depths.

Cries burst forth anew from within the pit. But the sound of the voices retreated as if something pulled them in, and for a brief moment the whole cave fell silent except for the echoes of small rocks hitting the floor.

Then the cyclone inverted, and souls burst upward toward the light and streamed into the beyond. Echoes of cheers and cries of joy reverberated through the cave. With Satan's deception broken, many now saw God's reality.

"Amma!" I cried out upon seeing her soul rising to the light.

Amma's face turned down and she smiled. She mouthed the words, "I love you" before she resumed her ascent to the light.

Then another soul broke free from the stream and headed for the tunnel toward the Dying Tree. I recognized the face. "Crystal!" I smiled knowing Nathan would soon have Crystal whole.

Josh fell upon the rubble as the ground shook again and the wind from the exiting souls swirled around them.

I realized he didn't have the strength to transport us out. God remained my sole hope. "Lord, I know I don't have the ring, and normally you don't even answer for my benefit if I did, but I ask as Your servant, save us!"

The ground shook and more of the ceiling fell in. A flood of souls continued to stream upward. I fell as the ground jerked to the side from under me. Jagged rocks ripped the skin on my upper arm, staining them red. The floor rolled in waves as everything moved from side to side.

Then I noticed a pair of feet walking toward me, as if the shaking ground didn't even bother them. I raised my eyes.

"Joel! Am I ever glad to see you!"

He smiled and reached out a hand. "I feared you'd never ask for help."

"You mean you knew I needed help and held back?"

"I operate under—"

"Restrictions. Yes, I know. But seriously."

He glanced at Satan, still screaming curses as the inferno enveloped him. "You figured out who gets the ring. Well done."

I reached out. He pulled me up and helped me navigate the crack toward the door. Josh and Joel locked arms and we surged toward the opening.

I glanced back. "Joel, can we get Cole's body?"

He frowned.

"Please? I'd like to give him a proper burial at least." I stared into his eyes, pleading.

He nodded and cast his hand to where Cole's body lay buried. Rocks flung to the sides. Cole's body rose from the debris and floated through the air until it landed on my shoulders. I grabbed him firmly and followed Joel through the tunnel. We struggled with the ascent at first, but the way grew easier as the shaking and falling rocks faded like a bad dream into the distance.

Cole's body felt cold and his limbs had grown stiff. It saddened me that what could have been would never be. I kept thinking there must have been some other way. Two of the people I most cared for no longer resided in this life.

I stared at the light emanating around Joel as we climbed the steps. "Joel, did I do the right thing? What would have happened if I had put the ring on?"

He glanced back; a smile spread across his face. "If you had, you would have been buried in Hades until the final judgment. No, you did good. You fulfilled the final destination of the ring as planned."

"You mean, it couldn't have been done any easier?"

One corner of his mouth turned up higher. "Sure, you didn't have to sin for the ring to come off. But God can work all things out anyway for your good." He laughed. "Ironic, isn't it. The very thing Satan thought would destroy and hide God from him forever, ended up sending him into a fiery Hell. He's blind that way, you know."

I nodded. "I understand all are who can't see God's reality."

Joel nodded. "Well spoken."

We continued the climb back to life.

39

The climb out of Hades took forever. I felt the end would never come, but then daylight burst forth above us. My pace quickened and Joel led us into the light.

I fell upon the ground and let Cole's body roll to my side. But I recalled my mother's condition and sat up to find her. She lay on the ground; dried blood stained her clothing. I let my head sink with my stomach.

Joel pointed at Amma's body. "Look again."

I did, and Amma's stomach moved. "The baby! Could it still be alive?" I leaped to my feet, and Josh also hobbled over to her.

Joel nodded. "The entrance into Hades distorts time as you know it. Several hours there passes in seconds here."

Josh felt her stomach. "The baby's still alive, but we'll have to take it out ourselves. You have a knife?"

I shook my head. "No."

He frowned, then reached into his cloak and pulled out a ball. He tossed it three feet away. "Expand to a knife."

A blade fell to the ground. I grabbed it and gave it to Josh.

Josh slid the knife along her lower stomach, cutting skin back. Deep-red blood oozed out. He cut deeper and deeper until he broke into the womb. Then he plunged his hands inside and pulled out a baby boy.

A wave of joy flood over me. Out of all this death, a new brother had entered the world. Josh helped me clean the baby. But the baby didn't act normal. It didn't cry. Yet it breathed fine. The way its eyes darted around, it appeared to be more aware of its surroundings than one would expect of a newborn.

I met Josh's eyes. "Who's the father?"

Josh stared into the sky. "Well...that's an interesting story."

"Josh! Who is the father? Since Amma has died, he'll have to take care of the baby."

"Honestly?"

"Yes. Please."

"Your father."

"My father!" I swallowed hard, attempting to digest the statement.

He nodded. "Like I said, long story."

I stared at the baby I held in my hands. No wonder he didn't act like a normal baby. This one was different.

The baby's hands jerked up, and he appeared to point behind me.

I turned my head in the direction he had pointed and saw Cole's body lying on the ground. I frowned. Certainly the baby couldn't be telling me anything.

Joel stepped beside her. "What makes you assume that?"

I shrugged. "Yes, I suppose I've seen stranger things." I hauled myself and the baby to Cole's body.

Did I dare hope anything could be done? His body, cold and stiff, gave little hope. Without the ring, what chance did I have of raising him back to life?

Joel knelt beside her. "Yes, by yourself, you don't have a chance."

I frowned. "You're being a little too free with this mind reading trick of yours. But you're going to say God does have a chance."

He rubbed her back. "Yes. But God does tend to work through people." He bobbed his head toward the baby.

Did he indicate the baby could do something? I checked Cole's lifeless body, then returned my gaze to Joel's searing eyes. "You mean, I can ask, without the ring?"

He nodded. "Faith doesn't require a ring to heal."

I motioned toward Amma's lifeless body. "What about her?"

Joel stared into the sky. "You saw her soul ascend, did you not?"

I nodded.

"Cole has taken a different trip, much like your father's. He can return. Your mother cannot."

I reached out a hand toward Cole's body, but paused. Did I not do this for myself? Would he not be happier in Paradise if such is where he went. Or did he need more time to change things?

Joel sighed. "It's all right. Pray!"

The baby in my arms reached out and placed his tiny hand on the back of my own. I felt a surge of power flow through me from his touch. I met the baby's eyes and saw an awareness in them. The baby knew what he was doing! I squeezed the child and focused on Cole's lifeless body. I rested my hand on his chest as the baby's hand lay on mine. "Lord, please heal Cole and raise him back to life in this world."

Seconds ticked by, and nothing happened. But his color? His pale blue skin turned into a vibrant pink.

Cole blinked his eyes open; they darted around. Then they locked onto mine and grew wide. "I should be dead."

"You were, but now you're alive!" I fell upon him and hugged his neck with my free hand. "Oh I'm so glad you're alive."

He squeezed back, then drew my ear near his mouth. "I've been to Paradise. You were right."

I pulled back and saw a wide smile below his beaming eyes. But his expression vanished. "Can you ever forgive me?"

I placed a finger over Cole's lips. "What happened, happened to accomplish God's will. I forgave you before we entered Hades."

"I'm not talking only about sacrificing you, but the deception, the fake reality I tried to drag you into. And for a time, I thought I had. But now I've experienced another reality. The reality."

I couldn't help but smile. "And that is?"

He grinned. "The freedom to live in the fire. Paradise."

I forced myself to frown and set my jaw. "You'll have to promise me one thing, however."

Cole nodded. "Name it."

I allowed the smile to return to my face. "To marry me, help raise our kids, and live the rest of your life with me."

His smile blossomed into a full grin. "Yes, yes, and yes!" He shook his head. "You really are an amazing woman."

"Ga gaaa," the baby cried out.

Cole stared at him, apparently noticing him for the first time. "Whose child?"

"Amma's and Dad's, or so I'm told. But seeing how I'm one of the few people left in the family, I guess I'll be raising him."

"What's his name?"

I stared at the child whose eyes searched me over. They peered deep into my mind. A strong power resided in him. I jerked my head back. "I hadn't thought about a name yet." I skipped through a list, but one popped its way into my thoughts.

"I'll name him Colbert. He just saved your life, after all. Or God did through him."

"Colbert." Cole winked. "Sounds like a fine name."

Josh cleared his throat. "I'm going to make another flying horse right after we eat. I'm starving. Then we can all head back to Octum."

I nodded. "Thanks, Josh." I held Colbert in front of me. "Welcome home, little brother."

"Ahhh gaaa." He patted his stomach.

"Hungry are you?" I stared at my breast. "Nothing will come from there." I called to Josh, "I think we'd better hurry, Colbert's getting hungry. Can we stop at Shore Cliffs for some milk?"

"Milk?" He pulled a ball from his cloak and then tossed it. "Expand to a jug of woman's breast milk." A jar bobbled on the ground until it rattled to a stop.

I rolled my eyes. "I don't think we'll need that much!"

He shrugged. "I wanted to make sure it was enough."

Joel stepped in front of me and held me by my shoulders. "I'm fairly certain, now that the ring is no longer your concern, you'll not see me again."

"Ever?" I stared at his bright, blue eyes.

"Well, maybe in the next life. But in this one, I seriously doubt it. Restrictions and all, you know."

I nodded and buried my face into his chest. His arms enclosed me and his warmth enveloped me. I felt something very familiar about him.

I pulled back and locked onto his eyes. "I sense Paradise in you."

He nodded. "And I in you as well." He smiled. "You do know, I love you."

I grinned. "And I you."

"As a brother, you understand."

I chuckled. "Oh yes, of course."

He smiled. "Besides, you have Cole. You will make each other better people for being together, which is what becoming one is all about. To save each other."

"I will miss you." I hugged him one last time.

"And I will miss our conversations. It has been a joy aiding you, even if sometimes tricky."

I smiled. But the smile faded as he pulled away and then vanished into thin air like an object sinking into murky waters.

Cole stood beside me. "Who was that?"

"Joel. Without him, I doubt I would be here now. I'd probably be stuck on a sky island being chased by a crazed wizard-mouse for the rest of my life."

"But what is he? I felt a different kind of magic from him."

I shrugged. "A prophet, a purveyor of fine teas, a friend, a brother." I sighed. "He's been like an angel to me."

The corners of Cole's mouth turned up. "Like you've been to me. My personal angel."

He pulled me into his arms and kissed me. His warmth, his love, his joyful exuberance poured from him. The only thing I didn't find this time was a vision, which suited me just fine. I could finally live a normal life.

"Gaa goo gaga!" The baby wrapped its short arms around my arm as well as he could and hugged me.

Well, maybe not a normal life. This baby wouldn't allow that to happen.

I enjoyed the trip back. I figured it might be one of the last times I would ride a winged horse. Maybe Josh would consent to let me keep one. The trip flew by, in more ways than one.

We landed outside the gates of Octum and rode in. Several stared as we trotted down the street. A woman with a baby, and two men wearing torn clothing, oily and dirty hair, and riding on winged horses apparently attracted attention. Including Nathan's, who burst from the inn doors and nearly knocked me over as my feet hit the ground.

He beamed. "Oh, Kaylee, you did it! You did it!" He pulled back and waved his hand behind him. "I'd like you to meet the real Crystal."

Crystal stood in the doorway of the inn. A sweet smile graced her face, and her black eyes sparkled with light from inside. She scurried to me and pulled me into a strong hug.

Crystal gazed into my eyes. Tears fell from hers. "I owe you my life, several times over. Thank you doesn't begin to say what I feel inside."

Nathan put his arm around Crystal. "And she's accepted my proposal. I'm marrying the real Crystal this time." Nathan's eyes blossomed with joy.

I smiled. "Great! We can have a double marriage. Cole and I are getting married too."

Nathan's expression darkened and he stared at Cole through narrow eyes. "Him! He ought to be strung up!"

I placed an arm on Nathan's shoulder. "No, he's changed." I glanced at Cole who nodded his head. "He's becoming a Christian now."

Nathan's red face relaxed and his forehead wrinkled. "He is?"

Cole nodded. "And it's about high time too." Cole's eyes grew wide. "Oh, I almost forgot." He reached into his pocket and pulled out Kaylee's bracelet. He smiled apologetically. "I'm afraid I broke it. Sorry." He handed it to Kaylee.

She turned it over, examining the latch. "It's just bent out of place. The latch is still intact."

Then Nathan's eyes caught sight of Amma's body lying limply on the back of Cole's horse. "Mother?" His eyes returned to me.

I nodded. "She sacrificed herself to save me."

He gritted his teeth as he buried his face in Amma's hair and smashed his fist onto the horse's rear, causing it to lurch to the side. He threw his head back and screamed at the sky a long wail before plunging his face back into her hair. A minute passed as everyone remained silent, giving Nathan the space to grieve.

I placed my hand on his back and rubbed. "I saw her soul ascending to Paradise. She's with Dad now."

He wiped the wetness from his eyes and faced her. "But your ring? Couldn't you have saved her?"

I held my hand out. "I no longer have the ring."

He blinked his eyes. "Who has it then?"

I smiled. "Satan."

His jaw dropped open, he tried to speak but no words left his throat.

"It's not what you think. I put it on his finger and it has cursed him big time. He can't even take it off. He's literally in Hell now."

Nathan sucked in a breath. "Oh, wow. I would have never thought to do that."

"Me neither, if it hadn't been for Joel."

Nathan raised an eyebrow and held his arm up, pulled back his sleeve to reveal his bracelet. "Remember? Joel said the bracelets were to support the purpose of the ring. Now that the ring is no longer yours, maybe my bracelet will come off now." He reached up and placed his thumb on the clasp. He glanced at me before focusing on the bracelet. Then he pushed. The latch flipped and the bracelet snapped open. Nathan slid it off his wrist and held it before me.

I stared him in the eyes. "I guess this means no more winged horse for us. That makes me sad."

He nodded. "Me too." He glanced at Crystal. "But probably for the best. Even if you are my sister, I have another woman now to focus my time on. My high-flying days are over."

Crystal beamed. "What winged horse can compare with me, anyway?"

I then remembered, "Oh, one bit of good news." I turned my back toward Nathan. "We did save the baby. I've named him Colbert."

Colbert stared at Nathan from the pouch on my back.

Nathan remained silent. I turned back to see his face.

He shook his head. "Amazing. This is my baby brother?"

"Our baby brother. I guess Cole and I will raise him."

He frowned. "He gets to visit us, doesn't he?"

I laughed. "Of course."

Josh, who had remained silent, lifted his hand. "I get to visit too, don't I?"

Our eyes turned to him. He smiled weakly. "Not that I'm the father, you know. But I feel I did have a part to play in the whole affair."

Nathan's eyes widened. "Affair!"

"No, no, that's not what I meant." Josh's shoulders sank. "It is Sisko's child. Honest."

I didn't think Josh would lie about such a thing. Yet Josh was probably the father. Dad returning in physical form to conceive a child with Amma? Pretty hard to believe. Whatever the case, the child existed, Amma had gone on to be with Dad in Paradise, and I would marry Cole.

I met Josh's eyes. "I'll take your word for it. But we'll be living in Reol, so you'll have plenty of time with Colbert."

Josh smiled and nodded. "That's good, because I think he'll need some...uh...training when he gets older."

All in all, events had turned out well. I'd miss Dad, Amma, and now

Joel. But Cole and I would share our lives together, I gained a new sister-in-law and a new baby brother to care for. I'd have my hands full.

We flew back to Reol, enjoying the fellowship and catching each other up on our parts of the adventures we'd experienced. Weeks passed before we arrived to the streets of Reol.

Cole, true to his word, entered the baptistery. Father Jonah dunked him under three times as he spoke the prayers, and Cole rose to a new life. His face beamed with joy as he told me that God had saved him through me. A big celebration drew a large crowd from around town. The whole village feasted with us late into the night.

The next day, under the sunlight of a March spring, I stood hand in hand with Cole, while to my right, Nathan and Crystal recited "I do." When Josh and the priest's wife placed the crowns upon our heads, I felt I couldn't be happier. We would share our own little corner of Paradise on earth as living martyrs, giving our lives for each other.

I thought of Dad and Amma in Paradise, perhaps watching the proceedings through some window like he did the first time. Maybe St. Valentine and Love watched with them. The thought forced me to smile. I glanced into the sky and waved. I knew they would appreciate the thought. They would be proud.

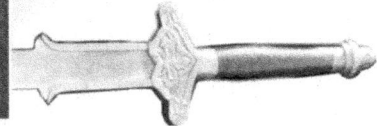

Diane M. Graham

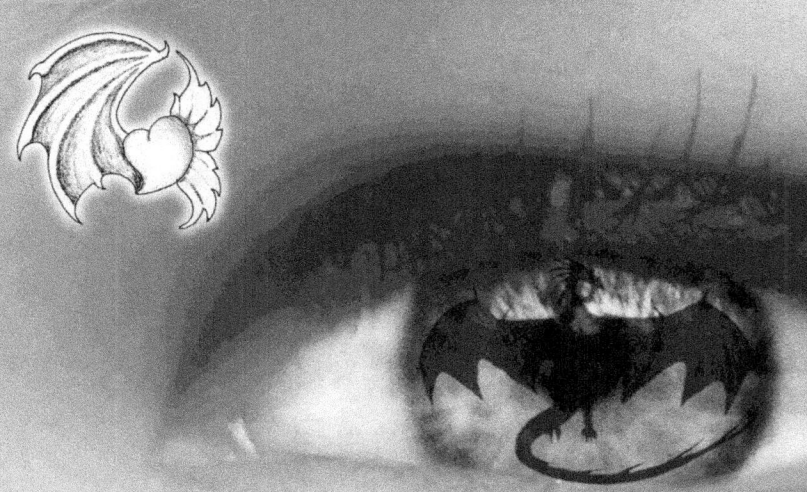

I know only my name. Beyond that is confusion, a
void where fantasy and reality swirl together.
Fairies, Giants, Elves, Dwarves,
ancient Keepers, and...Dragons?
A dark soul threatens the Five Kingdoms, but I am
powerless to stand against him, overwhelmed by
phantom memories, broken and lost.
Somehow, I must live. I must find my purpose.
There are friends to love and battles to fight.
I know my name. Perhaps that is enough.

I Am

Ocilla

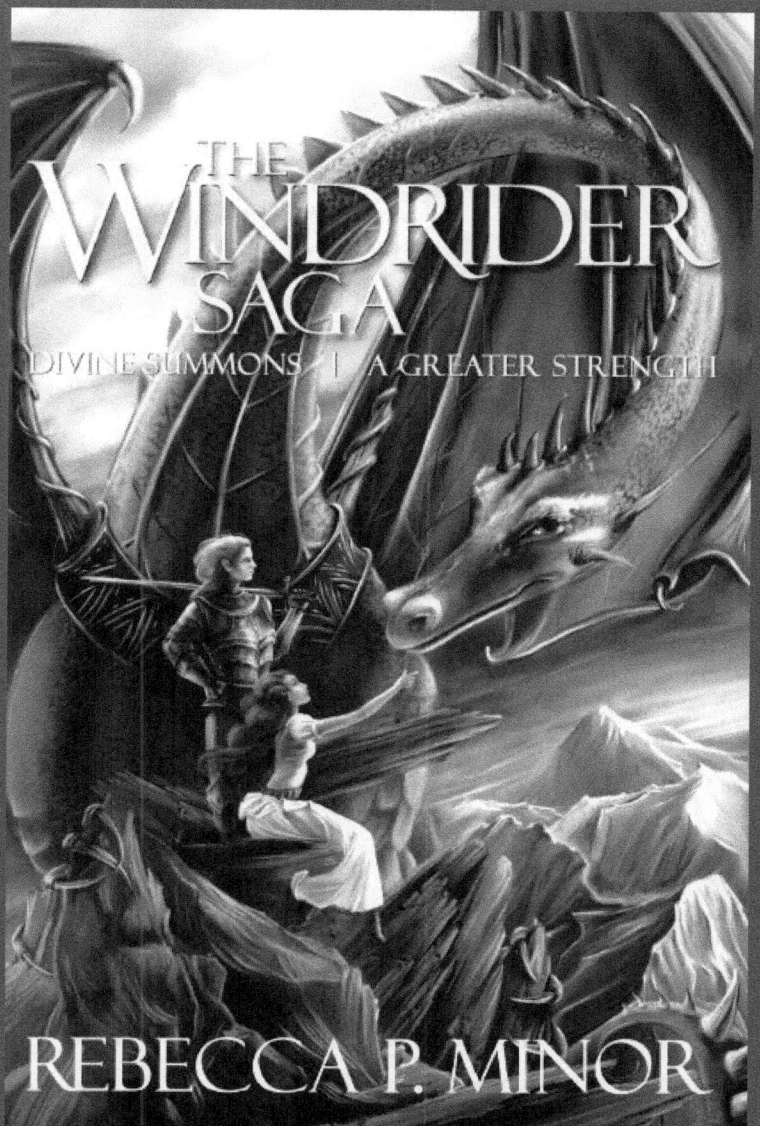

www.ingramcontent.com/pod-product-compliance
Lightning Source LLC
Chambersburg PA
CBHW070918180626
46817CB00003B/1118